Safe Haven: Ice

Christopher Artinian

DEDICATION

To Humphrey: The funniest, cheekiest, maddest bastard I've ever shared my life with. His body is gone, but his spirit will always be with me. Love you boy!

ACKNOWLEDGEMENTS

Without Tina (the missus) there would never be a Safe Haven for me. Thank you for everything you do, I would be lost if you weren't here to keep me on the right path.

Thank you to the members of my fan club. Your support always blows me away. I doubt if I can ever express how much of an honour it is to have you on this journey with me.

Thanks to my editor Roma Gray and a very big thank you to the amazing Christian Bentulan, the designer of this truly chilling cover.

And finally... A massive thank you to all of you. Even after four books and two novellas, I still find it difficult to believe that people want to spend their time reading my work. It is as magical as it is humbling. Thank you all.

1

Mike stood in the doorway for a moment looking at the small, frail figure lying in bed. He cast his gaze out to the grey clouds in the distance, and suddenly a familiar feeling crept over him. He turned and ran down the stairs, jumping the last five, hitting the hallway floorboards with a heavy thud.

"We've got to do something!" he said bursting through the kitchen doorway. "It's the flu, for fuck's sake, people don't die of the flu."

"Mike, they do. Flu is a virus, but it can lead to bacterial infections. Without running proper tests, I can't tell you what exactly, but there's a whole load. Hell, *Streptococcus Pneumoniae* has about ninety different variants alone. The flu that's hit us is the worst I've seen. It's a variant that is more potent, more virulent than any I've read about, and for Sammy, it's gone further," said Lucy.

"I need to do something," said Mike.

Lucy looked up from the mint leaves she was carefully slicing in order to make some tea. She hoped

Sammy might be able to take a sip or two in between bouts of delirium and sleep. If nothing else, it may help clear her airway a little. "Mike, sweetie, without the right antibiotics we can't do anything else," said Lucy as she reached out and closed her hand around his.

"Then we get the right antibiotics," replied Mike.

"Mikey, we've exhausted everywhere within eighty miles."

"Then we go further," he replied.

A short time later, the pair of them were back upstairs. A mug of steaming mint tea sat on the bedside table, and they stood watching Sammy. Lucy clenched Mike's hand tighter. Sammy, Mike's younger sister, had sweat pouring down her forehead, but at the same time was shivering under the covers. She was barely conscious; her eyes were fluttering as the fever consumed more of her with each passing second. Mike and Lucy raised their heads as they heard cries from the other room.

Mike closed his eyes tight. The winter had been harsh. It had taken twenty citizens of Safe Haven. Now, it threatened to take his own flesh and blood.

"Babe," said Lucy, "It's like looking for a needle in a haystack. We've used up everything we've found. Most of the pharmacies were robbed before we even got to them. We need strong stuff at this stage. We need something like Levofloxacin or even stronger. The chances of us finding that aren't great."

"I won't give up on her. I'll never give up on her."

"I wouldn't want you to. Sammy's like you. She's strong. She'll fight. That's what we want her to do, fight."

"You sound like any other fucking quack right now. You honestly think I won't tear every village, every town apart to find this stuff?"

"Stop! Please, stop this," said Lucy putting her hand to her forehead.

"I won't let her go. I won't allow it!"

"Mike, you can't control everything. But knowing that isn't going to stop you, is it?" She paused and looked to the snow-laden sky. "You're heading out again in this, aren't you?" said Lucy. "It's dangerous and irresponsible. People look to you for strength and leadership. Your family needs you right now."

Mike stared at Sammy. The last thing he wanted to do was leave her, but it was his only choice. They had raided every surgery, every pharmacy since the flu outbreak started a few weeks earlier. Lucy knew that with outbreaks of flu often came a host of infections that needed antibiotics to clear them up, and she wanted to be prepared. Now though, the stocks had run dry and there was just one option left.

"The longer I stand here, the worse it gets for her," he said.

Lucy didn't say anything. In her heart, she believed it was eighty-twenty that Sammy would not pull through. She hated lying to Mike, but she knew he would never forgive himself if he ran off on a fool's errand, and missed the last hours of his little sister's life, however horrible they would be to witness. "I can't stop you," she said, "but I'm telling you now, I think it's a mistake."

"I'm going too," said Emma, Mike's older sister, who was standing in the doorway.

Lucy looked up. "Emma…"

"We need to try Lucy!" said Emma interrupting her in an emotional outburst. The two of them had become like sisters over the last few months. The treacherous journey from Leeds across a wasteland filled with reanimated corpses, RAMs, hell-bent on adding to their ranks, had bonded them more than blood or name. Ninety-nine times out of a hundred, Emma would have sided with Lucy as she tried to talk Mike out of some 'Hail Mary' play, but right now, she was in Mike's camp. She knew the chances of success were slim. She also knew she couldn't just sit around and watch it happen.

"Right then," said Mike, "let's get a move on."

"If you're going, I'm going," said Lucy.

"Not a chance," he replied.

"Mike. You don't tell me what I can or can't do," she said.

"Luce," he said, taking hold of her upper arms. "You're the only one who can give me the time I need. You're the only qualified doctor we have. It would be mental for you to head out."

"Look at those clouds, Mike," she said, "It's mental for anyone to head out. They don't have snow ploughs and grit trucks clearing the roads anymore."

"We'll take the Land Rover," he replied.

"I'll start getting ready," said Emma, as she disappeared down the hall.

Lucy turned from Mike, taking a step towards the window. Her eyes misted over as she looked out towards the wintry clouds. "One of these days, you're not going to come back."

Mike moved close behind her and wrapped his arms around Lucy's stomach. "I have to do this."

"I know," she said, placing her hands over his.

"I won't take any risks," said Mike.

"We both know that's a lie straight off the bat," she said.

Mike released his arms from her stomach and turned her around to face him. He took Lucy's face in his hands and brought her lips to meet his. Their kiss lasted some time, but they both wished it could go on forever. "I love you," whispered Mike.

"I know," she replied. "I love you too."

He looked back towards the bed. "I know you're trying to protect me, Luce. How long does she have if we don't find this Levo... stuff?"

"Hard to say...a day...two. I really don't know," replied Lucy. "Mike. You do realise that there are no guarantees? Even if you get this stuff, it might be too late for her."

"She's my blood. She'll keep fighting."

"I know."

When Emma walked into the kitchen, Sarah, her partner, was sitting at the table sobbing. Emma went to sit beside her and placed a loving arm around her shoulders. She leaned in and kissed her face. "It's okay, we're going to get what we need to fight this thing," said Emma.

Sarah blotted her tears away with the heel of her palm. She sniffed loudly. Her crying wasn't just for Sammy, she had lost one of the pupils from her school for the deaf two weeks earlier, and now another had gone down with the flu. "What do you mean?" she asked sniffing back more tears.

"Mike and I are going out. We're going to get what we need to treat Sammy..."

"No!" said Sarah. "You can't. Look at the clouds. You'll get trapped out there."

"This is my sister. I need to do this. Mike and I need to do this," replied Emma.

"Em. Love. You know she's…"

"Don't!" replied Emma. "Just don't."

"I won't lose you too," said Sarah, standing up.

"You won't lose me," she replied. "We'll be back before you know it."

"I want to come with you," said Sarah.

Emma looked deeply into Sarah's eyes and kissed her. "No. You're needed here."

"No, I'm not. I want to be with you."

Part of Emma was happy and proud, part of her remembered back to their last battle. Sarah had been weak, a worrier. If push came to shove, she would fight, but by then it might be too late. "You should stay here. You're needed here."

"You don't want me to come?"

"Sarah," said Mike from the doorway, "we need you here. My sister is fighting for her life. Em and me are going to get her the meds she needs. I've got Lucy with her upstairs, but she can't be here twenty-four-seven. We need to know when she's not here that there is another member of our family here with her. You're the only one."

"Erm...okay. I erm..." said Sarah, on the verge of becoming emotional again.

Mike turned and left. Emma squeezed Sarah tight. "Love you."

"I love you too," replied Sarah.

Barely a moment passed and Mike returned, placing a heavy holdall down on the table with a clatter. The zipper fell open, revealing an array of hand to hand combat weapons as well as four pump-action shotguns and several Glock Seventeen handguns. The rucksack he had carried with him from Leeds was already around his shoulder. Protruding from the back of it were two crisscrossed handles belonging to hand-crafted machetes. Those weapons had saved him and his family countless times, now they were going back to work.

There was plenty more inside the rucksack, but Mike proceeded to take one of the Glock Seventeens, a spare magazine, and one of the shotguns as well as a handful of spare shells. He placed them carefully into his backpack and nodded towards the holdall on the table for Emma to select her weapons.

A few months earlier, Emma had been a timid girl, terrified of this new world. Now she had changed, almost beyond recognition. Circumstance and necessity had delivered her from her past. She still did not possess the same cavalier attitude to danger or recklessness that her brother did, but nonetheless, she had become a fierce and intelligent fighter. She made the same selection as her brother but dipped back in to pick out a crowbar and hatchet, in case she got into a situation where she had to fight hand to hand. She also removed a hunting knife and sheath. She undid her belt and looped it through the hole.

"Okay, ready!" she said.

"Right, let's get going. Every second counts," said Mike.

Lucy entered the kitchen just as Mike turned. She placed a hand on his chest, and he stopped in mid-stride. "Be careful," she said, before giving him one last kiss.

Mike smiled. "Course I will, careful's my middle name, you know that," he said, before heading into the hallway, picking the car keys off the telephone table, and walking out into the cold, grey morning.

Lucy looked at Emma. "Don't worry, I'll keep him under control," said Emma.

"Oh yeah, that always works. Listen, I don't think you should head out alone. Mike wouldn't listen, but I'm sure Hughes would go with you if you asked him," said Lucy.

"That would be good, taking one of the soldiers," said Sarah.

"I'll talk to him," said Emma, as the car horn beeped twice. "Subtle, isn't he?"

"Be careful," said Sarah, giving Emma one last kiss.

"Look after him for me," said Lucy, handing Emma the small sheet of paper with the name of the meds on that could help. "Take care," she said, giving her a kiss and a hug.

"I promise. Please do what you can for Sammy. We'll do our best. If that stuff's out there, we'll find it."

"I know you will."

2

The Land Rover sped through the picturesque Highland scenery. It didn't slow for the small villages on the way. Mike had been to every single one of them in the past few months. All living residents were long gone. They had either turned or were now members of the Safe Haven community. All useful resources had been procured for Safe Haven. Everything from gardening equipment and fuel, to polytunnels and solid fuel stoves had been relocated to make Safe Haven a functioning and thriving community. Their one big downfall had been medicine.

They had found bulk supplies of all sorts of painkillers, anti-inflammatories, antiseptic creams, and a whole host of other over-the-counter meds, but the more specialised ones were a problem. The strong antibiotics that Lucy had managed to bring with her from Leeds had been used some time since, and they hadn't been able to find any in the pharmacies or Doctor's surgeries. Mike blamed himself. He should have planned further ahead. He should have seen this coming, and now it affected him directly. He had put not just his people, but his family at risk.

"Can you please slow down?" asked Emma, sinking her nails into the car seat.

Mike looked across at her. "You do understand what we're doing? You do understand the sooner we find this stuff, the better chance Sammy has?"

"Of course I do, we're just not going to be able to help Sammy if we're at the bottom of a ravine, dead."

Mike ignored her comment and continued along at the same speed. Emma looked out of her window. The grey day cast a wintry darkness over the woodlands. It gave her a sense of doom, of foreboding. Mike had made trips like this dozens of times. He had become blasé about it, but she felt this was different, she felt there was something he was not telling her.

"Oh shit!" he said, and Emma turned to look at him.

"What is it?" Mike's eyes were staring dead ahead. Emma looked through the windscreen. At first, she had no idea what could possibly have rattled him, but then she saw it. A single snowflake drifted, then splattered on the glass. "Oh shit!"

***

"Oh shit!" said Hughes.

"What's wrong?" asked Lucy.

"This is why they didn't come for me."

"What are you talking about?" she asked.

Hughes was Mike's closest friend. He was one of the soldiers they had travelled with from Candleton in

17

Yorkshire. Hughes and Mike had hit it off from day one and bonded quickly. But as much as Hughes cared for Mike, he knew there was a dangerous unpredictability about him. "The last scavenging mission we went on for meds... Mike said then, the next one would have to be to Inverness. I told him he was crazy, that the small village medical practices were our safest option, but he just went quiet. You know the way he goes when he doesn't want to listen to what you're saying?"

"Oh shit!" said Lucy. "He wouldn't. He wouldn't take such a risk."

"Lucy, this is Mike we're talking about."

"But he's taken Emma," said Sarah. "He's a lot of things, but he wouldn't put Emma's life at risk."

Hughes combed his fingers through his hair and shook his head. "I'll get a group together, we'll go after them," he said.

"There's no way he'll come back without what he's looking for," said Lucy.

"I know...I know. The least I can do is give him some back-up, the bloody idiot. How's Sammy doing?"

"Raj and Talikha are up there at the moment. We're using every known natural remedy we can think of. We're keeping her warm. We have bowls of steaming water to help her breathe. When she can, she's sipping ginger and honey, or mint tea; I'm giving her paracetamol, but she hasn't really been conscious for some time now. I can make her as comfortable as I can, but without those antibiotics, the prognosis isn't great."

"Can I go up and see her?" asked Hughes.

"Of course you can, I'm just down here boiling another pan for Jake's hot water bottle, then I'm heading back up myself," said Lucy.

"How's he doing?" asked Hughes.

"Better than Sammy, but this is a bad strain of flu."

Hughes looked into Lucy's tired eyes. He knew she had hardly slept these last few weeks since the first cases of flu broke. He knew she would be worried sick about Mike and Emma, and he knew she was doing her best, but every time a citizen of Safe Haven died, she took it personally, as if she was responsible. It was a massive burden to carry. He hugged her, "It's alright love, I'll bring him back to you safe and sound." He pulled away, and she kissed him on the cheek.

"Thank you," she said with the start of a smile.

Hughes left the kitchen and headed up the stairs. As he reached the landing, he heard thundering feet, and within a second, Humphrey, Raj and Talikha's Labrador Retriever came bounding towards him with a familiar wild look in his eyes and a tail that wagged powerfully, destroying anything delicate it came into contact with. "Eh up! boy," said Hughes, crouching down and giving the dog a ruffle around his neck and ears, for which he received a wet lick across the face. Hughes spluttered and laughed, Humphrey always managed to put a smile on the soldier's face. He got back to his feet and passed Jake's room. The boy was asleep. That was good, rest was important. He went along to the next room and as he walked in Raj and Talikha stood.

Raj had been a vet down in Candleton and was one of the most well-educated people Hughes had ever met. He was also a good man, honourable and loyal. He had been a great friend to Mike and his family. Talikha, his wife, was beautiful, quiet, but able to turn her hand to anything. She had been the veterinary nurse at Raj's practice, but in recent times, the two of them had spent most of their days assisting Lucy and helping to establish trading partners with communities on some of the Scottish islands that had remained free of the reanimation virus.

"It is good to see you as always," said Raj, shaking Hughes by the hand.

"You too mate. How's she doing?"

"Her breathing improves with the steam," he said, pointing to the numerous bowls situated around the bed.

Hughes looked at the little girl under the quilt. Her eyelids fluttered as her body continued to shiver despite the fever. He looked towards Raj who had a resigned look on his face. Hughes thought he saw the slightest shake of Raj's head as if to say she's not going to get better, but he was not sure, and it was not something he was going to ask.

"Take good care of her," he said as he turned, nodded at Talikha and left.

***

The snow began to fall like dandelion parachutes floating on the breeze, but the whimsical gliding became heavier as the snowflakes formed battalions, then legions as they charged at the car windscreen. Mike flicked the wipers on, bypassing the intermittent and normal settings, going straight to fast, as the visibility deteriorated in a matter of seconds. The large flakes fell heavily, settling on the road and the surrounding trees, bushes and grass, painting everything white in a quick flurry. They passed a sign that was only just visible. In a few more seconds, snowy flakes would cling to it and hide the black lettering until the thaw began. It read Inverness twenty miles.

"Mike," said Emma, "You didn't actually tell me where you were planning on taking us."

Mike began to shift down the gears as they approached a bend. He had driven in snow plenty of times. He knew the dangers of braking too fast, but he knew this was different too. There were no police and ambulance services now. There was no gritting. There would be no snowploughs clearing the roads, so if he did have an accident, they were completely alone. There was no chance of being found or rescued. All of that was there in his mind as he shifted down the gears, but what was right at the front of it, what was making his grey matter pulse, was the fact that this snow was not like any other snow he had seen.

It was heavy, the flakes were big, and it was settling faster than anything he had witnessed before. The winter had been a lot colder than any he had remembered, and there had been talk about it being a result of the de-industrialisation of the planet. There was no more factory farming or air travel polluting the atmosphere with methane and carbon dioxide. There were no more factories pumping millions of tons of pollutants into the atmosphere; so, was this the result?

He took the bend slowly, but still the vehicle skidded on the quick-freezing snow. It was an old Land Rover, but it had been kept in good working order. Many a time had it crossed wet farmer's fields and negotiated dirt tracks with no difficulty, but this was something new.

"Mike!" said Emma again.

Mike suddenly snapped out of his thoughts.

"What?"

"Where are we going?"

"We're going to Inverness," he replied. "It'll be fine, trust me."

Emma put her head in her hands. "Oh, God, not again, not again. Mike please, don't do this. Of all the times I need you to be rational... Please, let's just stop and think a minute."

"We don't have a minute. Every second that passes is one second closer to the point of no return for Sammy. It's one layer of snow deeper. We need to get in, do this and get out again."

"Mike, please. Going into Inverness, just the two of us, it's suicide. That place is teaming with RAMs."

"Em! We've checked every pharmacy; every village practice we could find. We've emptied them. There will be a stockpile in this city that can get us through this winter, the next and maybe the one after that too. I'm not going to let our sister die," he said, looking at the white blanket laying down ahead of them.

"We can bypass the city. There must be some smaller places on the other side of the town we've not tried yet."

"Do you honestly think I would take a risk like this if I thought we had options?"

"Actually, yes," replied Emma. "You don't seem to have an inbuilt navigation for safety or danger. To you, it's all the same."

"If it makes you feel any better, you're not even

going to need to get out of the car. I know just the place. I saw it the last time we were here. You can keep the engine running, I can do a quick smash and grab, and we can be out of there in no time."

"It's all so easy in your crazy fucking head, isn't it? Not even getting into the fact that they may not have what we're looking for, what about the fucking RAMs, Mike? The place is teaming with them. You got out by the skin of your teeth before," she broke off, nearly in tears. She remembered back to her and Lucy's first encounter with Jules and the group she was leading at the Home and Garden Depot. She remembered how Mike and Jules had acted as decoys to lead hundreds of RAMs out of the city so the rest of them could escape. She remembered how she felt knowing he was putting himself in the firing line once again to save them. Emma looked across at her brother. There is nothing he wouldn't do for his family. He had proved that time and time again. Suddenly the venom left her argument.

"I won't let her die either," she said almost to herself.

"Huh?" he asked. "I didn't hear you." Mike was concentrating hard on his driving. The closer they got to Inverness, the more obvious it was that the snow had been falling for quite some time on this road.

"I said, I won't let her die either."

He looked across at his sister. Even though she was older than him, he always felt like the older one, the protector. He took his hand off the gear stick for a moment and placed it over hers. "I won't let any of us die, sis."

***

"I swear to Jesus there is something wrong with that boy," said Jules in her Belfast accent.

"You've only just figured that out?" asked Hughes.

Jules and her brothers had moved into the Old School House just up the road from where Mike's family lived. "So what's the plan?" she said.

"The plan is, I'm going to take Shaw, Barney and a couple of others, and go find the bloody idiot."

"Knowing the way Mike drives, he'll probably be there already," she said.

"That's true, but if anybody will be able to look after himself for a while, it's him. I just don't think he realises, there's a world of difference between a couple of us raiding a village surgery, and two people heading into the heart of a city."

"He did it before. He went into Inverness alone before and got all of us out," replied Jules.

"That he did, but let's face it. That wasn't a walk in the park, was it?"

"True enough," replied Jules. "So you want me and my brothers to come with?"

Hughes and Jules looked across at her three siblings. Andy, the eldest was wrapping a large plaster over his hand where he had just sliced it instead of a carrot he was meant to be chopping. The other two were giggling like children.

"Fuck no," said Hughes.

"Yeah! Can't say I blame you," she replied. "So, what do you need?"

"I need you to keep an eye on things here. Lucy, Raj and Talikha, are all going to be tied up. I need someone I can trust to look after the place."

"And that's me?" asked Jules with a toothy grin.

Hughes immediately blushed. He had developed a crush on Jules, but hid it well most of the time. He looked across at her brothers to see the younger two burst out laughing as they noticed their older brother had actually given himself a papercut from opening the box of plasters. "You sure you weren't adopted?" asked Hughes.

"Trust me, I wonder that myself every single day."

3

"I'm going to have to get back down to the hospital," said Lucy.

Raj began to stand, "I will come with you," he said.

Lucy put her hands up gesturing for him to sit back down. "Actually, it would give me a lot more peace of mind if you'd stay here." She walked across to the bed, sat down and placed her hand on Sammy's perspiring forehead. Lucy looked towards Raj, and he immediately looked down. "It breaks my heart to see her like this. I remember the first time I met this little sweetheart, her pop had passed away, her whole world was falling apart around her, but she still had this loving, caring warmth for others, even strangers. Life is so unfair." Lucy leaned in and kissed Sammy on her cheek. "Keep fighting baby," she said, standing up again.

"I will come," Talikha said. As she stood, Humphrey got to his feet too, thinking it might be time for his exercise. She put a single finger up, and he laid back down. "Raj will look after Sammy and Jake, I can come and assist you.

Lucy didn't argue. She knew there were people down at the hospital helping out, but she had worked with Talikha a lot since they had first met. The former veterinary nurse was very proficient and always an asset. Lucy was so tired, she needed all the support she could get. "I'll meet you in the car," said Lucy, and headed out.

Talikha kissed Raj. "I will see you later this evening." She looked down at Sammy. "Stay strong little one." As Talikha left the house, Lucy started the engine of the Vauxhall Corsa. George, one of the people who had joined them from the Home and Garden Depot in Inverness, had managed to maintain a fleet of vehicles for Safe Haven, to make sure essential services were catered for. Lucy covered more miles than anybody as she travelled the coastline dropping in on those who needed medical care, so she had a vehicle that used less fuel. It was not luxurious, but it beat cycling.

As Lucy drove the seven miles down the road to the hospital, she looked up at the snow-laden sky. It had not begun to fall yet, but it was threatening. "I really don't like the look of that at all," she said.

"Lucy," said Talikha, "If any man is safe in this world it is Michael."

Lucy smiled. Even now, Talikha was the only one who called him that. She let out a breath. "One day, though, his luck's gonna run out."

"There was a great spiritual teacher in our religion called Sivananda Saraswati. He said, *Put your heart, mind, and soul into even your smallest acts. This is the secret of success.* I believe that Michael is the very embodiment of his words. I think luck is for those who do not follow the path of

Sivananda's words."

"That's a really sweet sentiment, honey, but I don't know if I have your faith."

"You do not need it. I have enough faith for both of us. Michael only has one thought in his mind, and that is to protect his family. I believe he puts his heart, mind and soul into every action to do that. It is for this reason I know he will be successful."

Lucy took her eyes off the road for a moment and glanced across at Talikha. She was looking straight ahead. There was no false reassurance in her words. There was no bravado. She really believed it. "Tell me. You had the chance to go with the soldiers and the rest of the villagers when we were back in Candleton, but you chose to stick with Mike and Emma. Why?"

"You do not follow those running away. You follow those running towards. It is a far nobler thing to live your life and risk death in the pursuit of something than in the avoidance of something. As well as being our friends, Raj and I saw in you, Emma and Michael—hope and a future. That is why we chose to share a path with you rather than the others. And see, it was right, it brought us here, to this wonderful place."

Lucy looked again towards the sky and then out to the dark grey waves. "I don't know how wonderful it is right now."

"Our present circumstance is no reflection of our surroundings. The sea, the woods, the earth around us gives us bounty. The cliffs, the landscape give us protection. Michael chose the perfect name for our community. Safe Haven. We are going through a dark time, but we will see light again Lucy. I have faith."

Lucy smiled. "You really do, don't you?"

***

The burnt-out vehicle husks that Emma and Lucy had been responsible for several months earlier were now covered with thick snow. This venue, the bridge into Inverness, had been the prelude to a gigantic showdown between two enemies. It had been the first strike in a war that lasted a matter of days, but shaped the very fabric of their future.

"Ooh, nice flashbacks there," said Emma.

"Like I could avoid it. It's not like there are a lot of ways into the city," said Mike, having to slow the Land Rover right down as it skidded. "Erm, sis."

"What?"

"I think we're going to have to go on foot from here."

"What the hell are you talking about?"

"The snow's drifted either side of the pile-up. I'm not going to be able to get around."

"You are kidding me," she said looking at each side of the wreckage.

"No."

"Fuck!"

"Yeah!"

Emma looked down at her feet. "These were my favourite boots too. They're going to be ruined."

"That's why I was worried about telling you. I didn't want you to have to think about ruining your boots."

"Fuck off!"

Mike shut the engine off. He reached across and pulled a pair of gloves from the glove compartment and put on his Yorkshire County Cricket Club beanie hat. "Right then," he said grabbing his rucksack from the back seat. "Better get to work."

Emma zipped up her brown leather pilot's jacket, wrapped a scarf around her neck, put on her bobble hat and slid on a pair of tight brown leather gloves. She reached down and picked up her shotgun. The Glock Seventeen was already in a shoulder holster underneath her coat, but she patted it to make sure. "Okay then," she said with a little less confidence than her brother.

Their doors opened simultaneously, skimming the surface of the deepening snow, and the rush of cold air hit them both like a wall of icy razor blades. Mike's face contorted into a snarl of determination. Nothing would stop him. Mother Nature could give it everything she had, but while he had a breath in his body, he would not give up.

Emma closed her eyes tight. The second she was out of the warm and comfortable confines of the vehicle, she was that girl again. The quiet nerdy girl from years before who was scared of everything and depended on her younger brother to save her time after time, even though she should have been the one protecting him. The snow hit her face and began to melt against the soft warm flesh of her cheeks. She heard the slushing of feet and whipped round to see her brother standing beside her. The crisscrossed handles of the machetes stuck out from behind each shoulder like they were a part of him.

"C'mon sis," he said, placing his arm around her back and beginning to guide her through not so much a winter wonderland as a winter wasteland.

The pair of them trudged forward as the wind began to pick up. Mike powered through the thick white cold, but for Emma, as strong as she had become, it was an effort. By the end of the bridge, she was breathing heavily through her mouth. She sucked the occasional snowflake to the back of her throat and spluttered. Mike paused. He pulled Emma around towards him and tugged the scarf up to just below her eyes. The warmth of her breath against the fabric made breathing a little easier. "Thank you," she mumbled.

"Try breathe through your nose sis," said Mike. He brought a pair of swimming goggles out of his rucksack and placed the elastic over her head, pulling the plastic cups down to cover her eyes. Right then, right that second, they were kids again. He remembered back to how they used to go to the local swimming pool with each other, just to escape their nightmare of an existence for a couple of hours. He leaned in and kissed her on the cheek. "Love you."

"Love you too." She tapped the goggles. "You think of everything don't you?"

"Always best to be prepared," he said with a smile. "To be honest, I'd almost forgotten about them. I used them in the summer when me, Hughes and Barney were scavenging the wreckage in the bay."

The pair of them turned and began to battle through the white desert that continued to deepen in front of them.

***

"There's not a chance we're going to make it to Inverness," said Beth, correcting the steering of the minibus with another hard pull of the wheel.

"It's my fault," said Hughes from the seat behind her. "I should have seen this coming. There was no way Mike wasn't going to do something like this where his family was concerned."

Shaw got to his feet and steadied himself on the headrest of the seat in front of him. Since his accident, he was not able to sit for long periods without feeling pain in his leg. "Can't blame yourself, Hughesy, we should have all seen this coming."

"Yeah," added Barnes, turning around in the passenger seat. "We've all been together long enough now. Sammy got bad a lot quicker than anyone thought. There wasn't a chance we could have predicted this."

"Oh fuck!" shouted Beth, and all eyes immediately shot to the front as the minibus began to spin out of control. Shaw hung on to the support strap with all his might, while Hughes and Barnes gripped onto whatever they could to steady themselves. Beth didn't hit the brakes, she turned into the spin while moving down through the gears. The minibus felt like it was going to tip over for a moment, and their hearts rose up into their throats as they heard an unhealthy clunk come from the engine, but then the vehicle came to rest and just stalled while the sheets of white continued to fall. Beth looked around at the others. "Is everybody okay?"

"Yeah!" said Shaw, looking at his clenched fist as he gripped the leather strap like a vice. "Are you?"

"I think so," said Beth.

"What happened?" asked Hughes.

"Just lost control," replied Beth. "I think it's too deep to drive in.

Hughes looked at the other soldiers, then back to Beth, and then through the windscreen. The snow was in no danger of stopping. "Try starting her up again love."

Beth turned the key, the engine spluttered, then spluttered some more but was a light year away from ever starting. She stopped, then did the same again, but with the same result. "Shit," she said.

"Erm… yeah," said Hughes. "That about sums it up."

She twisted the key back and the windscreen wipers stopped working. Snowflakes mosaicked into a white rug against the glass and the four of them shot glances towards each other. This was like nothing any of them had seen before. The speed and thickness of the snowfall was unprecedented.

"This is bad," said Shaw.

"You're not wrong," said Hughes looking out of the side windows into the whitening woods. He paused for a moment. "Look! We don't have another choice. We're going to have to get going on foot." he said.

"What the hell?" said Barnes. "We shouldn't even be thinking about going out in this. If we all stay in here, we can keep the temperature up with the camping stove."

"Yeah, and assuming we avoid the carbon monoxide poisoning, how long do you think that will last? By that bloody time, the snow could be over our heads," said Hughes. "Look Barney, we don't really have an option mate. We either set off now, or we all freeze to death," said Hughes.

4

"There seems...to be...a real lack...of RAMs," said Emma as her teeth chattered.

"These are the outskirts. Hopefully, we'll avoid any big build-ups, but you can be sure there'll be some kicking about," replied Mike. "Fuckers are never that far away." He looked across at his sister. "You okay, Em?"

"C-cold," she said.

"You want to get inside for a few minutes?" he asked.

"C-can we?"

"Course we can," he said and put his arm back around her, guiding her into an alleyway by the side of a large abandoned carpet warehouse. He remembered back to the last time he had been here. He had come before on a motorbike and left it in the bus shelter nearby. Now the bus shelter was covered in white, just like the pavement and roads. The laid snow was easily eighteen inches now, and each stride took more effort than the last. Mike struggled to guide Emma up the alleyway as their feet dragged in the thick white carpet.

They eventually made it to the back of the store, and Mike found a small window to a downstairs toilet. He wiped the snow from the top of a recycle bin and dragged it across to below the window. He clambered onto it and then swiftly elbowed the glass. It smashed immediately, and Mike got to work removing the shards before climbing in. He was greeted by deathly silence and headed to the delivery area of the building. All the staff had clocked out long since. This warehouse was a husk even before the outbreak. He reached into his pocket and brought out a small penlight, and then traced his way into the back storeroom and to the emergency fire exit. He ran at it and barged against the panic bar. The mighty force displaced just enough snow to open the door wide enough for Emma to squeeze in. As soon as she was through, Mike pulled the door back in place. He held the penlight in his hand and the two of them watched as a few thick snowflakes that had followed Emma through the gap floated to the ground.

Mike placed an arm around his shivering sister and guided her down a corridor, looking at the signs on the door. One of them read *staff canteen*, and he pushed it open. It was a room about the size of a standard Portakabin. Snowy windows allowed the grey-white emptiness of a never-ending winter to bleed depressing light into the room.

Emma went across to one of the couches and sat down, immediately removing her gloves.

"Em, I don't understand. We've only come a few hundred metres. It's cold, but you're wrapped up well. What's wrong?" he asked, crouching down in front of his sister. He watched as his breath turned to frosty air in front of him.

She took off the goggles and proceeded to untie her boots with shaky hands. Her teeth chattered and her nose and face twinged with pain as she pulled off her right boot. She panicked as she saw a look of horror sweep over Mike's face, then she looked down to see her white sock dripping red with blood. Her teeth chattering stopped for a few seconds as she drew in a shocked breath. Mike gently stretched out her leg and looked at the underside of her foot. There was a jagged hole in the sock and blood was slowly pumping out of a wide gash. He picked up the boot and saw something had daggered through the thick sole. "Is it bad?" asked Emma.

Mike brushed his hand over his face. "Erm...it's not good," he said and began to look around the room. "Look, I need to bandage this and get your leg raised."

"I'm so cold Mike," she said.

"Okay sis," he said, laying her down on the couch and raising her leg and foot onto the arm so it was higher than her body. He took off his gloves, then unzipped his coat and placed it over her, before rummaging through his rucksack. He always kept a small first aid kit in there. It wasn't meant for a situation like this, but he would do what he could. He removed Emma's sock and she let out a cry of pain. The extreme cold numbed her to the full extent of what she would feel in normal circumstances and that was one thing Mike was grateful for. It made him feel physically ill to think of his sister in pain like this. He rinsed her foot with water from his flask and saw that the gash wasn't as bad as he had thought, but he still needed to stop the bleeding. He took out a large hip flask from the side pocket of his backpack. "This might hurt a bit," he said, taking a quick swig, then pouring some of the amber liquid onto the wound.

"Arrrggghhh! Fucker!" she yelled.

Mike handed her the hip flask and she took a healthy shot herself. He grabbed some gauze from the first aid kit, placed them over the wound and wrapped a bandage around tightly before threading a safety pin in place to secure it. He watched for a moment to see if blood seeped through, but it didn't. "Okay!" he said standing and looking around the room again. There was an electric cooker, and beside it, a fire blanket, he thought about that for a second, then he headed across to the windows and pulled the orange, flowery curtains down that looked like they had been there from the eighties. There were four of them, one for each wide window. He sniffed them. They were old but clean enough. In the absence of a blanket, they would have to do. He went across and placed them over his sister.

"Ugh! Gross!" she said. "What a horrible design."

"Funny, that was my main concern too," he said, cocooning her in the fabric of three of the curtains. Her feet stuck out at the bottom. Her right foot was still raised, her left dangled over the side. He pulled up one of the matching chairs and rested her still booted left foot on its arm. "How's that?"

"Okay," she said through chattering teeth. "Still freezing."

"Here, have another drink," he said, passing her the hip flask. "I'm going to have a quick look around."

"What for?" asked Emma.

"Don't know yet," he said, opening the door and heading out into the dark corridor.

***

"I can't really make it out. But they're the closest thing to tyre tracks we're going to see in this," said Barnes looking through the scope of his SA80 rifle. He brought the sight back down from his face and slung the rifle over his shoulder.

The four of them looked at each other. As the snow continued to fall. "This is mad," said Beth. "We could be trapped here for the rest of the winter." She looked up to the sky. There was no sign of the snow stopping, and what had settled already was up to their knees. Nobody said anything in reply. There was nothing they could say. None of them had seen or felt a winter like this before.

"We need to find shelter as fast as we can." said Hughes.

"Easier said than done in this," replied Beth. "We're probably at least another two miles out of Inverness still."

"Then we'd better get a move on before it gets any worse," said Shaw, already grimacing as the cold began to play havoc with his bad leg.

***

Mike scanned the dingy showroom. Despite large windows at the front of the store, a combination of painted window signs saying *closing down sale*, dirt, and an ever-increasing build-up of snow meant that not much light was left to illuminate the sales floor. There were thick cardboard inner tubes from carpet rolls, metal racks, floor tiles that someone had begun to peel up only to give it up as a bad job halfway through. There was a counter with a thick wooden top covered with dust and an old cathode ray tube computer screen sat there, long disconnected from the actual computer.

Mike stepped behind the counter and saw piles of

sales leaflets in boxes and a sturdy metal thigh-high waste bin. He picked up the bin, and his eyes shot open wide in surprise. It was much heavier than he thought it would be. "Okay," he said, heaving it up and carrying it back into the canteen.

"What's that for?" asked Emma.

"Back in a minute," he said disappearing again.

He returned with two boxes of leaflets and dumped them.

"Mike? Mike?" she called as he left the room once more. Emma took another drink from the hip flask and suddenly, her breathing became a little easier for a moment. Then she heard clattering, battering and chopping echoing down the hallway from the showroom. "What the fuck is he doing?" she muttered to herself.

"There, that should keep you going for a while," he said, walking back through the door with slices of a heavy wooden countertop.

"What? What are you doing? What are you talking about, keep me going for a while?" She was cold, in pain, and now she was confused as well.

Mike walked across to the emergency fire blanket and pulled the chords of its protective wrapping to unfurl the heavy, flame retardant material. He opened the grill door in the oven and pulled out the large grill pan. He took out the rack, putting it to one side, then picked up the blanket and grill pan and headed back across to where Emma was laid. "How you feeling sis?" he asked as he laid the folded blanket down about a metre back from the couch. He placed the grill pan on top of it, then went across and collected the metal bin. It was perfect for what he wanted. It came with a decent sized hole in the metal for people to place their rubbish and the top was removable so the inner lining could easily be taken out and emptied. Mike discarded the top and the lining and placed the bin upside down with the rubbish hole facing the couch.

"Will you please tell me what you're doing, Mike?" she begged.

"Patience." Mike pulled the hatchet back out of his belt, and raised it, before powerfully bringing it down at an angle, on the base of the metal bin. Despite its sturdiness, a deep indentation appeared and Mike went into his rucksack again for a straight-edged screwdriver. Now the metal had been weakened, it did not take him long to make a small hole using the screwdriver and the flat edge of the hatchet as a hammer. He repeated this to create another puncture in the bottom of the metal bin. When he was done, he could just about fit his middle finger through each hole.

Emma looked on in confusion, baffled as to what he was trying to do. The cold and the pain had been momentarily forgotten. She took another drink from the hip flask as Mike walked across to the sink. He crouched down, reached to the back and proceeded to pull and wrench the lengthy copper pipes that had long since run dry away from the wall, making the taps and whole sink unit judder violently. He went back to the couch, flinging one of the pipes on the floor, while he squeezed the other into the first hole he had made. There was an eardrum piercing metal on metal screech that made both him and Emma wince, but eventually, the pipe wedged comfortably into the hole. He repeated the exercise for the second pipe and the second hole, then stood back with his hands on his hips. He grabbed a chair, stood on it, and levered open the ceiling tile just above the pipes.

"It's not perfect, but you should be able to have a small fire without choking on smoke," Mike said, climbing back down from the chair. He twisted some of the sales leaflets into kindling and assembled some of the broken and chipped pieces of wood into a wigwam shape in the mouth of his newly created chimney stack. He pulled out a lighter from the rucksack and third click lucky, it ignited the paper which slowly began to catch.

The pair of them watched as the small flames gradually grew larger and glowed brighter. Mike went to the end of the couch and looked at Emma's foot. Blood had still not seeped through the gauze which meant the bleeding was stopping. Regardless though, there was no way she could head back out with a wound like that, and with nothing to protect her foot apart from a boot with a hole in it. Mike picked up the remaining curtain and carefully wrapped it around Emma's lower leg and injured sole, making sure she was insulated from the cold as well as she could be.

He moved back round to her side and added some more kindling and wood to the fire. "I'll get this going, then I'm going to have to get off."

"What?" she said in a disbelieving whisper.

"Em. You can't walk on that foot. You don't have any cover for your feet. You're going to have to stay here while I go out and find the meds," he said, twisting some more of the leaflets into kindling.

"But Mike, you can't. You can't leave me...here...alone...like this."

"Listen. I won't be long. The chemist wasn't far from here, and there was another one just a bit further down the road. One of them is bound to have what we're looking for," he replied, placing the wadded paper through the gap and watching the flames grow higher.

"I don't want you to do this alone. What if something happens to you?"

Mike smiled. "We all run that risk every single day. Nothing is going to happen though. I'm getting pretty good at this whole staying alive thing now."

"Don't be a smart arse. It's dangerous out there at the best of times. We're in the middle of a city. We don't have a quick out. This could get very bad, very quick."

Mike edged onto the couch and placed his hand on his sister's cheek. "This is what's going to happen. I'm going out there to get the antibiotics we need to save Sammy. Then I'm coming back here to get you, and the pair of us are going back home." he leaned in and kissed her on the forehead.

The fire was starting to take hold and crackle away. Mike moved the bits of wood in reach of Emma, so she could keep feeding it in his absence. He pulled a packet of rice crackers from his backpack and slotted the bottle of water in between Emma and the couch cushion so she had easy access. The heat from the fire was starting to warm the air around them. "Okay Em, I'm going to need my jacket back," he said, loosening the curtains so he could take it off her. She reached across for her gloves and put them back on, while Mike tucked the curtains back around her. He kissed her again. "I promise, I won't be long. Keep the fire going." He got up and started walking out, then he noticed a red fire extinguisher bracketed to the wall at the other side of the room. He went across to get it and put it in easy reach of Emma. "Just in case," he said, winking.

"I love you, Mike," she said for the second time that

day. Her words and the look in her eyes transported him back to a different time. She was fourteen, he was ten. It was the middle of the summer holidays from school. Their father had been cut to part-time hours that summer. He spent a lot of his afternoons out drinking, and often when he came home from the pub, he would want to take his frustration out on one of his children, which always ended up being Mike. If he ever went near Emma, Mike would pick a fight with him deliberately. This day, his father had been particularly vicious, and he had battered Mike brutally. When it was over, the young boy had retreated to bed, pulling the covers over himself as if he was a wounded animal trying to retreat from the world and die. He had been in so much pain. The betrayal he was used to now, but this level of pain was something he had felt only once in a while. That night, Emma had stayed with him. She had laid on top of the covers with her arm draped over him, praying that they would both be left alone. Just before he went to sleep, she had said, "I love you, Mike," in exactly the same way as she just had. There would never be anything he would not do for her.

"I love you too, sis."

5

The 'hospital' had developed since the early days of the settlement. Now it consisted of four static caravans, which Lucy always called trailers. Dora, one of the girls from Sarah's school, was an excellent caregiver and a very quick learner. Although she was deaf, she could lip-read, and Lucy never hesitated to give her responsibilities many would shirk. She had been tending to the patients in the doctor's absence. In reality, there was not much that could be done for them other than making them comfortable. Their life or death was in the hands of God right now.

Dora insisted on writing notes which she added to the clipboards at the end of the bed. Initially, Lucy humoured her, saying they were useful when really, they were not. However, as Lucy spent longer periods away from the hospital, she found the notes to be of more and more help, and she realised just how perceptive and intuitive Dora was. Now, each time Lucy arrived back, she would make a point of reading every sentence as she did her rounds.

Nothing was unexpected. Most of the patients were

in there with severe cases of the flu. They were nearly all older people, but one was a bit of a puzzle to Lucy. Jonathan McGregor was in his thirties. Other than suffering from really bad hay fever in the summer, he had never had any problems. It was strange for someone in his general good health to be so ill with the virus. Strange, but not unknown. Lucy looked at his notes. *Asleep most of day. Woke up for a while. Complained of scratchy, dry throat. Gave him water and lozenges, felt a little better, fell back into deep sleep soon after.*

She looked at the patient. He was still in a deep sleep. His brow was slick with perspiration, and his eyelids were fluttering just like Sammy's had. Sammy! God how she hoped for a miracle. If Mike lost her it would kill him. He had made a vow to Alex, his stepfather, that he would look after the family. It was something beyond his control, but she knew he felt responsible. That's why he'd gone on this mad mission.

She placed the notes back on the bed and looked out of the window. The snow that had been threatening to fall had finally begun its descent. She opened the door and stepped out into the freezing air, just as a car pulled up. The driver's door opened and Jules climbed out.

"Hi," she said.

"Hi, sweetie," replied Lucy.

There was a pause as the two of them let the snow fall and melt on their faces for a moment. "How're things going here? Y'need anything?" asked Jules.

"I just need Mike and Emma to come home safely," she said.

"Bloody hell. If there's one thing I'm sure about, it's that gobby shite will be back," she said, and the pair of them laughed. Jules walked around the car and gave Lucy a hug. "Seriously. I joke a lot, but Mike is special. He will do everything to get those drugs and get back here."

"I know he will. It's just one thing going on a scavenging mission in this weather. When it's into the centre of a city full of RAMs, that's something else entirely."

"I know what you're saying, but have a little faith," replied Jules.

"You're right. I know you're right."

"How is Sammy, anyway?"

"She's not good Jules. She's teetering on the edge. I've left Raj with her because I genuinely don't want to be the one there if she passes. I don't want to be the one who says to Mike, I was there and there was nothing I could do. Because there is nothing I can do. Other than administer the drugs if he gets them. The rest of it is just trying to make her comfortable." A tear appeared in the corner of Lucy's eye. And Jules took hold of her hand.

"Sammy is just like Mike. She's a fighter. She'll keep going and going. You watch," said Jules, giving her a reassuring wink. "Right, I'm off. Doing my rounds, making sure everyone's okay."

"Thanks for dropping by," said Lucy.

"Sure thing," replied Jules before climbing back in the car and heading off again.

It had only been snowing a short time, but a thin film of white had already settled in the stone chipped car park. "Please, God! Look after them," said Lucy, before heading back inside.

***

The wind had begun to pick up as Mike squeezed back through the fire door. Snow had drifted at the opposite side of the courtyard. This really was like nothing he had seen before. He retraced his steps, even though they had a healthy white covering since they had been made originally. When he reached the alleyway, the full force of the freezing air and snow cut into him, and for a moment he faltered, before pushing forward again. He had borrowed Emma's scarf which comforted him more than he would ever let on, and he had taken back the goggles. Pulling them down over his eyes and dragging his beanie hat down to his eyebrows, he battled forward. He was on a mission and there was no way he was going to fail.

He reached the end of the alley and saw that the snow was drifting high against the front of the carpet warehouse. Even though the landscape resembled something from a Christmas film now, he remembered back to a few months earlier when he had been here looking for Emma and Lucy. That had been an insane time, they had been at war. Now, they were at war again, albeit the enemies were microscopic germs. As he got closer to the end of the street, he realised the snow had funnelled and drifted much more on the road he needed to head down. "Son of a bitch," he muttered into his sister's scarf.

It was slow going as he climbed the white incline and turned onto the street leading to the ring road that encircled the heart of the city centre. In turn, this would take him to the pharmacy that he hoped would be the answer to all his prayers. The one saving grace as he fought on was the wind was now at his back. It whistled around his ears, urging him to go faster, but it was tough work. For the time being, the snow was supporting his weight, but he was ready to hit a hollow patch at some stage and have to climb his way out. *What he wouldn't give for a pair of snowshoes right now.*

A ghostly hymn continued to whistle in his ears as he journeyed further and further into the frigid wasteland. Another hundred metres and he would hit the ring road. Then, there would be a turn, and the wind and icy flakes would bombard his left side as he continued his trek.

He felt high up as he walked across the drifting whiteness which had massed on this one street like no other. An anomaly, a quirk of design meant that he was walking on snow five feet above ground level. The shops and buildings that lined the road he was on had even deeper arcs of snow riding up their sides creating a wintry valley.

He turned his head to look behind him and got a freezing blast in his face for his efforts. He turned back around again and wiped his goggles clean with his gloved fingers.

"Shit!" he growled as his foot caught on something. He had no idea what he could be walking on top of. It might be discarded shopping trolleys, husks of vehicles, it could be anything. He tugged again, and this time, his foot broke free. With the cold whoosh of winter laying thicker flakes of white every second, there was no time to investigate. He would just make a point of avoiding this side of the street on his way back.

His progress was slow, but it was progress. "Son of a bitch!" he said as his boot got caught again. This time, he could not pull it free as easily, and he bent down to brush the snow from around it. "Fuck!" he shouted, as he sprang up. He tugged his foot free with all his might and staggered back two paces. It was still visible...a hand...a child's hand. Only it wasn't a child's hand anymore. It was grey and necrotic. It was the hand of a RAM. It reached higher, desperately grabbing at the freezing air, catching snowflakes as it rose, hoping to catch something else...someone.

Mike span round and saw the hand from the other creature that had snagged his boot before. He scanned the white blanket around him and as if magically sensing the presence of a live human, more grasping hands began to rise. Then, a cascade of snow revealed a head as a creature frantically began to fight and struggle free from its icy shackles. Mike looked around quickly, there were eight of these things. All of them were now beginning to battle their way free. Air pockets formed due to the creatures' continued efforts to rise, making the whole icy bridge to the ring road unstable. Suddenly, the snow collapsed beneath Mike's feet, and he was stuck in it up to his thighs.

"Oh fuck, no!" cried Mike, as he tried to scramble out; but each movement he made, just meant more snow tumbled around him. At the exact same time, the first RAM shuffled free and began to crawl towards Mike. Invigorated by the promise of fresh blood, the creature glided across the icy surface on all fours like a hockey puck. Mike shot a quick glance around him. All of the beasts were making progress. "Oh shiiittt!" he shouted as he pulled the machetes from his rucksack.

As much as he wanted to use one of the guns, that would alert every RAM in Inverness to his presence, and right now, he was in enough trouble without doing that. The first beast was almost on him. A teenage girl in life, still in her school uniform. Her matted long black hair swung from side to side over her windswept grey face as she bounded towards Mike on all fours. The snow lashed against her, but she had no concept of pain or discomfort. All she saw was fresh meat, and it was dinner time. Mike raised one of the machetes and swung down, slicing through the air. He heard the whistle of the blade even over the sound of the freezing wind, and that familiar smashed coconut crack as the stainless steel broke through bone. The RAM immediately collapsed; its head dropped face down in the snow, and a slow seeping pool of blood turned the surrounding area pink, then red.

Mike struggled, managing to free himself a little. He turned in time to see the first creature that had snagged his foot. It was another girl, still in uniform. Her progress was slower than the first, and he noticed her trailing leg. Chunks of flesh and muscle had been ripped out of it. He leant forward, freeing himself a little more, and ended her suffering with another loud whoosh and a bloody crack. She stopped, a frozen monument in the icy landscape. This time there was no blood; the cold, almost instantly cauterising the wound at the top of the creature's head.

The harsh conditions were forgotten now, even as the sharp pricks of snow stabbed his face, Mike only had one focus. With a huge grunt, he dragged himself completely free in time to stop a boy this time. The child's white collar was torn where a gristly chunk had been ripped out of his neck. The creature freed both its arms and started to pull itself from its snowy confines when Mike plunged a machete blade straight through its eye. Mike turned to face the strengthening blizzard full-on as he battled towards two more RAMs, swiping at them both simultaneously with samurai like grace. The young heads fell forward. Small globs of goo leaked onto the snow before stopping just as quickly.

Mike turned again, and suddenly, the wind was behind him. "Four down, four to go," he muttered, as he headed towards the beast that looked most likely to gain freedom from its icy cocoon first. His foot snagged, and he immediately looked down. It was another hand clasped around his boot. The rest of its owner still beneath the deepening snow. Mike raised his machete, and the world fell from beneath his feet once more, as the snow collapsed.

"Fuck!" he growled, but then it was growling of a different kind he heard. The familiar guttural growl of a RAM. As the cascading snow settled around them both and the flurry of surprise ended, Mike jolted back to the moment just as the beast, who had suffered the same disorientation as her captor, lunged. Mike leant back, feeling a wall of ice supporting him, as he pushed the blade up through her chin, brain and skull with lightning force. The familiar grey eyes, with those eerie shattered pupils blinked shut one last time, and Mike let out a relieved breath. He could not pause though. He took hold of the creature's school jacket and pushed the beast to its knees, creating a stepping stone for himself, back out onto the icy battleground.

The other four creatures were making headway as their grey fingers clawed and pulled at the snow around them. Mike pushed all thoughts about these being youngsters to the back of his head; their school uniforms, their bead bracelets, one of them even had a satchel around her neck. He could not allow his sadness for these lost children to impede his actions. There was a child, still very much alive that he was doing all this for. So as the young hand of a teenage schoolgirl reached out to grab him, he grimaced, placed his foot firmly over it, pinning it down, then unleashed another deathly strike as his machete sliced through the girl's skull. For a split second, she wasn't a RAM. Her dead grey eyes were a sparkling blue, and her pallid face was a rosy pink in the cold air. She did not look at him with ferocity and malevolence but with sadness and pleading. She was just a young girl, innocent and lost; afraid and sad.

He stood there for a moment, locked in his trance;

the metal blade wedged in the girl's skull holding it unnaturally off the ground like her head was floating in the wind. He whipped the machete back out, making the head drop like a deadweight, face down into the crunching whiteness. How many now? How many daughters? Sons? Husbands? Wives? Brothers? Sisters? How many had he killed? Killed wasn't the right word, but how many had he...finished off?

It felt like legions. Then he remembered back to his little sister. His Sammy, feverish on the bed. Was he too late already? He twirled around and in an instant, the pity, the humanity was gone. He trudged towards the next creature. Swipe! Then the next. Swipe! Then the final one. It lunged towards him, its lower half still trapped in a freezing prison. Mike stamped on its head. It's dirty, matted blonde hair falling around his boot. He dropped to one knee plunging the machete blade into the back of the beast's skull, rendering it still. He brought the blade back out and wiped it on the grey woollen school blazer, before placing it and the other machete back into his rucksack.

The blizzard was blowing even harder now. He looked at the downed beasts, and with each second that passed, another small piece of them was laid to eternal rest under a veil of winter. Mike took in a breath of icy air and continued his journey. As the wind blew at his back and the large wet flakes sped by him like arctic butterflies, he kept his eyes fixed firmly on the ground. He would not feel comfortable until he was back on a lower settling of snow, and the only demons he would see would be heading straight towards him, not trying to drag him down to Hell.

6

"Bloody 'ell it's cold," shouted Hughes as the four of them marched into the blizzard head-on.

"I think I see their car," shouted Beth, whose scarfed face was now covered in thick snow.

"What?" said Shaw.

Beth realised the futility of trying to communicate verbally in such adverse conditions, and so she stopped and pointed. The three men halted too and squinted as the snowy shards cut into their faces.

It was the Land Rover Mike and Emma had set off in. "At least we know they got this far," shouted Hughes.

"What?" replied Shaw.

Hughes just shook his head, hitched his collar a little further up and carried on marching through the thick snow.

The other three did the same. Their breathing was

heavy and laboured. Despite the scarves around their faces and mouths, the freezing conditions sliced into them like a thousand sheets of razor blades. They were all thinking the same thing. They had never known conditions like this before.

They got to the car and all climbed in. The temperature inside was the same as the temperature outside, but the respite came from not having endless rounds of white, wet bullets firing at them. Beth clenched her hands together a few times before daring to take her gloves off. She leaned forward in the back seat and pulled the rucksack from her shoulders. Reaching into it, she brought out a large blue flask and twisted the top off causing a geyser of steam to rise into the air. Within a few seconds the smell of pea soup filled the small enclosed space.

"C'mon then," said Beth, "Pass us your mugs."

The three men, who had been clasping their hands in their armpits in a vain attempt to warm them up, swiftly dragged their mugs out of their backpacks and offered them to Beth like they were playing the lead in a stage production of "Oliver Twist". The creamy, green, hot liquid poured into their cups, and they inhaled the steam like it was some magic elixir. The aroma filled the car and suddenly, the pain and discomfort of the journey they had just undertaken were forgotten for a few moments as rich warmth coated their insides.

"God, that tastes good," said Barnes.

"Yeah," replied Hughes, "but what I wouldn't give for a bit of ham in there as well."

Beth dipped her hand back into the rucksack and pulled out a cob of bread. She tore it into four pieces, handed one each to the soldiers, then kept the final piece for herself. For a while, the only sounds that could be heard in the car were slurps and chewing. Each of them saved a good-sized chunk of bread to wipe away the soupy residue from their mugs before savouring the final mouthful.

When they had finished, they all put their gloves on, pulled their scarves back above their mouths and noses, and prepared to fight mother nature head-on once more. Shaw opened his door, and immediately the comfort of the last few moments was lost in a melee of storming snow. Their hearts sank as they resumed their journey, noticing the snow was now twenty minutes thicker, and twenty minutes heavier against their advancing feet.

"We're going to die here aren't we?" said Beth.

The thought had passed through all their minds. They had no transport, virtually no supplies, and they were trapped in a city full of RAMs.

"Over my dead body," said Hughes.

"I kind of think that's the whole point," she replied.

***

"Hi Ruth. How's it going?" asked Lucy as the librarian walked into static caravan number three, or Ward Three as it was known.

The librarian smiled. "Are you serious?"

"No. Not really. How are David and Richard?"

"They're both full of the flu, but bearing up. They're at home in bed. I came down here to see if I could help with anything."

Lucy looked at the older woman and smiled. She remembered how she had been the one responsible for getting Mike back to them safely when he was in Candleton. She had given him her car - a completely selfless act for a total stranger. Ruth, Richard and David were all socially awkward. The Library in Skelton had been their home, their life. They had wanted to end their days there because they thought they would be of no use in this new world, but Mike knew differently. He knew they were intelligent people, and in a world of barbarism, they would be vital to help restore order.

"Lucy?" asked Ruth, a little worried that she hadn't received a response.

Lucy snapped back to the present. "Sorry...miles away. No, thank you. I want you to get home before this snow gets any worse. I've got Dora, Talikha and myself to look after things here. To be honest, there's not much we can do," she said in a quieter tone, leading Ruth out by the arm, back into the cold air. "If Mike gets some decent antibiotics, we might stand a chance, but this is the worst case of flu I've seen, it really weakens the host, making them susceptible to all kinds of bacterial infections. Making people as comfortable as possible, that's pretty much it right now. Hopefully their bodies will be strong enough to fight."

"Jules told me about how Sammy was and Mike heading off. You don't really think he'll have gone to Inverness, do you?"

Lucy looked at her as a steady cascade of snowflakes fell between them. "This is Sammy we're talking about. For her, he'd walk into the depths of Hell."

***

"Mike? Mike is that you?" called Emma, as a sound woke her from a deep sleep. She looked at the fire. It was burning well, but she leaned down and threw another couple of pieces of wood onto it. "Mike?" she called again after getting no response.

Had it just been her imagination? Had the sound been in her dream? She held her breath. The only thing she could hear was the gentle crackle of the fire. "Nice work girl, you're starting to imagine things now. That's all you bloody need."

The fire was heating the room well, and with heat came pain. The numbness of the cold had stifled a lot of it, but now her foot was in agony. She delved into her pocket and brought out a hip flask full of her gran's homemade plum brandy. It was warm on the throat and even warmer on the insides as it went down. She looked at the silver vessel for a moment and raised it a little, "Miss you Gran," she said, before taking another drink. Emma replaced the cap and put the flask back inside her jacket pocket.

There was a clatter from another part of the warehouse. "Oh shit!" she said and immediately reached for her Glock Seventeen. "Mike?" she asked, with a slight tremble in her voice.

There was no response, and Emma's heart began to pound harder. She heard shuffling in the corridor outside, and suddenly the pain in her foot was gone as adrenaline surged through her body. She struggled free of the curtain cocoon Mike had wrapped her in, and sat up, pointing the Glock straight towards the door. The shuffling stopped and a few seconds seemed like an eternity as the crackle of the fire popped through the air like an irregular clock ticking a countdown. Something nudged the door to the canteen and it creaked open on its hinges. Emma gulped and tried to steady her shaking hands.

"Hello?" she said, but it came out as nothing more than a whisper.

***

Mike felt the stab of each icy missile as they splattered into the small portion of his face that was left uncovered. He had reached the ring road, and the snow, although deep, was nothing like the deadly bridge he had just crossed. As he struggled forward, kicking through deepening mounds of the stuff, he looked over to his right. There stood the Home and Garden Depot where he had found Lucy and Emma, and where he had met Jules, her brothers and their group. The entrance had been blown apart by Andy, Jules' idiot brother, and snow entered the store unencumbered. There wasn't that far to go now. He had recalled seeing the green cross of a pharmacy up a side street, just opposite the neighbouring store.

The last time he was on these streets he remembered hearing the angry growls of hundreds of RAMs, now all he heard was the whistling whoosh of winter. He clenched his gloved hands together, three, four, five times. He could barely feel his fingers in this cold. Finally, the pavement led to a post office building, and he was able to take a few minutes respite from the rampaging storm attacking his left side. He leant up against the wall, slid off his gloves and blew into his hands. It was no good, no sooner had he warmed them up then they were cold again. He blew warm air from his lungs into the gloves before weaving his fingers back inside. He could actually see the black tarmac of the pavement here. Small amounts of snow still painted patches on it, but the rest had drifted away. He took a deep breath of cold air and coughed. This was where it was going to get tough. He had to take a left turn, straight into the blizzard. If his memory served him, the pharmacy was about a hundred metres up the street. This was going to hurt.

Mike repositioned his goggles, clapped his hands together and set off. "Arghhh!" the snow and wind hit him like a freezing wall, making him feel naked against the elements. He had never felt cold like this. Immediately, he noticed he was climbing as the snow was deeper on this street. He saw the sign for the pharmacy, "Thank fuck!" he yelled into his scarf, but even if someone stood by his side, he would not be heard in this storm.

Then he noticed them up ahead, right at the end of the street, five RAMs. He let out a groan. For the time being, he had gone unseen, but his luck never lasted. He continued, and the white deluge came head-on, but he kept going. He had no option, and when the RAMs saw him, he would have no option but to deal with them too. He was on a life or death mission, and he was prepared to pay the latter if it came to it in order to try and save his sister.

The cold, harsh, biting, freezing snow had no effect on the creatures. They just wandered aimlessly searching for prey. Then one turned in Mike's direction. Mike stopped. The snow kept coming at him like a hail of bullets, but he just stood there, ready to fight.

The beast then turned in the other direction and carried on down the street and out of sight, its four companions joining it.

Mike continued to stand there, confusion reigned on his face. He was sure the RAM had looked straight at him. *Why had it not attacked?* After a moment, he continued into the blizzard, the freezing air tore at the back of his throat despite the scarf. Mike was a very fit guy, but these conditions, this hike was making him gasp for breath.

Finally, he reached the pharmacy. The steel roller shutters protecting the two large windows and front door were both locked. The last time he had been here, he had only seen the sign, never the storefront. He closed his eyes, and for a moment the snow and wind were forgotten. "Why is everything a fight?" he sighed. He dropped to his knees and started digging the snow like an excited dog digging sand at the beach. Handful after handful he scraped behind him, burrowing deeper towards the pavement and whatever lock was stopping the shutter from pulling open. Finally, he reached the bottom. He could feel the sweat pouring down his back. The lock was part of the shutter. He was hoping there would be a hasp and padlock, but this made it more difficult. *Why would it be easy? Nothing else was.*

The snow continued to drive against him, freezing him, impairing his visibility, but he carried on. He removed a long-handled crowbar from his rucksack and slid it under the roller shutter, then he pulled with all his strength. Mike felt his muscles straining. "Fuck!" he shouted, releasing the crowbar. He rested his hands on his knees for a moment to catch his breath, before trying again.

"Damn you!" he shouted, and this time unleashed five heavy punches against the roller shutter. "Well you're not gonna keep me out," he said, throwing the crowbar back into the rucksack and pulling out his shotgun. He looked up, then down the street, it was all clear. This was a risk worth taking. He pumped it and fired where the lock was, a big hole appeared. He tried lifting the shutter but to no avail. He fired another round and this time, most of the bottom of the shutter disintegrated. He pulled it up revealing a reflection of himself in the glass door. He let out a small laugh. No wonder the RAMs didn't see him. He was white from head to foot. The snow had clung to his clothes, his hat, his scarf, only leaving his plastic goggles and the small section of his upper cheeks clear. He put the shotgun back in the rucksack, removed the crowbar once again and in a single, powerful blow, shattered the glass.

Mike dragged what remained of the shutter down behind him, flicked on his torch and stepped inside. It was icy cold, but at least for the time being, he was not being bombarded by snow. He stamped his feet and patted his coat and trousers heavily, making a white pile on the carpet in front of him. He took off his gloves and put them in his pocket before blowing into his hands and rubbing them almost as if trying to start a fire with two pieces of wood. Mike raised his goggles and unzipped his coat reaching into his inside pocket for Lucy's note.

LEVOFLOXACIN.

"Okay," said Mike, watching his frosty breath dance in the torchlight. The pharmacy didn't appear to have been touched. The shelves were still stocked. At the counter, there was an array of cough syrups, tablets, all in one flu powders, pain relief gels, and if he had time and space, he would have grabbed all of them to take back. He went behind the counter and into the back room. Lucy had told him that the different categories would be laid out in sections. Injectables would be in one, drugs to use externally in another and so on. He looked at the header boards at the top of the shelving units. "Stupefacients? What the bloody hell's a stupefacient?" Then he saw it "Oral use. Bingo!"

Lucy had told him that once he found the right section, everything should be laid out alphabetically. Mike panned his torch down the shelving unit. "Levothyroxin, back, back, back. Ha! Gotcha!" he said pulling twenty long thin boxes from the racks. He retrieved a folded plastic rubble sack from his inside pocket and placed the boxes carefully inside. Then he shone the torch around again, looking at the header boards. He walked across to the injectables section and found four phials of Levofloxacin there too. Lucy had told him, if Sammy got any worse, injecting it into her system might be the only way to help her. He pulled some packs of disposable syringes from the shelves and put those in his bag as well. When this winter was over, they would come back here and empty this place. This could stock the Safe Haven hospital for years.

Mike stopped again at the back of the sales counter. He got a few packets of the strongest over-the-counter pain meds and anti-inflammatories he could. Then he threw some antiseptic creams, TCP and bandages into the bag. He wrapped the ample plastic of the rubble sack around his supplies and placed it in his rucksack, before heading back to the entrance.

Mike looked at the hole in the base of the roller shutter. Snow had started to come in from outside already. He put his gloves back on, pulled his goggles down, lifted the shutter and stepped out into the furious storm once more.

No sooner was he outside than he heard something other than the whistle of the wintry conditions that had been his constant companion since he left Emma. He looked up the street. At least twenty RAMs were battling through the snow to reach him, the sound of the shotgun had alerted them to the proximity of living prey. He turned to head the other way and stopped mid-stride as double that number were racing towards him from that direction.

"Oh fuck!" was all he could say.

7

"Who the hell is it?" demanded Emma, focussing all her attention on the gap in the door.

"Em?" asked a familiar female voice.

"Beth? Is that you?"

The door swung wide open and Beth rushed in. Even though she had tried to shake herself free, snow still clung to many parts of her outer clothing, but she could not stop herself running to Emma and flinging her arms around her friend. She kissed her on the cheek and pulled back, looking down at Emma's raised foot. "What the hell happened? And where's Mike?" asked Beth looking around the room.

Just then, Hughes, Barnes and Shaw all entered. Their faces lit up for a moment, but then the happiness dipped as they saw Emma's foot.

"What the hell happened?" demanded Hughes, brushing snow from his clothes, and heading towards Emma to give her one of his famous bear hugs.

"How the hell did you find me?" asked Emma.

"A while longer, and we might not have done, but we could still make out prints in the snow. There aren't exactly a lot heading from the bridge into the city," said Shaw.

"I can't tell you how good it is to see you," replied Emma.

"Don't tell me soft lad's out there by himself in this?" asked Hughes.

Emma nodded, "Yes."

"Bollocks!" replied Hughes.

***

"Are you two alright there?" George asked Annie and John, Beth's sister and brother.

"Yes, thank you," replied Annie in a broad Yorkshire accent as the two children continued their task of sorting screws into different sizes and jars.

George had grandchildren in the world before. How he wished he had never moved to Inverness. His life had been lonely after his Susan had passed away. Then he met his old childhood sweetheart at a school reunion and moved to the city to be with her. Childhood memories are always painted in sweet pastel colours, but sometimes they are stark and painful. George found out the hard way, but by then it was too late.

Oh! how he hoped his son and family were okay. He remembered back to the last conversation he ever had with them. He was on speakerphone, and he just managed to tell them that he loved them before the line went dead.

What he would not give to tell them that to their faces now. He took a deep breath. He could not let himself get upset in front of Annie and John.

"How about we go wash our hands and go have a bite to eat?" he said.

Annie and John were used to staying with Sammy and Jake when Beth was not around, but they were sick, so Beth had asked George instead. Annie thought it was going to be boring, but it was quite a lot of fun. Beth had made them pack books they had already read and games they could not stand the sight of. George, though, had different plans for them. He ran a big workshop that fixed cars, motors, nearly everything that was broken, and Annie and John were helping him. Sorting screws was very important.

George looked out at the settling snow. "Maybe we should shut the doors early today, eh?" He walked to the front of the large workshop, closed the double doors and guided the two children through the back doors and into the attached cottage. The heat from the black wrought iron solid fuel stove hit them like a wave as they walked in, and they all immediately discarded their outer layers of clothing. The children went and sat on the couch, while George headed to the kitchen and started making sandwiches.

Just then, there was a knock on the door. It was Lucy and Talikha. "Beth asked me to check in on Annie and John," said Lucy.

"Come on in," said George, "I'm just making a cuppa and a sandwich. Could I interest you ladies in one of each?"

"Actually, I wouldn't say no," replied Lucy.

"That would be very nice," said Talikha.

"You'd better come in then," said George with a smile on his face. The two women stood with him while he made the sandwiches. "I thought you'd be down at the hospital."

"To be honest, there's not a lot I can do down there until we get some proper meds. Dora and a couple of her buddies are doing a great job. Plus, they live at the campground, and the way this snow is coming down, I don't really want to get stranded there when Sammy is the way she is," said Lucy.

"I'm guessing that means she's not getting any better then?" asked George looking up from the sandwich he was cutting.

"If Mike doesn't get these meds, I don't see her getting through this," said Lucy in a voice barely above a whisper.

George put the knife down and rested his hands on the counter. "Oh, dear god," he said. "Poor little mite."

"I know."

"But this is Mike we're talking about. If anyone can get this medication it's him," said George.

"I hope you're right, I really do."

***

Mike stood there frozen, not because of the cold, but because of his choices. Going back into the pharmacy would seal his fate. He would never escape, but what else could he do? His speed and agility were rendered useless in these conditions. The thick snowy carpet and vicious blizzard slowed him to the same pace as anyone...or anything.

Suddenly, he was deaf to the growls, the wind, even his own laboured breaths beneath the scarf. He watched the snow, but he didn't feel it any longer as it whipped and lashed at his skin. If he could not this medicine to his little sister, she would die. If she died, that would be the end for him. He would have broken his promise to Alex. "Fuck it!"

He marched into the middle of the street, pulled the rucksack from his shoulders and placed it down on the ground. He pulled the Glock Seventeen out of the bag and put the spare magazine and a handful of shotgun shells in his pocket. He really wished Lucy was with him. She was an amazing shot. Mike was average at best, but anything was better than nothing. The creatures were still too far back to hit with any degree of accuracy, especially in these conditions, so he waited. Moving in either direction would do nothing but exert his own energy. This was his last stand, and that's just what he was going to do...stand.

***

Hughes and Barnes ploughed through the snow as fast as their legs would carry them. It wasn't difficult to see evidence of Mike's movements. Although the RAMs in school uniforms had been pretty well covered by a fresh layer of snow, Hughes and Barnes shot each other relieved glances. They were all down and there was a trail of footprints heading away from the carnage. The snow had done its best to cover them, but to the two soldiers, it was obvious who they belonged to. If nothing else, it meant that Mike was okay, for the time being at least. The wind at their backs had begun to ease slightly, and the snow was falling straighter now. The cold was still biting and harsh, but both were military men and knew how to dress to conditions.

"You ever wonder how the hell he's still alive?" asked Barnes.

"He doesn't know how to give up," replied Hughes. "That's the reason we're all still here. The day Mike dies, that's the day hope dies for all of us."

"Well, let's pray to God that's not today, because this is fucking mental."

The two of them continued in silence, stretching, leaning, negotiating their way through the drifts. They controlled their breathing. They remembered back to their training. It was a long time ago now, but some things they would never forget.

"You do realise, somebody's going to have to explain to him that there is no way he can get back home," said Barnes.

"Yeah," replied Hughes. "I think we might draw straws for that one."

Suddenly, shots rang out.

"What the fuck?" cried Barnes.

"That sounds like a Glock," replied Hughes.

"Where's it coming from?"

"Dunno, but when those shots stop, we're going to be too late."

***

Mike fired, hitting the first RAM in the neck. There was a red splat on the snowy mound behind the creature and a momentary pause as its momentum was interrupted, but then it carried straight on towards its prey. Mike steadied his hand and fired again. This time, it hit the beast in the middle of the forehead. Another red blotch appeared on the snow long before the RAM hit the ground.

Mike fired again at the next RAM, missing completely, then again, hitting its shoulder, then again, hitting its head. *Five bullets used, two RAMs down.* "Fuck!" At this rate he'd need more than three hundred bullets, and including the shotgun shells, he might have forty at the most.

The progress of the creatures was slow. It seemed like mother nature was the great leveller. Mike turned to look at the RAMs heading towards him from the opposite end of the street. They were still not an imminent threat. He turned back and in all the madness, had not noticed the wind had calmed, and the icy flakes were not as cutting. He aimed and fired at the next creature, no more than fifteen metres back. Lucky shot. Went down in one. The next, two shots, the next one, the next three. Before Mike knew it, he was changing magazines.

He started again, one down, two down, three down, four down, five down, six, empty. "Fuck!" he growled, and quickly replaced the Glock with the pump-action shotgun. It boomed like a cannon, and just then he noticed more RAMs had started coming around the corner at the far end of the street. He turned and saw the other group getting nearer and nearer. They would have to be dealt with soon too. He looked beyond them and saw more creatures appearing at the other end of the street.

This was it. This was how it was going to end.

***

"Get down," hissed Hughes, and he and Barnes dived onto their bellies, losing themselves in the snowy landscape.

The ring road was in view now, but so was a procession of RAMs heading towards the sound of a booming shotgun. The two soldiers rolled over towards a large snowdrift and sat there for a moment while they collected their thoughts.

"What are we going to do?" asked Barnes.

Hughes slid up and twisted around, inching his head over the top of the drift. The creatures had slowed from their usual sprint because of the thick snow, but they were relentless, and there was a steady stream. "Honestly, Barney, I don't know."

He slid back down and looked across at his friend. "That's his shotgun," said Barnes as another thunderous boom echoed. "It sounds like he's a couple of streets away."

"I know."

"He won't have many rounds left."

"I know," said Hughes, barely audible now as he sank into his thoughts.

"Even if we could do something, by the time we get there, it will be too late."

"I know, Barney." Hughes turned to look at his friend with tears in his eyes.

Barnes had known Hughes a long time. Hughes was a real tough nut, a real fighter, nothing phased him, so when he saw his friend crying, he knew it was to mourn, to honour the death of one of their own.

The blasts from the shotgun stopped. The two of them sat with their backs to the snowdrift, listening to the increasing volume from the growls of a legion of RAMs.

***

"Bollocks!" shouted Mike, as he realised he had used his last shell. He crouched down, placed the shotgun into the rucksack and retrieved the two machetes. He took hold of the rucksack and threw it over towards the entrance of the pharmacy. The last thing he needed was to be tripping up if he was at least going to put on one final show.

The RAMs continued to come at him from both sides. The first, blade through the eye. The second, sliced through the temple. The third, straight beneath the chin. Each time a creature fell, the snow turned a little pinker. Each time a creature fell, Mike felt more drained. He had expended a lot of energy just negotiating these conditions, but now he was in a battle for his life with untold numbers of these things.

Two came at him at once. He managed to dispatch one with a fast swipe, cutting straight through the brainstem as he ducked its attack. The second lunged, and Mike lost his balance. He went over in the snow with the creature on top of him, snapping like a starving piranha. He used all his strength just to stop the teeth from ripping into the flesh of his face. He was holding his machetes in front of him, pushing the creature up, and not getting enough momentum, to push it off and make a decisive blow. Mike began to growl in anger, out-matching the beast's own sounds for volume.

Suddenly, he was aware of many more growls as the

procession of RAMs from both sides got nearer and nearer. The sounds of the beast on top of him and those of the advancing hordes were vibrating through the freezing air with more ferocity than ever. The crunch of the icy snow beneath their feet sounded like a single vast machine, crushing, destroying everything in its path. After all, these creatures seemed to have but one purpose, to infect the living and to that end, they were one.

Everything slowed down as Mike looked up at the RAM he was fending off. It's snarling face, its filthy yellow and brown gnashing teeth, its opaque grey eyes with those eerie shattered pupils; if there was a place such as Hell, then these things were born there. He shifted as the beast thrust a grabbing hand towards his face, and in an effort to misdirect its blow, the machete handles fell from his hands into the snow. He felt the cold wind of the movement as the RAM's grey fingers plunged into the icy white carpet inches from him. He looked back at the ghoul's face as it closed in on him once again; it's heavy frame, the snow, and the beast's violent jerky movements all contributed to Mike's inability to shake it off.

Suddenly, another creature joined them on the floor, down on all fours, trying to barge its way into the action like a clumsy dog. Mike turned his head slightly and caught sight of more and more feet not far away now. He took one of his hands from the first attacker and brought his fist down on the head of the other with all his might before it could shuffle fully into position. It fell on its face dazed for a moment before beginning to scramble to its knees once more.

The first creature swiped at Mike again, burying its other hand in the snow, and now Mike was pinned between its two arms. He heard the crunching trudge of a thousand more feet begin to close in as his final breaths drew nearer.

The second creature's growl rose in its throat, and Mike caught even more movement out of the corner of his eye. Then everything went silent.

8

"Come on," said Barnes, "We're going to have to head back mate."

"Head back?"

"We can't stay out here, there are hundreds of those bloody things...more than hundreds," replied Barnes.

"Barney," said Hughes, still with tears in his eyes, "we've just lost Mike. He's gone."

"You and me have lost mates in battle before, Hughesy. This is no different. If we don't want to end up like him, we need to get moving," he said putting a hand on his friend's shoulder. "Mike would want us to protect Emma. Get her back to Safe Haven."

Hughes sat for a short while and wiped the warm tears from his face. The last shot had sounded several minutes ago now, and although they could not see how many RAMs were massing, they could hear their deathly chorus rise into the wintry sky. "We're going to lose Sammy as well," said Hughes, not to Barnes, but to himself.

The snow continued to fall around them. The bleak iciness penetrating their very souls. Neither of them doubted for a moment that if it was not for Mike, Safe Haven would not be. With great certainty, both of them believed things would never be the same again, and now, hearing the words out loud... *we're going to lose Sammy as well*—neither of them doubted that this could be the end of a chapter. "Maybe not," said Barnes. "There's got to be some way we can get back. There's got to be some way we can find those meds and get back Hughesy. This is down to us now. You, me, Shaw. We can't have come so far to lose. Look what we've done. Look what we've fought for and achieved. We have to keep on fighting."

Hughes turned to look at him. His eyes were still wet, and when he spoke there was an unfamiliar resignation in his voice. "Look around you," he said, gesturing towards the fast laying snow. "We're going to be trapped here until this thaws, and who knows when that will be? Christ! I've been on exercises in Estonia in the dead of winter and I've not known anything like this. We could be here for bloody weeks."

"Mike wouldn't give up, neither should we, we owe him that."

"Mike didn't give up. Now look where he is, look where we are." Hughes swivelled around and slid up the drift again. "They're not looking in this direction, they're heading towards where they heard the noise. Let's get back, we're going to have to tell Emma."

"Shit, Hughesy, we tell her Mike's dead, and we're stuck in this bloody city, then we're telling her Sammy's dead too."

"Jesus, don't you think I know that? Don't you think I know what's going on? It's not just Sammy. We're going to lose a lot of people to this, young and old. Things were just getting good for us too. People were just starting to get a little more positive. This will set everything back. We destroyed an army of vicious marauders, but we can't kill some microscopic ones. People are going to start losing hope again," said Hughes.

***

Raj sat by the side of Jake as he watched the youngster struggle to breathe. Short, sharp snatches passed to and from his mouth, almost as if the air was being sucked from the room. Raj put his hand on the child's head, he was burning up. All this time, the big worry had been Sammy, she had been the one struggling, wearing her body out the fastest as the infection took hold with an iron grip, but now it was Jake who looked at bigger risk. Raj sat there on the bed as the grey afternoon sky was barely visible through the thick snowfall. Humphrey came across and rested his chin on the vet's knee. Raj gently stroked the Lab's golden head. Nothing was surer to relax him in hard times, nothing was surer to help him think. He looked down into the dog's big brown eyes.

"In that young head, there is a wise old brain my friend," he said looking down at Humphrey. "You are right, we must go. We must take them to the hospital. There is oxygen there. At the very least we might be able to help him breathe." Raj wrapped the damp quilt tightly around Jake's feverish body and carried him out of the room, down the stairs and out into the cold air.

"It's f-f-freezing," said Jake, still stuttering for breath through chattering teeth. He had not had the same drugs Sammy had been given, and he remained semi-conscious, albeit delirious a lot of the time when he had spoken. "Where are we going, Mike?"

Raj looked into Jake's eyes. They were dancing. His pupils focussed on nothingness as false truths engraved themselves into his memory. "It's alright Jake. It's me Raj. Remember? Your friend Raj."

"Cold. So cold. Can't breathe," he rasped.

"It's okay Jake, we're going to see Lucy. She's going

to help you with your breathing." Raj opened the back of the Range Rover where Humphrey normally sat during journeys and placed the little figure down gently. He tapped the carpet next to Jake, and the Labrador jumped up and nestled down next to the child like he knew it was his job to keep him warm. Raj noticed for the first time how deep the snow was getting as he made his way back to the cottage to get Sammy. He looked up to the sky. There was still plenty more to come if he didn't get the children to hospital now, it was possible he might not be able to later.

Sammy's condition had not changed since Lucy had left. She was a fighter, just like her older brother. Her eyelids fluttered as her body battled with everything it had. The drugs had left her unconscious, barring the odd few moments of lucidity here and there. In his life, Raj had never seen a flu like this. Not in India, not in the UK.

Raj laid Sammy down in the back seat of the car and jumped into the driver's seat. The wheels started to spin as he set off up the incline to reach the main road, but it was nothing that the four-wheel-drive vehicle could not handle, for the time being anyway.

***

Jules stood on the north ridge. A vast biting winter desert laid out in front of her, getting deeper by the minute. An older man and woman came and stood beside her. The three of them watched as the snowstorm of the century covered everything. Flakes of arctic cold landed on their faces, sending shivers through their bodies.

"I've sent my three idiot brothers to the west ridge, they're relieving Katy and Mac. Are you sure you're happy sticking it out here?" asked Jules. "It's not too late. I can radio in and get some cover out here to replace the two of you. It could be a long haul. This storm doesn't look like it's going to be stopping any time soon," said Jules.

"You've brought us enough supplies to last a month, we'll be fine," said Don lifting the tarpaulin from the back of the pickup.

"C'mon," said Mary, "We'd better get this stuff inside before it gets any worse. "You've got a distance to cover before dark," she said to Jules.

"It's a lot better up here now since we built the cabin. I don't think we would have lasted long in a tent," joked Don.

"That's our Mike. He's always thinking ahead. We were in the midst of summer. Fuckin' midges were biting the tits off us and he goes, *we need to build some log cabins for the lookout posts for the winter.* Right there and then I thought I was going to swing for him. We'd come out of that battle. We'd built polytunnels and prepared fields. We'd rebuilt homes, walls, fences, we were all knackered, and he says that to us," said Jules with a smile on her face.

"I remember," replied Mary, laughing. "It was at that barbecue we had at the beach that Sunday afternoon. It was the first afternoon we'd had off in weeks, and the Martins wanted to thank everyone for helping them with their roof…" she stopped and chuckled to herself. "I thought you were going to stab him with your fork."

"He has no idea how fucking close he came. But look," she said putting a box down on the sturdy wooden table and gesturing around the two-room cabin. "I'm willing to put my hand up when I'm wrong. Lookouts are vital for Safe Haven. They're our early warning system.

There's no way you guys could stay up here without this place." Jules looked towards the wood-burning stove crackling away and the pile of logs in the corner. There was a big pan of soup simmering, and the smell made Jules's mouth water. "He's got a gift for seeing what's needed for this community. I don't always agree with him, and sometimes the little pisser drives me mad, but we'd be lost without him."

"Very true," said Don, heading back outside with Mary to grab another box.

"I'd be lost without him," said Jules to herself.

9

Something cut through the silence like a knife. A whistle. Mike turned his head slightly as he caught movement from the corner of his eye. He bludgeoned the second creature on top of the head again as hard as he could, stunning it once more. He dug his left foot into the snow compacting it with all his strength and pushed, simultaneously grabbing the freezing cold handle of one of the machetes. Mike forced the creature pinning him down upwards with all his might. Its frigid, decayed hands grasped at the air next to his face as the momentum released them from the snow. Mike plunged the machete blade into the beast's skull, rolling over at the same time. The RAM flopped to the ground, and Mike had a secondary pause as he looked towards the others closing in on him. They were mere feet away now. He grabbed the other machete, arcing it down and slicing the top of the head clean off the second creature that had attacked him.

Mike looked to where he had seen movement. A rope hung down to the ground from the roof of the empty store next to the pharmacy. On the roof itself stood a hooded figure looking straight towards him. Light snow fluttered around her.

There was no time to lose, the creatures were upon him. He ran into two of them, palming them off like he was on a rugby field. He booted another one off its feet, then, hearing a growl behind him, turned and swiping through the air at the same time with his machete, cut a gory trail through its head, causing it to drop to the ground. He swooped down and grabbed a strap from his rucksack, flinging it over his shoulder.

Another RAM came at him and got a blade thrust up through its nose straight into the brain. Then another attacker appeared, he was about to raise his machete again, and suddenly, he heard a different whistle, and a split second later, an aluminium bolt cracked through the top of the beast's skull.

Mike looked up and down the street. There were hundreds of RAMs. Far more than he could fight alone. He looked towards the rope, then at the hooded figure on the roof. Whatever lay in wait at the end of that rope had to be better than this. He began to climb, pressing his booted feet hard against the brick surface of the wall. The growls intensified below him, and he heard more whistles as a second and third bolt rained down.

Mike felt the rope begin to sway as a hand from below grabbed it, but he kept his fists gripped tightly around the coarse woven fabric. After what seemed like an age, he clambered over the ledge and onto the flat roof. A teenage girl pointed two one-handed crossbows straight at him.

"Drop your weapons and bag on the floor," she said.

Mike looked at the aluminium bolts. She had

managed to take out at least one RAM with a bullseye shot at thirty feet, he was pretty certain she could make the same shot at ten feet with no problem. He dropped the machetes and slid the rucksack from his back.

"You're not going to try anything stupid?" she asked.

"Erm...no!" replied Mike.

She regarded him for some time, holding her weapons steadily. The snow continued to fall around them.

"Who are you? What are you doing here?" she demanded.

"My name's Mike, I needed medicine for my sister," he said.

"Where's she?"

"Back home."

"Where's home?"

"The coast."

"Whereabouts?"

"Wick," he lied.

"Is it just you and your sister?"

"Yes."

"What's wrong with her?"

"She's got an infection. She's bad."

The crossbow wavered for a moment, and for the

first time Mike looked beyond it to the girl asking him the questions. She wore a three-quarter length hooded coat with a tied belt around the waist. Her black zipped boots went up to the knees of her skintight blue jeans. Covering her eyes was a pair of ski goggles. Those and the hood meant he could not see much of her, but the impression, from the skin and bone structure he could see suggested that she was a striking-looking young woman.

"What's her name?"

"Emma."

"What's your name?" asked Mike.

"We're not making friends here," the girl said. "I'm just figuring out if you're with them or whether you're for real."

"What are you talking about? With who?"

The young woman continued to look at him. "Back up," she said, and Mike took a few paces back. She walked forward and crouched down, placing one of the crossbows on the snow while beginning to search through his rucksack. "Your accent. You're not from around here." She stood up again. "Well?"

"Well what?" asked Mike.

"I said you're not from around here."

"I know, I heard you. What do you want me to say?"

"I asked you a question," she said raising the crossbows once more.

"No you didn't. You made a statement. Where are

you from? Is a question. You're not from around here is a statement," replied Mike.

"You try to piss off a girl who's got two crossbows pointing at you, not very smart is it? Now that's a question."

"Look. I don't know who these people are that you're talking about. I came into the city for medicine for my sister. Believe me, don't believe me, I don't really care. I need to get back to her," he said.

"To Wick? In this?" she asked. "What are you going to do, fly?"

Mike looked out across the white city below him. "I've got to find a way," he said to himself more than the girl.

"Those medicines in the bag. There's a lot there for one person don't you think?"

"I don't see any new chemists opening soon, do you? If one of us gets ill again we may not be able to find any. Thought it made sense to stock up while I could," said Mike.

"How do you know to get those drugs? I've never heard of them."

"My sister...she's a qualified pharmacist. She told me to get them," said Mike. "Now who are these other people you're talking about?"

"There's a gang, twenty or so. They took my dog, but I managed to get him back. They live on the outskirts, on the other side of town in some luxury flats, but they come into the city now and again. If they catch you, you're done for." she said.

"How do you know?"

"I've seen them. I've seen them kill a man, and they took his woman off kicking and screaming," she said, suddenly looking sad.

"How did you get your dog back?"

"I tracked them, and when night came, I sneaked in," she said, looking even sadder. "That woman, I heard her cries. I wish I could have done something, there were just too many, and she was in somebody's flat, Wolf was tied up in the entrance."

"Wolf? Is that your dog's name?"

The girl nodded. Suddenly, the frost within her melted and she placed one, then the other single-handed crossbow into the bag that hung at her side. "Yes."

"What breed?"

"German Shepherd."

Although he could not see her eyes, he maintained contact with where he thought they were as he bent down to retrieve his rucksack and then the machetes. He put the rucksack on his back, crisscrossed the machete handles into it, and took off his right glove. He offered the girl his hand. "As I said, I'm Mike."

She paused for a moment, took off her right glove and shook it. "Wren. I'm Wren," she said.

"Okay Wren, thank you for saving my life," said Mike.

"You were an idiot to use a gun to get through that shutter," she said.

"I thought the sound might be masked by the storm," he replied.

"That worked well didn't it?"

Mike smiled. "So where do we go now?"

"We?" she said.

"I'm guessing you know a way down from here that doesn't involve us climbing into a crowd of bloodthirsty zombies."

"Is that a question?" Mike smiled again. She smirked, pulling her scarf up over her face. "C'mon, it's this way," she said, heading across the snow-covered rooftop. The row of retail units had one continuous flat roof, punctuated only by the odd ventilation or heating duct. Wren walked to the edge and picked up a large ladder which she turned and stretched across to the next building, making sure the brackets fell into place so it would not slip off the edge if there was a jerky movement.

"Be careful, it can be a bit tricky the first time," she said, kneeling down on the frame and starting to shimmy over the rungs. She got to the other end and signalled for Mike to head across. He mimicked her movements. The area below was an empty white courtyard. A small alleyway ran off it, but there were no RAMs and even though their growls could still be heard, he could feel his heartbeat beginning to settle to a more normal pace. He climbed off the rickety bridge and Wren retrieved the ladder carrying it across to the other side of the building.

"You're pretty strong," said Mike.

"What, for a girl you mean?"

"No...I know plenty of strong girls. I mean, you are

strong," said Mike.

"Whatever," she said, stretching the ladder across to the opposite rooftop. "I was in training for the next Commonwealth games when all this went down."

"What was your event?"

"Heptathlon."

"Bloody 'ell," replied Mike. "Impressive."

"Yeah...well...lot of good it did me," she replied.

"You've survived this long out here. I'd say it's served you pretty well," replied Mike.

"Maybe."

"You were pretty handy with those crossbows too. Don't remember that being an event in the heptathlon," said Mike.

"You can either teach yourself the skills you need to survive or you can die. There isn't really another option is there?"

"Suppose not," said Mike, climbing onto the horizontal ladder and shimmying across.

Wren reached the other side and a wave of guilt hit Mike. He took her by the arms and stared through the green ski goggles. Look, I'm sorry, I've not been honest with you."

"Duhh!" replied Wren. "You talking about the girl you left in the Carpet warehouse? Was that your sister or your bird?"

Mike laughed and spluttered at the same time.

"How long were you following me?"

"Long enough," replied Wren.

"So all that stuff about the others?"

"Might have been a setup, but the more I spoke to you, the more I realised you were pretty clueless," she said, heading towards an external fire escape. She started to descend, and Mike walked across the snowy roof to follow her.

She went down one flight then climbed through an open window into an apartment. As Mike climbed through, he noticed a mound of snow on the beige carpet. "Leave a crack in the window," said Wren as she turned on the Calor gas heater. Heat and fumes began to mix with the frigid air within the flat as the two of them sank into a deep, luxurious two-seater sofa.

"She's my sister," said Mike.

"She's sick?"

"No. She's hurt. My other sister's sick," he replied.

"You have two sisters."

"And a brother."

"And?"

"And a girl who I'd kill or die for."

"And?"

"And a family, I didn't realise I had. They just kind of crept up on me."

"I see," replied Wren.

"And I really need your help to get back to them."

10

"I'm back!" shouted Sarah as she walked through the front door. She kicked the snow from her boots and headed into the kitchen, putting the large bucket of mussels down on the table. "It's bloody freezing out there, but I got a good haul from the rocks." She bent down and opened the door to the range. The glow immediately warmed her face, and she put her hands out too. "I'm going to make a cuppa," she shouted. "Anybody want one?" She waited for a response and when none came, she went to look in the living room. There was no sign of anybody there.

"Hello?" she called as she headed up the stairs. "Raj? Anybody?" She walked first into Jake's room and saw not only was the child missing, but his sheets as well. She felt her heart begin to beat faster as she rushed down the landing to Sammy's room. Once again, the bed was empty.

"Hello?" she called, more desperately now. "Hello?" She ran back down the stairs two at a time, and nearly stumbled as she rushed out into the cold. It was only then she noticed Raj's Range Rover was gone. "Oh shit!"

***

The narrow road became even narrower with the snowfall. Despite the Range Rover being a four-wheel drive, it still careened all over as it headed towards the village. Raj looked at Sammy resting peacefully in the back seat, then looked beyond, only being able to hope that Jake was managing to hold on.

He negotiated a bend and suddenly, another vehicle was on top of him. He jammed on the brakes and the wheels instantly locked. He watched as the other car suffered the same fate and both vehicles slid towards each other shovelling snow into the air, spinning side on and smashing metal against metal as Raj's left side collided with Lucy and Talikha's right side.

He waited until the Range Rover came to a stop and then climbed out into the freezing snow. He walked to the other car and opened the passenger door, crouching down next to Talikha.

"Are you alright my love?" he asked her. For a moment she seemed dazed, but then she came to her senses and her eyes met his. He smiled, that's all he could ever do when he looked into her eyes. He looked across to Lucy who was rousing herself. "Are you okay Lucy?" She waved her hand as if to say *give me a minute*, and then he turned and went to the back of his car. He opened the hatchback and Humphrey looked up towards him. Jake's eyes were fluttering, not as a result of the collision, but due to his illness.

Lucy opened her door as the snow kept falling. She looked flustered and shaken, but staggered around the front of the vehicle and headed across to the Range Rover.

"What's going on? Is Sammy okay?" she asked, joining Raj.

"Jake has taken a turn. He is struggling to breathe. Sammy is the same."

"What?"

"Yes."

Lucy immediately put her hands around Jake's face. "He's scalding."

The child continued to stutter for breath, gasping for gulps of freezing air like a fish out of water.

"I think oxygen would help, yes?" asked Raj.

Lucy looked at Raj. "Right now, I think anything would help," she said, shaking herself out of her daze. "You okay to follow us back to the hospital?"

"Of course," replied Raj, "This is the finest British engineering," he replied.

"Uh-huh," she replied, "that's why I'm asking you."

Raj smiled. "Yes Lucy, we will meet you at the hospital."

Lucy returned to her small car. She would not be able to travel much further in these conditions. It didn't even have winter tyres. There were dents and scrapes all up one side, and as she got in and turned the key, she heard a clanging sound like something had dislodged in the engine. She managed to stutter the car to the snow-covered verge.

"C'mon, we're getting a ride," she said, reaching into the back seat for her doctor's bag.

Talikha climbed out of the car and slid on some compacted snow. Raj was just setting off, but pulled on the handbrake and immediately got out to help her to her feet. "Are you alright?" he asked.

She got to her feet laughing a little. "I am fine. Just clumsy." The pair looked at each other and Raj leaned in to kiss her.

"We're going to have to ride with you Raj. I think my car has gone to that great junkyard in the sky."

"Very well," he said nodding, and guided his wife by the arm around to the passenger side of the Range Rover, before rushing back around to help Lucy into the back seat with Sammy.

"Thank you. Always a gentleman," she said, placing her bag in the footwell.

Raj returned to the driver's seat, released the handbrake and the car began to move off. Lucy looked into the back of the vehicle. Jake was still struggling to breathe, Humphrey was lying nestled beside him. She looked down at Sammy, whose face was bright red. "Oh Sammy," she whispered and gently stroked her head.

Lucy looked out of the window at the grey sea. White waves crashed as more snow fell. The wind was coming in fits and starts and a real blizzard was threatening to unleash itself. She looked beyond the waves...thousands of miles beyond them, to her homeland, to her home. She thought of happy summers, she thought of country fairs and freshly made lemonade. She thought of the drive-through theatre and the first time she rode a horse. She thought about her mother's homemade jam and helping her dad repair the family pick-up. She thought about all the happy times. She needed to fill her head with happy times, because right now all she could think about was the future, and the future looked bleak.

Even if Mike found the antibiotics Sammy and Jake needed, there was no chance he was going to get them back here in time. The roads were becoming more impassable by the minute. Sammy and Jake were going to die, as were many in Safe Haven. Mike would never forgive himself, and for a guy who was always on the edge, this would be the final push.

A tear ran down her cheek, and she wiped it away, before checking to make sure Raj had not seen her in the rear-view mirror. Lucy resumed her gaze out across the ocean, but now, she could no longer see the days of happiness she had lived. Everything was sad and grey. Winter had come to Safe Haven, and it was going to last a lifetime.

***

"There was no way you could get to him?" asked Emma.

"The whole place is rotten with those things. We were lucky to get back here without being seen," replied Hughes.

"But you didn't see his body?" asked Emma.

"No," replied Hughes.

"Well, how do you know he's dead?"

"Em, love, there were hundreds of those things all heading towards him. We heard his weapons run dry, I'm all for living in hope, but…"

"He'll find a way," replied Emma.

Beth sat down on the couch next to her and took her hand. She remained silent, convinced her friend was in shock. Denial was often a stage in the loss of a loved one.

Barnes, Shaw and Hughes all looked at each other. "We need to come up with a plan to get out of here," said Shaw, leading the other two men out of the room.

When they were in the large showroom out of earshot, Hughes whispered, "She won't go anywhere if she still thinks he might turn up."

"She's just in shock, that's all," replied Shaw.

Beth came out to join them. "How is she?"

"She reminds me of how Sammy was when we thought Mike was gone back in Skelton. She refused to believe he was dead. Turns out she was right," said Beth.

"This is different though," said Hughes.

"How?" asked Beth.

"Because...you weren't there. There's no way he could have survived."

"You might be right. She might be right. We'll know soon enough. In the meantime, I think we should get comfortable," said Beth nodding towards the huge display window at the front of the showroom. The snow had drifted against it leaving just the slimmest of gaps at the top for daylight to fight through.

Beth turned around and headed back to the canteen. The three men watched her go. "She's got a point, I suppose," said Shaw.

"Yeah," replied Hughes, we'd better get some more

wood chopped up and try and get comfortable for the night."

"No, I mean about Mike," replied Shaw.

"Jesus, not you as well. Mike is my friend. It's the last thing I want to believe, but I know what happened," said Hughes. "Now come on, let's get to work."

***

"So, what is this place?" asked Mike looking down at the empty street below.

"This is one of my hidey-holes for when I come into the city and need to catch a breath," replied Wren.

She walked through the flat into the kitchen where she pulled a small camping stove and gas canister out from under the sink. She opened a cupboard and took out two tins of spaghetti hoops. "We'll eat, then I'll get you back to your sister."

Mike leaned against the wall and watched as she took out plates and forks. "So, this is how you live? You keep coming in for supplies like this?"

"There are still plenty to find. I'm okay as long as I stay clear of *them*. But there seem to be more of them than there were," she replied, emptying both tins into a pan, putting it on the stove, and turning on the gas. She retrieved a plastic bag from her inside pocket, pulled out a bag of matches and struck one, causing a blue flame to ignite. She bent down to check it was an even burn, and then leaned back against the sink to look at her guest. She peeled off her hood and ski goggles.

It was only then that Mike realised he was still wearing his and removed them. "So you've got ropes and ladders on the rooftops all over the city?"

"I've got a few," replied Wren.

"That's pretty smart."

"Yeah well, you need to be smart to stay alive these days…which makes me wonder how you've lasted so long."

Mike laughed. "You remind me of someone,"

"Good or bad?"

"Good. But she's a gobby shite too," he said.

Wren's face lit into a smile. She really was striking. "Seriously, though, you can fight. You took out a lot of them."

"When you've got something to fight for it's amazing what you can do. Where's your family?" asked Mike.

"You ask a lot of questions, don't you?" she said pretending to look at the flame again, but knowing there was no need. "We lived in Edinburgh. Things went bad quickly. I'd spent a lot of time up here with my grandad. I hoped he'd still be around. Less populated and all that. No such luck. His neighbourhood was overrun with those things. It was like a war zone. Didn't see the point going anywhere else, so I found a place in the sticks, found Wolf roaming around the next day. Been doing this ever since."

Mike sensed the avoidance, she didn't want to talk about what had happened to her family. "How old are you?"

"You don't stop do you?" said Wren smiling. "I'm

sixteen. My favourite colour is Teal, I'm a Maiden fan, I loved English, hated maths, and all of my time out of school was spent training. That enough, or you want more?"

Mike smiled again. "No, that's enough for now. You're quite...something."

"Yeah...I've got abilities," she said smiling.

"You don't seem sixteen."

"I get that a lot. Well, I used to anyway," she said, taking a fork and starting to stir the spaghetti hoops. She looked out of the kitchen window. She had avoided thinking about the past as much as she could. She had put Edinburgh behind her, but now, it was all raw again. She let out a heavy sigh.

"Is it easy to get back to the carpet showroom from here?" asked Mike.

She snapped out of her sad reflection, this time grateful for the question. "Yeah! Won't take us long," she said. "But you're not going to get any distance in this."

"I'll figure it out," said Mike.

"Figure what out? Unless you've got some superpower you've not told me about, there's no way you're getting back to Wick.

"Actually, it's not Wick we're heading to, it's the west coast," said Mike.

Wren smiled. This guy was a little smarter and a little more paranoid than she had given him credit for. She put the fork down and turned to look at him. "Look out there Mike. I'm assuming that's your real name?" she said with a smile. "I've got what I came in for this time. The two of you can come and stay with me until this storm settles down."

"I have to get back. My sister needs to get these meds."

"Screw it. Do what you want. Die on the road for all I care," said Wren turning her attention back to the pan.

"Come with us."

"What?"

"Come with us to Safe Haven. We have a community. We grow our own food. It's safe. We have defences and lookouts and we live next to the sea. You should come with us. You should be with us. We've even got a hospital and a vet," said Mike.

"I've got my own place," she said, stirring the spaghetti a little faster.

"Okay. Then come visit. Come visit us for a little while," said Mike.

"Wolf too?"

"Of course, Wolf too."

"Family is more than blood, Wren. I know that better than anyone," said Mike.

Wren did not take her gaze away from the pan of spaghetti. She angled her head over it and sniffed the food almost as if she was a chef creating a new signature dish. It took everything she had not to reveal her excitement.

"Well…I could, just for a while. See what you're up to there."

Mike smiled. "Good then."

Wren looked at him and nodded. "Good then."

11

"It's starting to get dark out there, but it looks like the snow's finally stopping," said Beth, walking back into the canteen. Over the past half hour, Emma had got quieter, and as Beth looked at her now, Emma's eyes were closed. Beth doubted that she was asleep, but she knew that with each minute that passed, the likelihood of Mike returning safely diminished that little bit more. Emma closing her eyes to the world was probably all that helped.

"Right," said Hughes, dropping two armfuls of wood and kindling onto the floor. "This should keep us going for the night. Shaw and Barnes came in behind him and shut the door. The temperature in the room, although not scorching, was warmer than the rest of the building thanks to the makeshift stove Mike had built.

Beth and Barnes started pushing two couches nearer to the stove. Shaw and Hughes both slouched into armchairs. "We'll kip here for the night and then figure out what the hell we're doing tomorrow morning," said Shaw.

Emma remained silent. Her eyes remained closed.

The darkness crept into the room, and despite how early it was, the five of them drifted off to sleep.

It was Shaw who awoke first, in a bit of a daze. The room was not in total darkness. The huge amount of snowfall guaranteed whatever small amount of light was given off by any stars that managed to peek through the clouds, reflected.

It was a sound that had woken him. At first, he did not know if it was part of his dream, but then he realised, as he heard more sounds, and voices that he was not dreaming. He reached for his SA80. The glow from the fire revealed the outlines of his friends. He could see Emma's face clearly. Her eyes looked dark. They were open. She was perfectly still, just looking into the glowing embers as they hissed and crackled.

The handle of the canteen door began to turn slowly, and Shaw raised his rifle. The door opened and for a short while, all Shaw could see was blackness in the gap. Then a figure came out of the dark.

"Mike?" said Shaw.

Emma sprang up. "Mike?" she asked excitedly.

Mike looked quizzically towards Shaw who flicked on a lantern. The others roused as they heard Emma almost squeal with excitement. "I knew you'd be okay," she said, clumsily staggering to her feet. She flung her arms around him and kissed him on the cheeks again and again, as more torches and lanterns were switched on.

"What are you guys doing here?" asked Mike, looking around the room towards Hughes, Shaw, Barnes and Beth.

Hughes beamed, "What do you think we're doing.

We've come to help."

"Great job," replied Mike. He squeezed Emma tightly, and helped her back down onto the couch, before embracing the rest of the group with equal vigour.

The door squeaked again as Wren came into the room. "Guys," said Mike, "This is Wren. She saved my life today."

Wren was nervous. Mike had only mentioned his sister and now there were these other people—armed people. But Mike had seemed genuine when he was surprised to see them.

"Saved your life?" asked Emma.

Mike noticed Wren's trepidation and beckoned her to come further into the room. He gently put his arm on her back and moved her forward from the shadows, and into the glow of the fire and lantern light.

"Erm...hi," said Wren.

"Wren lives outside of the city. She comes in for supplies, and lucky for me, she was here today, otherwise, I'd have been well and truly screwed."

"We heard the gunshots, then it all went quiet. Well, as quiet as it gets with hundreds of RAMs kicking about," said Hughes.

Mike sat down next to Emma and held her hand. "Yeah well, that's where Wren came into the equation, it's a long story, but now's not the time. We need to come up with a plan to get the hell out of here and get these meds back."

"Erm, Mike, I don't know if you've seen it outside,

but we'll be lucky to make it a hundred yards in this," said Shaw.

"That's why we need a plan. I've not gone through all this to give up now," he replied.

"Mike!" said Emma. "Think about it. We can't get back while the roads are like this. We're going to have to let them thaw at least a little before we try. Even with a four by four, there's no way we can make the journey."

"She's right, Mike," said Hughes. We had to abandon the minibus coming here. It's snowed a hell of a lot more since. We're stuck here, for a while at least I'm afraid, mate."

"I can't accept that. I won't accept that. If I don't get back, Sammy won't make it. I won't allow that. If I have to walk back, I'll get there," said Mike.

"Mike," said Beth, "think about this. What good will it do for you to go on a suicide mission? Let's just hope, Lucy can stabilise her long enough for things to get a little better for us to travel."

Mike looked around the room. All faces were on him. "This is our sister," he said turning to Emma.

Emma looked at him for a moment, and her eyes welled up. "I know Mike. I know."

***

"This is the last Calor gas canister we have," said Raj, attaching it to the heater.

"Make sure you keep that window open a crack. I know it defeats the object a little, but we can't afford this place filling up with fumes," said Lucy.

Each of the four static caravans that constituted the Safe Haven hospital had been fitted out as self-contained wards. There were two beds in each of the two bedrooms and two more beds in the living room area. Supplies had been scavenged since the founding of Safe Haven from doctor's surgeries, local clinics, in fact anywhere that had anything they could use. They'd even plundered houses for shower curtains that they had fitted on polls around the beds to give patients privacy if needed.

Sammy and Jake had been put in a room to themselves, and this particular static caravan, like two of the others, was now at capacity.

Lucy stood in the doorway and watched as Dora put a cold facecloth first on Jake's head, then on Sammy's. They had given Jake oxygen which had helped, but now he was breathing by himself once more, and although it was laboured, it was not as bad as it had been.

Both children were battling hard, but there was no more anybody could do without the right antibiotics, and with the snow still falling, and a long night ahead, Lucy felt a familiar feeling of hopelessness rise within her. Dora smiled at her as if sensing what she was feeling. Lucy tried to smile back but without success.

"You are doing a great job, Dora," she said, over-emphasising the pronunciation more than she needed to, to make sure the deaf girl could read her lips well enough.

Dora nodded and smiled gratefully in reply, before brushing past her and into one of the other rooms to see how the rest of the patients were getting on.

The familiar thud of Humphrey's feet pounded down the hall, he barged past Lucy, almost taking her legs from under her as he swept into the room, first looking at

Jake, then Sammy's bed before jumping onto the latter and curling up beside the frail-looking girl.

"They seem to be a little more comfortable now, and at least if Jake has difficulties again, he is in the right place for it to be dealt with," said Raj, joining Lucy in the doorway. "I am happy to try and take you home, but you are more than welcome to spend the night at ours. There are plenty of free berths on the yacht."

"Thanks, guys, but I'm going to stay here. I shouldn't have left them before. This is my family, but y'know, the oath and all that. This makes more sense, I can keep an eye on them and everyone else who needs help this way. I've not been thinking straight," said Lucy.

Raj took hold of her hands. "My friend, it is clear to me what is going through your mind. You are thinking that if something happens to Sammy or Jake, it is down to you, it is your responsibility, and that Mike will never forgive you."

Suddenly, Lucy swallowed hard. She tore her eyes away from Raj and looked back into the room, at the two children lying in bed. "I'm scared," she said turning towards him again with a film of tears coating her eyes.

"Lucy, you are a great doctor. You have done everything you can, and you will continue to do so. What happens from here is in the hands of the Gods," said Raj.

"I'm begging you, for all our sakes, don't say that to Mike."

***

Mike sat in the darkness of the showroom by himself. The windows were still covered by the frozen drifted snow, and the cold silence encircled him while the others slept in the canteen. His sister and each of his friends had told him it was impossible to get back to Safe Haven before the snow began to thaw. Each one of them told him he would be a fool to try. Fool or not, doing nothing was not an option. Staying put while his sister withered away would haunt him for the rest of his life. He would rather die trying than live with the alternative.

"I thought I heard you get up," said Wren.

"Bloody hell!" said Mike, "you're like a ninja."

"I'm sorry about your sister."

"I'm trying to wrack my brains, Wren. There's got to be a way to get back to her. There's got to be," said Mike, swivelling around to look at the girl. The pair of them remained in silence for a moment before Mike asked, "will Wolf be okay by himself?"

"When I come here, I keep one of the outbuildings open. I leave plenty of food and water just in case." She paused looking towards the windows. "I don't go out there in the dark. Those things see better than us at night, it's too much of a risk. We should all set off at first light and get back. At least we'll be out of the city and much safer then, while you figure out your next move."

"Thank you again for what you did today, Wren. You really did save my life."

"Don't mention it. That's my good deed for the year," she said smiling. "My place is two miles out of the city. There's fresh running water, fish, it's off the beaten track," she said proudly, before noticing the look on Mike's face. "What is it?"

"I'm not staying. I'm going to get back to my sister," said Mike, "but it would be good for the others to go with you."

An uneasy smile crept across Wren's face. "You're a bit of a psycho aren't you?" she said. "Don't worry, it's not a criticism, but what I mean is you don't give up. You can't give up. I know how that feels. I know where you are coming from. It's what got me so far with my training. It's what drives us to keep going when others stop."

"How old did you say you were again. Sixteen or sixty?" asked Mike.

"Remember, girls develop faster than boys."

"Funny."

"What's your plan then?"

"Haven't got one yet."

"Y'know I told you I was out in the sticks? Granted, I'm not too far out, but there's a big farm near me. I went there once. It was deserted, but they had a huge barn with loads of tractors and stuff. Maybe something there could help?"

Mike jumped to his feet. "Tractors? That's genius. I bet a big tractor could make it through the snow. The tyres on some of those things are massive." He took Wren's head in his hands and kissed her forehead, before walking straight past her and back into the canteen.

Wren stood there for a second with an excited smile. Other than the flat dwellers, who she never wanted to see again, these were the first people she'd had real contact with since she moved here. She liked them, they were good people. She liked Mike. Wren turned and followed him to the canteen. The rest of the group were all sleeping in the dim glow of the fire. Wren watched in the doorway as Mike crouched down by the side of Hughes. He gently roused him and signalled for him to follow. Hughes looked confused at first but then headed out of the room with Mike.

"What is it?" whispered Hughes, as he rubbed his eyes.

"Bruiser, I need your help," said Mike, using the nickname he had given Hughes way back in Candleton.

Hughes used the nightlight function on his watch. "It's quarter to two in the bloody morning, what the hell do you need help with?"

"Wren says there's a farm next to where she lives. They've got a big barn with loads of tractors and stuff."

"And?"

"And a tractor would get me home to Sammy."

Hughes rubbed both his hands over his face and sighed deeply. "Look, Mike, even if there are, chances are the batteries would be dead. You ever tried to push start a tractor in snow?"

"We could take the battery from the Land Rover," said Mike.

"We…" Hughes paused and his brow creased for a second. "Actually, that'd work." He looked back into the room, and the comfortable chair he had slumbered in moments before. "I suppose you're wanting to go right this minute, aren't you?" Mike said nothing. "Stupid question. Okay, I'll wake the others."

"No," said Mike, grabbing hold of his arm. "They'll slow us down. Wren can draw a map, they can follow tomorrow."

"This is why you don't have any friends. Y'know that don't you?" said Hughes.

Mike smiled. "In fairness, yes I do."

The three of them tiptoed back into the room. Wren gripped her mini torch between her teeth, took one of the leaflets, and drew a simple map to her place with a couple of lines of instructions. She placed it on the table in front of Shaw who remained fast asleep. When she was done, she signalled to the two men, who collected their belongings and headed for the door.

"Mike," whispered a voice. Mike turned and Emma was holding her hand out. He grabbed it and sat down beside her.

"I'll meet you out there," whispered Mike to Hughes as he and Wren left the room.

"You're going, aren't you?" asked Emma.

"I think I've found a way. I think I can get back home. Then when things get a bit better, on the roads, you can head back too," said Mike.

Emma looked down at her foot. "I suppose I'd only slow you down."

"Wren's left a map. Head there tomorrow morning. She's got food and supplies. You'll be safe there until things thaw out."

"I love you, Mike."

"Love you, Em."

"Be careful."

"I will."

"Now go save our sister," she said, pulling herself up a little from the couch to kiss him. The two clutched each other for a moment, then Mike laid Emma back down. He looked at the glowing fire and put a heavy chunk of wood into it along with some kindling. The flames caught quickly, and it started to glow brightly once more.

He left the room, pulling the door behind him, making sure not to click it shut and wake the others. "C'mon then," he said to Hughes and Wren, leading the two of them down the hall to the fire exit. He pushed the panic bar and the door opened a little. The three of them felt an arctic breeze brush past them, before Mike pushed the door a little more, displacing enough snow to make a big enough gap for them to squeeze through one by one.

The gentle whoosh of the wind worked its way down the corridor, caressing the walls before pushing through the gap in the entrance to the canteen. The door creaked open a little wider and the flames fanned a little higher before returning to normal.

When the three of them were on the other side, he shoved the door back into place, careful not to make too much noise. He heard the click on the other side and relaxed. "Right then," he said, "lead on Wren."

12

A candle burned in the corner of the room allowing Lucy to see the outline of Dora sitting fast asleep in the armchair by Jake's bed. She was such a sweet kid. Really conscientious. She was an excellent caregiver, and was going to make a great nurse. Lucy's arm draped over Sammy. The young girl's body was still burning up, and her breathing continued to be strained. Lucy lifted her head to look across at Jake, he was the same. She sniffed the air and smelled menthol, then noticed there was a bowl still steaming a little on the bedside cabinet. Dora must have popped some menthol crystals in it to try and ease the children's breathing.

Neither of the children had roused in hours. Without the proper equipment, there was no way of telling, but she was confident they now had some kind of pneumonia. She turned onto her other side and noticed the curtains were open. She could have sworn she'd closed them before getting into bed. The window no longer had snow over it; the Calor gas heater had obviously melted any covering. The sky was now free of clouds. Hopefully there would be no more snow and a thaw could begin. She began to drift off to sleep again but suddenly caught movement and her eyes shot open once more. It was Dora's reflection in the glass, she was standing bolt upright and pointing at Lucy. Lucy swivelled back around onto her other side and felt something wet beneath her. She put her hand on it and saw blood glistening in the candlelight. She looked down at Sammy, who in turn looked up at Lucy with soulless grey eyes. Blood and flesh dripped from her mouth and her lips curled back as a godless growl emanated from the back of her throat, before leaning in to take another bite from Lucy's shoulder.

Lucy woke up with a start. It took her a moment for her breathing to return to normal. She had her arm draped over Sammy and Jake was in the other bed, but there was no sign of Dora. Lucy wiped her forehead, it was really hot, the Calor gas heater had some real power. She could feel her entire right side damp with sweat, so she turned over.

"You missed it! You missed it! You missed it! You missed it! Now they'll all die because of you," screamed Dora as she stood over Lucy accusing her with a pointing finger.

Lucy jerked awake. Her arm was draped over Sammy. She took a deep breath and looked behind her. Nobody was there and the curtains were closed. She looked over to Jake and beyond to the candle. The bowl of water was steaming on the bedside cabinet and Dora was fast asleep in the chair. Lucy let out a deep breath. It was a while before her eyes began to close again.

***

The journey back out of Inverness was as uneventful as the journey in. The RAMs would still be in the hot zone, where live prey had climbed a wall earlier in the day. RAMs were not thinking animals. That was their last sighting, they would stay there until some other sight or sound lured them away.

The three of them reached the Land Rover, and Mike popped the bonnet while Hughes removed the battery. Wren, carefully shone a torch for him so he could see what he was doing, but he had done this so many times, he could have done it blindfolded. Hughes opened his backpack and placed it inside, swinging it back on his shoulders. "Bloody 'ell, that's just what I needed, more weight to carry in this."

"I can carry it if you're struggling, old man," said Mike.

"Laugh it up…cheeky little twat," said Hughes and suddenly realised Wren was there. "Sorry love, didn't mean to swear," he said.

"Erm, no, you're okay. I don't offend, I'm not eight anymore," she said with a smirk.

Hughes smiled. "Oh, you and her are going to get on like a house on fire," said Hughes looking at Mike.

The going was slow in the deep snow, but in places, drifts had cleared the road and Mike, Wren and Hughes were able to make good time. They headed over the bridge and a wave of relief swept over the three of them. Getting to the other side meant they were out of the city, out of imminent danger. Well, that's what it felt like. In actual fact, danger lurked everywhere.

"It's a really bad idea coming out in the dark," said Wren.

"I know, love. We avoid it whenever we can," replied Hughes.

"I've only ever done it twice when I didn't have any other option, and I swore I'd never do it again," she said.

"What changed your mind?" asked Hughes.

"It's not like I had a choice is it? Help you or a little girl dies."

They continued for a while before Mike asked, "How much further?"

"Not too far," said Wren, "We need to go cross country a little from here," she said, veering from the road and climbing over a waist-high barbed wire fence. "Watch your dangly bits," she said, "you don't want to skewer anything."

Mike and Hughes both winced. "Duly noted, thanks Wren," said Hughes.

While they negotiated the fence, Wren, removed the large rucksack from her back. It was mainly packed with weapons, packets of dried food and the odd tin, but she retrieved a red and white tea towel and proceeded to tear it in half. She tied one piece to the fence.

"What's that for?" asked Hughes.

"Your friends. It's a marker for them. To help them find us."

Mike and Hughes, both smiled. She was a smart kid. The three of them continued over the field. The sky was completely clear now and it was hard to believe they had been in the midst of such a terrible blizzard a few hours ago. The starlight reflected off the white blanket of snow enough to light their way until they reached the trees and hedgerows that divided the field from the next; then Wren flicked on her torch again. She pulled out the other piece of tea towel and tied it to the end of a branch.

"I doubt if there'll be any more snow to cover our tracks, but just in case," she said, before continuing through the brush, over the fence and into the next field. "That's my place up ahead," she said pointing to a large white cottage just beyond the boundary at the far end of the field.

"Nice," said Hughes.

"Yeah, it's practical. It's got a solid fuel range and a stove, so if nothing else I can stay warm and cook," she said.

"You're a smart cookie, Wren. We could use someone like you in Safe Haven," said Hughes. Wren carried on walking, but inside she was beginning to get excited again. These people could be the answer to her prayers.

***

The wood continued to burn in the stove, casting a warm orange glow all over the canteen. The heat and light even spread out into the corridor, bleeding the reflections of its dancing flames into the darkness. Just one gust of breeze, one errant wisp of wind was all it took. The group of RAMs had headed from the south. They were following the constant dirge being growled by hundreds of their brethren in search of food, in search of new victims. Now as they fought through the snow to find their own, an out of place orange glow caught their attention. Snow was piled against the window of the abandoned carpet showroom, but there were small gaps revealing something out of place, something unnatural, something human.

The creatures stopped in their tracks and headed towards the small snowless gaps in the otherwise whitewashed windows. Not knowing why, they fell to their knees and started to dig and scramble, churning the snow away, becoming excited, at the flickering light from within. Soon five RAMs became ten, and ten became twenty. Twenty became thirty, and in the end, there were nearly forty RAMs. They dug and clawed at the snow, flinging it behind them as they went. Before long, the beasts were pressed up against the glass, and much of the snow they had dug away had shifted and settled back around them. They did not feel the cold. They did not feel the wet. They did not experience discomfort like the living did. They could keep a happy vigil, at the same time as desperately trying to gain access to the showroom. Their genetic predisposition to spread the virus within them provided the only intelligence they had, but that was the only weapon they needed.

***

Wren, Mike and Hughes approached the final hedgerow before entering the croft on which Wren's house stood. She tore into a yellow and white tea towel, tying it to the end of a branch.

"You got a thing for tea towels?" asked Mike.

"Just thought they were pretty. Nice for my kitchen. You got an issue with that?" she said.

"No. All good," said Mike.

Hughes began to climb through the thicket but stopped dead in his tracks as a low-pitched growl began to rise into the otherwise silent night. Mike stopped too and began to reach for his machetes, but Wren pushed past both of them. "Come here then, come here my beautiful boy, mummy's home," she said crunching her knees into the snow and holding out her arms.

A second later an agile but enormous German Shepherd dog came bounding out of the shadows, kicking showers of snow into the air. It collided with Wren who laughed and began kissing the dog like she had not seen him in years.

The two men looked at each other in the dark. "I thought these things only came out on a full moon," said Mike.

"Close your ears. Close your ears, boy. What is he saying?" said Wren, fussing, and squeezing Wolf. "What is he saying about my boy?"

Mike and Hughes began to exit the thicket and Wolf's head shot round to look at them. "Erm, are we okay to come out?" asked Hughes.

"As long as your friend keeps his smart mouth shut. Wolf is his own man. I can't be responsible for what he does if someone upsets him," she said standing up and beginning to head towards the house.

Mike and Hughes remained still. Wolf continued to sit there, his head clearly pointing in their direction, watching their every movement.

After a few seconds, Wren looked back, "C'mon boy," she said giggling. The dog turned and began to carve a fresh track in the snow after her.

"Don't suppose you've got any silver bullets in your rucksack have you, Mikey?" asked Hughes.

"I heard that," called Wren, "so did Wolf."

The four of them continued to the house. Wren opened the door and lit three lanterns. Wolf went to a corner of the kitchen where a large bowl was filled with water. He lapped at it for a moment, then went to lie in his bed. He watched everything that went on, ready to spring into action if these strangers caused him concern.

The place was owned by someone with money, but a love of the traditional too. Slate covered the floor to the large kitchen and solid oak cupboards and cabinets lined the walls. A basket with logs in it stood by the side of a large black range. Wren opened the bottom door and placed in two of the logs and a little kindling. She twisted a few pieces of old newspaper and took a safety light from the countertop, depressing the switch and igniting one of the pieces of paper. When she was happy the flames were catching, she closed the door.

"That'll warm the place up for when we get back," she said, looking at Hughes. "C'mon then, we'd better get off," she continued, going towards the door. "Wolf, stay," she said and signalled for Hughes and Mike to leave, before giving one last smile towards the German Shepherd, and closing the door behind her. Wren moved past the two men taking the lead. They followed her around the back of the house and found she had a large enclosed garden surrounded by a healthy wooded area. "I love a good forage in here. There's all sorts of stuff you can eat y'know. Stuff that they ate in the olden days but we just forgot about."

"Sammy would love you," said Mike smiling. "She's always wanting volunteers to go foraging with her in the woods."

"Sammy? That's the one who's ill?"

"Yes."

"Then let's hope she gets better so we can," said Wren.

***

Emma's eyes opened slowly, and the heat from the fire made her shut them again straight away. She was in a deep sleep but something had disturbed her. Despite all her senses still being dulled by the depths of slumber she had just aroused from, she smacked her tongue and found she was thirsty. She reached into her backpack and pulled out a flask. Emma took a couple of drinks of the cool water, replaced the flask and put her head back down in an attempt to drift off to sleep once more.

She closed her eyes, but then that nagging sound dragged her back from the edge of dreams. She leant up a little, looking around the room. Barnes and Beth were snuggled up on two pushed together couches. Shaw was fast asleep in an armchair. She remembered Mike and Hughes had left with that girl. What was that noise? It was like old water pipes banging. Was it the plumbing? No, there had been no running water in months. The whole day she had only got up once to pee and her foot had been agony, but Mike had picked up some anti-inflammatories and painkillers for her at the pharmacy, and the pain was not as pronounced as it had been. She pulled back the curtains that were acting as her blankets and swivelled her legs off the couch. Her foot landed on something large warm and furry that let out a loud 'eek' and then scuttled away.

Emma screamed and Shaw sprang to his feet, Beth jumped up and saw a rat perched on the arm of the couch just above where her head had been.

"Aaaggghhh!"

Barnes scrambled to push the two couches apart and got to his feet. He turned his torch on, Shaw turned his on too, and they began to swing them around the room like searchlights at a prison break. There was another rat on one of the surfaces near the microwave, and the hind end of one was sticking out of Shaw's rucksack.

"Little bastard!" shouted Shaw, booting the rucksack and making the rat squeal loudly before it ran towards the open door. The other creatures panicked too. The one next to Beth tensed, then sprang through the air desperate to reach the light glow beyond Barnes's shoulder.

To Barnes, it looked like the creature was leaping straight for his throat, and he batted it hard with the back of his hand. The dazed rat hit Emma's chest and fell onto her foot causing her to scream like a banshee. "Fucker! Watch what you're fucking doing?" she screeched at Barnes, as the rat scurried after its friends through the gap in the door.

Barnes put his hands up when he realised what he had done. "I'm sorry! I'm sorry, Em," he said. The rat next to the microwave jumped down from the counter and sped across the canteen floor, terrified by the uproar and desperate to escape into the blackness.

"Are there any more?" cried Beth.

Shaw and Barnes scanned the room with their torches. They opened cupboard doors and did a full sweep like they were looking for an IED. "No, said Barnes, we're clear. I'm really sorry, Em," he said walking over to his friend and throwing his arms around her.

"We were lucky," she replied. "Jules had real problems with them at the Home and Garden Depot. They swarmed on a night and attacked people. And if any of those filthy little fuckers bit into a RAM, the residue on their teeth could infect you too."

"Well, that wasn't a swarm, thank God, and they were certainly a lot more scared of us than we were of them," said Shaw.

"Erm, speak for yourself there," said Beth.

"Hang on a second," said Barnes, "Where the hell is Hughes…and Mike…and the girl?"

In all the panic, they had not even noticed, but now things had calmed, worried looks swept over Shaw's and Beth's faces too. "Don't worry," said Emma, "they've gone to Wren's place. They've got a plan that might get Mike back home. We're meant to head out tomorrow to Wren's house, then when the thaw comes, we can get back home." The other three looked at Emma as if she had gone mad. "No, really. Mike, Hughes and this girl all went off together," said Emma.

"Why the hell didn't they wake us?" asked Shaw.

"You know Mike. He gets an idea, that's it, he doesn't want to discuss it to death, he just does it. I suppose he didn't want anybody telling him it wouldn't work, and he didn't want anyone slowing him down," she replied looking down at her foot.

"Bloody idiot," said Shaw.

The four of them stood there looking at each other in the dimmed light. "What is that sound?" asked Emma.

The others paused, they had jumped straight from sleep to sheer panic and nothing else had mattered but vanquishing the room of rats. "It…it sounds like banging, or thumping," said Barnes.

"Come on Barney," said Shaw, "Let's go take a look."

"Stay here," said Barnes to Beth, "we'll be right back."

The two of them left the room, concentrating their torch beams on the carpet. "We'd better make sure there aren't a load of those little...OH FUCK ME!" cried Shaw as his beam hit the window revealing the squashed bodies and faces of not rats but RAMs, desperate to get in, even more so now that light had been accompanied by movement.

The creatures began to hit the glass harder, with outstretched, clawed hands, tantalised by the feast that shone torches towards them. The dull thuds became thunderous bangs, as Shaw and Barnes looked towards each other, both thinking the same thing. Barnes said it first. "That glass isn't going to hold."

They both backed down the corridor, turning their torches off, but the damage was done, and the picture of those creatures was burned indelibly into their brains. They ran back into the canteen. "We need to go now!" said Barnes.

"Why, what's going on?" asked Beth.

"Beth, Em," said Shaw, "we need to go now!"

13

Hughes gave Mike ten minutes of training on the controls of the Massey Ferguson 135 tractor that they had chosen for Mike's journey. He took the battery from his backpack and lifted the section of bonnet directly in front of the steering wheel.

"How do you know all this stuff?" asked Mike.

"You'd be amazed at what I know, Mikey Boy," he said as he started to remove the contacts.

Mike jumped down from the tractor and went to stand with Wren who was holding another torch up to help Hughes.

"I want to thank you again, for everything," said Mike.

"You're welcome," she said smiling.

Hughes clicked the compartment above the battery

back into place and wiped his hands on his jeans. "Now for the proof of the pudding," he said, climbing into the cab.

He made sure the handbrake was up and the gear was in neutral before turning the key. The powerful engine rumbled to life and a smile appeared on Hughes's face. He and Mike spent the next few minutes doing a quick revision of the controls and Hughes also demonstrated the loader, which Mike would need to shift snow if he got stuck.

The large barn had remained untouched and there was a wealth of fuel and equipment that Hughes had every intention of utilising for Safe Haven. Most importantly, though, they had managed to fill two jerricans with red diesel for Mike's journey. "Now remember, do not under any circumstances let the tank run dry. You'll not be able to start it again. You've got a full tank and that's about ten gallons, that should get you a fair distance, but it's going to be slow going in this depth of snow, so just keep an eye on it, okay?"

"Yes, dad," replied Mike.

"That's right, make fun, you little shit, you'll see if you run out of diesel," said Hughes, smiling and giving his friend a hug. "Take care, Mikey boy, see you soon."

"Look after Em."

"You know I will," replied Hughes.

"Well, this is smell you later then," said Wren with a

hint of sadness on her face. She pulled a large bag of dry roasted nuts from her pocket and reached around putting them into Mike's rucksack. "In case you get hungry," she said, and nervously tiptoed up and gave him a peck on the cheek.

"Thanks, Wren," he replied giving her a big hug. The sadness left her face and she reciprocated, feeling his warm cheek against hers. "See you soon."

He pulled back, picked up the two jerricans, placed them behind the seat in the cab and climbed in. The engine rumbled too loudly for sentimental goodbyes, so Mike just waved his final farewell to the two of them.

Hughes jogged over to the large barn doors, unbolted them and swung them open. Mike remembered his tuition and the tractor pulled away, into the snow, into the night, into whatever fate laid ahead.

***

Emma's socks had dried, but there was still a large hole in the boot, the sock, she could swap over. Shaw took the boot and looked at the gaping hole. He removed his knife and cut an oversized piece out of the cushion from the plastic armchair and placed it inside.

"There we go, fastest repair you'll ever see. Not perfect, but it's better than nothing," he said.

"Thanks," said Emma, pulling the boot on. "Don't forget the map."

"What?" asked Shaw.

"Remember, the girl drew us a map of how to get to her place?" Emma's eyes scanned the room and stopped on the table in front of the chair where Shaw had been sleeping. "There," she pointed.

Shaw picked up the leaflet and shone his torch on it. He looked at it for a moment, committed as much as he could to memory and folded it before placing it in his jacket. "Come on then, we'd better get the hell out of here while we still can."

"You're forgetting one thing," said Beth. "You say there's a few dozen of those things out there. We have to walk right past them to get out of the city. The only way in and out of here is the alleyway."

Shaw and Barnes looked at each other, "You're used to being in charge, what's the plan?" asked Barnes.

"Yeah, made a great job of it, didn't I?" replied Shaw, pulling his Browning Thirteen out of his rucksack and placing it in the back of his jeans.

"How about we lure them in?" said Emma.

Barnes let out a nervous laugh. "You're Mike's sister alright. What do you mean?"

"We block the corridor. It's not that wide, we could break the window, and while they try to get to us through the corridor, we escape out of the back door. By the time they break through, we'll have made it out of the alley and we'll be on our way," said Emma, placing her rucksack on her shoulder and tentatively pressing down on her foot.

She grimaced a little, but she could suffer the pain to escape this nightmare.

"That's...actually...that's not a bad idea," said Barnes.

***

Mike looked at the watch Hughes had given him. It was just before five. The sun was still in hiding, but at least he was on his way. He remembered back to a few months before when he had travelled on this road on a bike at well over one hundred miles per hour. Now, here he was, negotiating snowdrifts and lucky if he could break ten miles an hour.

Sammy was still alive, she had to be. She was a fighter, she would hold on. Flu always affected the old and young, and even though it would be less common now the human population had diminished to a mere speck of what it was, it did not mean it was gone for good. Since they founded Safe Haven, their numbers had grown. Word had spread about the fortress by the sea, the community where a new life was possible.

Every now and then, there'd be an outbreak of a cold after some newcomers had arrived. Short of putting people in quarantine, there was not a lot that could be done about it, but they had not suffered anything as virulent as this. This was off the charts.

As Mike brought the tractor to a stop to deploy the front loader and clear a high drift of snow, something struck him. There was one of the flu victims who was neither young or old. He was a pretty fit guy in his late thirties. He was handy in a fight when it came to battling RAMs too. McGregor had been on a few scavenger missions with Mike and the soldiers, and he was one of the last people Mike would have expected to get really ill with this virus. Just a couple of days before, McGregor had been on a fruitless meds hunt to a clinic with himself, Barnes and Hughes. They'd run into a small handful of creatures, which was not uncommon, but all of them had been put down with ease.

Mike remembered that the four of them split up, and when they met back up, McGregor seemed a little different. When Mike asked if he was okay, McGregor said, he was fine. The next day he started developing flu symptoms.

Suddenly, Mike's memory drifted back to Joseph down in Leeds, and the time when he had been scratched by his turned son. He developed symptoms not unlike the flu then. Mike paused, the front loader was full of snow, but now, that was the last thing on his mind.

McGregor goes with them on a scavenging mission. He's fine, goes off by himself, comes back quiet. Next day has flu symptoms, then gets really bad and goes into deep sleep, practically a kind of coma. It was rare, not unheard of, but rare for healthy adults to be affected so badly by the flu. What if it wasn't the flu? What if McGregor had been scratched?

"Oh shit!"

***

Barnes and Beth pulled one of the heavy metal carpet rails in front of the entrance to the corridor while Shaw and Emma stood holding torches. The creatures were continuing to get more excited and the volume of the bangs and thuds grew greater with each passing second. For the moment, the glass and the seals were holding, but for how much longer was anyone's guess.

Barnes and Beth dragged another showroom rail across and tipped this one on its back in front of the first. They reinforced the barricade with some of the heavy cardboard inner tubes, office chairs and stools, before the two of them carefully climbed back over. They headed into the canteen and started dragging out the furniture, stacking couches, armchairs, the microwave, even the cooker to create as big an obstacle as they could for the RAMs. Sweat was dripping from the pair of them by the time they had finished.

The corridor was blocked well and truly. It was not impossible to negotiate the barrier they had created, but it would give them ample time to make their escape through the back, especially when it was set alight and the back door was wedged shut.

"Okay," said Barnes still trying to get his breath back, "so what do we do now?"

Emma and Beth were twisting leaflets and old bits of newspaper, and throwing them onto the couches and chairs. Shaw took the remainder of the wood that Mike had chopped for the fire and carefully positioned it to make sure there was a quick ignition when they set the structure alight.

"Erm, well, we could wait," said Shaw.

"That window could cave in any minute or it could last for hours," said Barnes.

"Fuck it," said Emma, taking off her coat, wrapping it around the Glock tightly, and firing four shots in the general direction of the windows. The crack of the gunshots was deafening in the narrow corridor.

"Fuck!" shouted Beth, "What are you doing?" she asked, holding her ringing ears.

"It worked in The Godfather Part Two," replied Emma.

"Fuck!" shouted Beth again, holding her fingers into the light of Shaw's torch to see if there was blood on them.

Suddenly, there was another sound like thick cloth ripping, followed by a thundering crash as the massive panes shattered causing the RAMs to collapse forward like zombie dominos, each one pushed by a massive invisible finger.

"Shiiittt!" said Emma, placing the Glock in the back of her jeans and quickly pulling her jacket back on.

"Great work Em," said Barnes as the creatures began to scramble to their feet and head towards their breakfast.

Shaw disappeared into the canteen and re-emerged seconds later carrying a baking tray of glowing embers from the fire. He had gloves on and had folded his coat sleeves around them too for extra protection from the heat. The wax from his jacket sizzled and filled the air with a smell as jarring as the cordite.

He threw the contents of the tray onto the couch with the wood and rolled up newspaper. A few of the pieces began to burn, but it was nothing like the inferno he had envisaged. "Fuck," he said, noticing the first of the creatures was just ten metres back. Now that the snow no longer encumbered them it took the beasts no time at all to tap back into their speed and strength.

A second, two, then the first RAM leapt, vaulting the carpet inner tubes and the front showroom rail, and landing heavily on the second with a crack that sent chills down the spines of the living.

"Holy shit! Did you see that?" asked Beth, as all four of them began to back down the narrow hallway.

"It shattered ribs there, and it didn't even miss a beat," said Barnes, raising his SA80.

The creature continued scrambling over the obstacles while others fell, others tripped, but still more began to climb. "Come on," said Shaw we need to move, he said putting a hand on Barnes's shoulder.

"You go, I'm right behind you," replied Barnes. "Take Beth and Em, get out of the back door and get ready with the wedge."

"I'm not leav…" began Beth.

"Now!" shouted Barnes.

Shaw pulled Beth back and the two of them helped Emma down the corridor. The creature landed on the couch with the scattered embers and paper, just as Shaw hit the panic bar of the fire door, sending an icy spiral of freezing air whooshing down the hallway. The influx of oxygen coincided with the ruffling of the paper, wood and embers as the creature landed, causing the threatening fire to ignite, and before the beast could jump back off, Barnes fired the rifle, stopping the RAM dead in its tracks. Its neck snapped back on the arm of the couch, leaving its body raised while the fire burned underneath it. Its wet clothes sizzled and smouldered as the couch around it began to burn.

Another two beasts started climbing over the miniature obstacle course, and the former British Army sniper put both of them down with a single shot to their foreheads. The arm of one lopped over the carpet rail and into the flames. The wet fabric smouldered and then caught fire. Barnes watched as the flames spread, then turned and ran towards the open door. Once outside, Shaw shoved it closed with a loud bang, and he and Beth wedged a pallet diagonally against the handle before piling snow against it.

"Okay," said Barnes, "let's go."

14

"Shit!" said Beth, pulling her head back around from the corner of the alley. "There are more heading towards the store."

"Shit," said Barnes, "It must have been the shots."

"Do you think?" said Beth.

"Hey, don't blame me, the boat had already sailed on that one," he replied, looking towards Emma.

"Yeah well, I didn't see anybody else coming up with ideas," she said, limping to the edge of the alley to peek around the corner. She stayed there for a minute watching four RAMs disappear out of view, then she waited a minute more.

"What do you see?" asked Barnes.

"I think they've gone into the store. I can't see anymore," she replied.

"Okay, so what should we do?" asked Beth.

"Well, we don't have too many choices," replied Shaw.

"I say we wait a while longer. It will be light soon enough, then at least they won't have that advantage over us," said Beth.

"There's way too long to wait before daybreak. With all this snow on the ground, there's enough light for us to get moving. We know we don't have any friends in town, so if something moves, we kill it," said Shaw. "We really can't afford to wait until that fire catches hold of the rest of the building."

"I like the idea of seeing what we're doing, but right now, we've got an advantage. We've got a lot of them trapped in the store. We should go for it," said Barnes.

"Okay, let's put this to a vote," said Beth. "Em what do you th…"

"Oh shit!" said Barnes as the three of them realised Emma had already decided. She was halfway down the alley. Calling to her would be out of the question as that would create too much noise.

Beth, Barnes and Shaw started to follow her. They saw her slow down and crouch a little. She pulled two weapons out of her rucksack before continuing. Emma reached the end of the alley and then looked back. She waved her arm beckoning them towards her.

"That was really bloody stupid," hissed Shaw as he

came up beside her.

"We're here, aren't we?" she said stepping out onto the street. She looked in both directions before turning left. The others followed her, and then took the lead, as Emma continued to struggle with her foot. She looked back, there was no sign of anything tailing them. "Wait up," she said, turning back to her direction of travel.

Beth dropped back a little and put an arm around Emma's waist, while Emma put her left arm around Beth's shoulder.

"You're getting more like him every day, y'know that?" said Beth.

Emma smiled. "I'll take that as a compliment."

"You do now. You wouldn't at one time."

The group was almost out of sight when the first RAM emerged from around the corner. It was some distance away when the gunshots sounded, but it followed the sound, and now it had arrived. It did not know what it had heard, all it knew was that sound was not made by one of its own. It was not alone. A dozen, two dozen, three dozen more followed, all in pursuit of the same echoing shots that had exploded through the creatures' own chorus of growls. There! Just a fleeting glimpse was enough. Suddenly, their excited song rose at the back of their throats again. It had been too long since they had last fed, and nothing was going to stop them now.

***

Lucy's sleep had been dogged by nightmares. When she woke, it was on the precipice of dawn. She looked across to see the candle had flickered away to practically nothing. Dora had left, and the children were still struggling to breathe. Lucy was cuddling Sammy. Even without touching her forehead, she could feel the child was burning up. She picked up the facecloth that had fallen from Sammy's head in the middle of the night and went across to Jake. She put her palm on his forehead. "Oh, Jakey, sweetheart." His eyelids still fluttered as he fought the infection with everything he had. She was trying to remember the last time she had seen him conscious, in full charge of his faculties. It was yesterday afternoon. He had a bad case of the flu, but it had not been as virulent as Sammy's. Now, though, they were both hanging on for dear life.

Lucy took the facecloth from his pillow too and rinsed it in the bowl of water infused with menthol that had been steaming last night, but was now icy cold. She repeated the process with Sammy's cloth. She then placed one of the cloths on Jake's head, and one on Sammy's, then took the bowl to refill it with boiling water. Steam was one of the few things that could help them right now.

She flicked on her torch and went to the kitchen. Some of the cupboards contained food, some contained meds. She checked the bottles looking for menthol crystals, then saw one marked *oxycodone*. She pulled out the bottle and held it in her hand. Maybe just one. They helped before. They helped with the stress, they helped with the loss. Just one pill and everything would numb a little. Everything would be that bit less painful. She put the torch down on the counter and flicked the lid off the bottle. It was almost full. She looked again at the label. These must have been gleaned on one of Mike's scavenging missions.

"What the hell?" she said and put a small tablet on her tongue, tipping her head back and swallowing it. She had depended on these pills in the past, they had become a habit, an addiction, but she had managed to beat it. This was a one-off, just to relieve the stress. She could not think clearly, and this would help. It was not like she would become dependent on them again.

Lucy put the cap back on, put the bottle in her pocket and closed the cupboard door. She turned to leave and saw a figure standing in the doorway. It was Dora. Lucy shone the torch in the girl's face and saw in her eyes that she had seen everything. It was like she was looking into Lucy's very soul.

"I was looking for menthol crystals," said Lucy.

Dora opened the cupboard Lucy had been in seconds before and immediately pulled out a small bottle labelled menthol crystals. It was two rows over from where the oxycodone tablets had been, but for some reason Lucy had missed them. It was like her eyes had zoned in on the oxycodone label and blocked out everything else.

"Thanks," said Lucy, before filling the kettle and walking out into what was once the living room of the caravan but now housed hospital beds. She went to the solid fuel stove that had been installed by George, and placed the final log from the basket inside, before putting the kettle on the hob. The stove glowed brightly, and Lucy threw a glance down the hallway to see Dora looking at her, judging her from the darkness. She felt an urge to escape. "I'm going to head across the village hall. See if they've got more logs."

Dora couldn't make out what the doctor had said, because if she had, she would have told her there was another sack of logs in the cupboard. Before she got the chance to find out though, Lucy was out of the door.

***

Light finally started to dawn on the long day ahead as Mike dumped another load of snow. The tractor began to move once again. The skiddy, bumpy ride had suddenly taken on a greater urgency as he had realised what other horror may befall Safe Haven.

The tractor chugged towards a small roadside café. This was one of the first places they had visited on their scavenging trips. It had long since been pillaged of any food, but the fittings, the plumbing, the windows, and more had become part of the Safe Haven community. Nothing was left to waste. Mike pulled up in the small car park and took the packet of dry roasted peanuts from his rucksack.

Wren was special. She was a really sweet kid. She had saved his life, then given up her time, her house, and her supplies to help them. He opened the bag and took out a handful of nuts, throwing a few into his mouth. He hoped she would come and join them permanently. They needed people like her. Mike munched on the nuts, taking another handful and shoving them in his mouth. They were tasty but salty, and they made him thirsty. He took out the flask of water from his backpack and had a drink, before folding the top of the bag over, placing it back in his rucksack and taking the handbrake off.

The tractor moved away again, it went around a long bend before going past a sign for Gravir. Mike rubbed his hand over his face. Gravir was quite a large village and they had always done the quickest of scavenges there as they had never gone with numbers to match the RAMs. It had one of the main schools in the area, they had been in three times and each time, run into more RAMs than they were prepared for.

Driving along the outskirts at sixty miles an hour was not a problem. Spluttering in a tractor at ten miles an hour was. He reached the bend and immediately saw signs of the creatures up ahead. A few had gathered at the service station on the main road. Not only did the canopy protect it from snowfall, but heavy tree cover on both sides prevented major drifting, so the RAMs were already running towards Mike when he spotted them.

"Fuck!" he hissed. "Eight of them". There was no way he could shake them off in the tractor, not even at the maximum speed, they would cling to whatever part they could until his tank ran dry. He had to deal with them sooner or there would be no later.

He stopped and pulled the handbrake on. He put his rucksack on his back and jumped out of the cab into snow that went up to his knees. As cold as it was, he found his thick jacket had restricted his movement back in Inverness, so he took it off and threw it into the cab.

Another twenty metres and the snow was thinner, the RAMs would be on him in no time, and eight would be a struggle for him on a good day, today was not a good day. This place gave him the biggest advantage. Mike strode forward a few paces, kicking through the icy covering. He stood with his legs apart to give him the best balance, and pulled the two machetes from his rucksack.

He watched the speedy creatures hurtling towards him, but then they reached the thicker snow and their movements became more laboured, almost like the zombies of the classic sixties and seventies movies. Instead of lightning-fast killing machines, they had been transformed into clumsy ghouls whose malevolence outmatched their physical ability to capture their prey. Their growls remained just as bone trembling and their pallid skin and grey eyes were still enough to freeze the soul of the bravest man or woman, regardless of the season. But now, with Mother Nature playing no favourites, the RAMs had to fight through the snow just like any other creature.

They struggled, but pushed closer and closer. Mike could not hear them any longer. He could only hear his own breathing. He could only hear the blood coursing in his veins. He did not feel fear, only rage. How dare these monstrosities, these abhorrent creations try to stand in between him and his family?

The first RAM was nearly on him when Mike flashed the blade through the air, slicing through its skull. It dropped to its knees and fell face down into the crisp icy blanket, staining it pink as its wound oozed. Mike pushed its body down hard with one foot, before climbing onto its back and using it as a springboard for the next two creatures who were nearly upon him. He leapt through the air, crisscrossing the machetes. Both RAMs turned their heads at the same time as they watched the blur of movement, and both were chopped through the bridge of the nose in perfect synchronicity. The blades cut through brain tissue before the beasts even had a chance to throw up a grabbing hand.

They had fallen still on the frigid ground before Mike had landed. His boots crunched into the snow and straight away, he brought one of his blades up for the next creature, pushing the already bloody metal through its open mouth and up into its skull. The large shattered black pupils became pinpricks in an instant.

Mike removed the next beast in an almost identical fashion, but then the final three were on him. He lifted his boot, smashing one backwards. The creature stumbled hopelessly and fell to the ground. It struggled like an upturned beetle trying to regain its footing, giving Mike enough time to crisscross his blades once more, chopping into the grey matter of the other two RAMs.

Not even pausing to watch them drop, Mike leapt on top of the fallen creature as it continued to toil on the ground. It reached for Mike, but before it could get close to touching him, he stabbed it through both eye sockets with the two machete blades. Mike paused for a moment, letting his breathing return to normal, and then stood.

He looked around. There was no further movement, all the creatures had been dealt with. Mike wiped off the blades and placed them back in his rucksack, before heading back to the tractor.

"Fuckers!"

***

The soup smelled good as Sarah poured it into the three large flasks. It was Sue's recipe, potato and onion. She really missed that woman. When Sarah had needed help the most, it had been Sue who was there for her. It was hard to believe that she was Mike's gran. No, that was not fair. Mike had a caring and warm side, in fact, he was a really good man, but when anyone or anything threatened his family, he had no qualms about turning to psychotic lengths to save them. But Sue, she could never have harmed anyone or anything. She had even built a nice lean-to for Daisy the goat, that had a small radiator piped through to it. Who did that kind of thing?

"I miss you, my friend," said Sarah out loud as she twisted the cap on the final flask. She took a towel and wiped the sides down before placing them in her shoulder bag. Sarah opened the cupboard doors beneath the sink and pulled out two large bags full of green leaves, cauliflower and cabbage hearts as well as scraps of all sorts. She opened the kitchen door and stepped outside into the thick snow. She crunched her way to the wooden construction that most people thought was a coal shed, and opened the door. Daisy was lying down by the radiator. She had no intention of getting up to greet Sarah, but did show her the courtesy of raising her head. Sarah distributed the leftovers evenly into the trough that had been built for the goat. There was enough food to keep her going for a few days or so at least, just in case the snow got bad again. Sarah stroked Daisy a few times to which the animal seemed indifferent, then got up and left, leaving the door ever so slightly open just in case Daisy wanted to venture out.

Sarah headed into the house, put on her thick coat, gloves and hat. She put the bag over her shoulder and walked back out into the cold. She did not have transport, and it was a seven-mile walk into the village, but she could not just sit at home not knowing Sammy and Jake's fate, not offering any help. Today she would not collect mussels, so what, she could make it up other days. When the snow melted, she would go foraging and maybe even take the small boat out and do some fishing, but right now, she needed to see her family. Her family—that's what they were. According to Mike's speech when they founded Safe Haven, they were all family now, but this was a little different. Sarah and Emma were together as a couple. Mike, Lucy, Sammy, Jake, they were Emma's family, so they were hers as well now.

She began her ascent up the hill that led to the main road. It was steep and on a clear day it was hard on the back of the legs, but this was agony. She grimaced as she fought against the incline and grunted like a woman giving birth on more than one occasion as she pushed against the deep snow.

Sarah finally made it to the road which for the time being headed downhill. She checked her watch. She had been walking over twenty minutes already and only just reached the main road. This was going to be a long journey.

***

When Safe Haven had been founded and word had begun to spread, the village hall had been key to accommodating refugees until they were found housing. The permanent housing was everything from abandoned homes to static caravans. New houses were built or converted from outbuildings, Safe Haven was a growing community.

The committee had deemed it prudent to install a kitchen into one of the back rooms of the village hall to make sure that refugees could be fed hot food and treated well until they were placed. The snow had caused no end of problems. Older people struggled to get to their logs and coal. Some homes had experienced structural damage due to the storm, so now, the village hall was operating in full vigour.

"Lucy!" called Ruth as she waved at the doctor across the small sea of camp beds.

Lucy headed across to the librarian who was behind a serving counter helping other good Samaritans to dish out hot tea, toast, jams, kippers and various other scrambled together breakfast foods.

"What's going on?" asked Lucy.

"The storm caused quite a lot of damage so we've got more guests here than usual," said Ruth looking around at the old and young faces alike.

"Hell, there must be fifty people here, can you cope?" asked Lucy, looking beyond Ruth towards the other volunteers and the serving trays.

"Of course," replied Ruth, grabbing Lucy's arm. "Come join me and Jenny in the back, we'll have breakfast together." Lucy did not argue, she allowed herself to be escorted by Ruth into a back room where Jenny, the former hotelier from Candleton was waiting.

"Hiya, love," said Jenny, "Long time no see."

"Hi, Jen," said Lucy leaning down to kiss her. "Yeah, Mike and I keep meaning to head across to see you."

"Ahh, don't worry. I know you're both busy. I'm busy myself now we've actually got booze in the place again," she said laughing.

"Yeah, who'd have thought you'd be running a small country pub after that hotel?" replied Lucy smiling.

"It is what it is. It keeps me busy, and I have help."

"Uh-huh! I've heard about your help. In his thirties; tall, blonde, handsome and stupid," replied Lucy.

"Yes. He can be very...distracting," said Jenny laughing.

"You are such an old tart," said Ruth, beginning to spread homemade jam onto her toast.

"Guilty as charged," said Jenny. All three of them

laughed.

"How are Sammy and Jake?" asked Ruth.

"Still the same. All we can do is wait and hope. We're very limited as to what we can do for them without strong antibiotics. They are pretty much sleeping all the time now. They're still feverish, they're still going through periods where they struggle to breathe. Part of me wants to be with them twenty-four-seven, part of me wants as much distance as I can get."

Jenny reached across the table to take Lucy's hand. "Whatever happens love, everybody knows you will have done everything you can, you will have given it your best."

Lucy pulled her hand away and a snapshot of Dora flashed into her mind. That look in her eyes when she had seen Lucy take the oxycodone tablet. She moved her hand down to her pocket. There it was, that hard plastic container. She could walk outside and tip them all into the snow right now, but...no. She could not. She needed them for emergencies.

"How are Richard and David," asked Lucy, looking towards Ruth.

Jenny moved back from the table, taking her cue. "They are improving," replied Ruth. "They started bickering again yesterday which is always a good sign."

The women laughed. "When this is over, the three of us, Emma, Sarah, Beth and Jules should all have a girls night in. Robert can look after the pub and we can head upstairs with a couple of bottles of Harris Gin that I've managed to procure for my own personal reserve. That stuff is to die for," said Jenny.

"Robert?" said Lucy.

"My toy-boy," said Jenny, grinning widely.

"You know his name, that's good," replied Lucy.

"Darling, I know lots of things," said Jenny laughing.

"That sounds like fun," replied Ruth.

"That sounds lovely, but a long way off right now," said Lucy, taking a first bite out of her toast.

Ruth took a pot from the centre of the table and poured the steaming brown liquid into each of their mugs.

"What's this?" asked Lucy sniffing at the liquid.

"This, my dear, is dandelion chicory, made by yours truly," said Ruth.

Lucy tentatively put the mug up to her lips and took a sip. "Hey, that's not bad. Could do with a sweetener, but I could get used to that."

Ruth smiled and produced a small plastic tube. She hovered it over Lucy's cup and pressed a button causing a small white tablet to fall from it. She took a teaspoon and stirred the concoction. "Try that," she said.

Lucy took another sip and a broad smile appeared

on her face. "Where did you learn to make this stuff?"

"Never underestimate the power of books or the knowledge of a librarian, my friend," said Ruth smiling. "Everything we need to know is in books."

15

Emma, Beth, Barnes and Shaw had been trying to outpace their pursuers ever since they had caught sight of them. They reached the bridge with the first group of ten just a few feet behind.

"It's no good," shouted Emma. "My foot's killing, I can't keep this up."

Shaw's leg was hurting too. It had never been right since the break and the cold weather made the pain acute. The pile-up from months before was a snow-coated rusty junkyard. There was no possibility of finding a working vehicle.

"What are we going to do?" asked Barnes.

"There's only one thing we can do," replied Shaw, unslinging his rifle. He brought the sight up and began pulling the trigger. Each one was a headshot, stopping the RAMs dead in their tracks.

Barnes began to do the same. Ten shots, ten downed creatures, seven to Shaw, three to Barnes. "Nice shooting," said Barnes.

"They're not exactly fast-moving targets in this depth of snow are they?" he replied, lowering his rifle for a moment.

The next group of RAMs were about twenty metres back, then another lot about fifty metres behind them, followed by a more or less single file stream from thereon.

"There's no way we'll have enough bullets for this," said Beth.

"Bullets, Beth…" said Shaw, raising his rifle again and taking six more well-aimed headshots, "are not the problem. We've just given away our location to every RAM in earshot. But it was our only choice."

"Come on," said Barnes, putting the SA80 back on his shoulder, let's keep going, that's given us a little bit of time."

"Seriously," replied Emma. "I'm struggling."

Barnes put Emma's arm over his shoulder, and his arm around her waist as the pair began to move forward again. Beth and Shaw looked at each other, then back towards the procession of RAMs that continued to appear.

"They'll be on us in a couple of minutes at that pace," said Beth.

"I know," replied Shaw letting out a heavy sigh.

The two of them began running, as much as they could run in the knee-high snow. They caught up with Barnes and Emma, and Beth placed her friend's other arm over her own shoulder and continued, speeding Emma's progress up only marginally.

Shaw brought up the rear, turning back to fire a few precise shots before changing his magazine.

"How many mags have you got left?" shouted Barnes.

"This is my last one," replied Shaw.

Barnes did not say anything, he turned his head round to look at the road in front of him and kept moving. "How many bullets is that?" asked Beth.

"Thirty," replied Barnes.

Beth turned back and looked down towards the bridge, and then beyond to the seemingly endless line of creatures trudging towards them. "Oh God," she said.

"It's no good. It's no good," said Emma. "Leave me," she said, digging her feet into the snow and releasing her arms from the grasp of Barnes and Beth.

"Don't be ridiculous," replied Beth.

"Look!" shouted Emma, pointing at the RAMs that were gaining all the time. "There's no way we can shake them at this speed. I'm going to get you all killed."

Shaw and Barnes brought the scopes of their SA80s

up to their eyes and began to squeeze the triggers. Explosions of red sprayed into the crisp morning air as they downed seven more beasts.

"Listen to me, Emma," said Shaw, still with his rifle up to his shoulder. He paused to take two more shots at creatures further back, causing a third one to trip, "we're all in this together. We either all survive or none of us survive, so deal with it."

"It's madness," Emma replied. "You're signing your own death warrants when the three of you could make it. I could hold them off long enough."

They were a quarter of a mile past the bridge, but the incline they were on gave them a clear view of the creatures still teaming out of the city. Shaw delved into his inside pocket and took out the map. There's not that far to go before we get off the road and head cross country," he said.

"And what then?" asked Emma.

"We'll lead them straight to that girl's house. What good will that do us? What good will that do anyone? You should let me fight for as long as I can. I've got two magazines for my Glock and I've got my weapons. I can stall them long enough for you to get out of sight."

"What the hell!" said Shaw, folding the map and placing it back in his inside pocket. "This is as good a place as any to make a stand." He brought up his rifle again and aimed, taking the next two creatures down. "We're sticking together, Emma."

Barnes brought the SA80's scope up to his eye and took out another RAM. "We've always stuck together. We're not going to stop now," said Barnes.

"Through thick or thin," added Beth, pulling the rucksack from her shoulders and taking out her Glock Seventeen. She looked at Emma, "You, Lucy, Mike... you saved me back in Leeds. I'm here because of you. If we die today, we die together."

Emma swallowed hard in an attempt to hold back her tears. "You're all bloody idiots, the three of you," she said, taking her own Glock from the back of her jeans and bringing it up to fire.

**

Mike had been on the road for just a few hours, but it had felt like days. Every so often he would come to a drift that was too big to drive through, and he needed to set about the tiresome task of using the loader to clear it before he could carry on. He still had a lot of ground to cover, and now he was alone with his thoughts, anxiety was beginning to take hold of him.

What if he was too late? What if Sammy had not held on? What if McGregor had turned? What if? What if? What if?

He battered the steering wheel with his outstretched hands. "C'mon y'bastard, move!" But the tractor did not respond. It just kept chugging away, clumsily digging trails in the vast white sheet that had covered the highlands.

Mike let out a sigh. He continued with one hand on the steering wheel and delved into his pocket with the other to pull out another handful of dry roasted peanuts. He stuffed them into his mouth all at once and as he brought his hand away from his face, a memory stirred.

The last Christmas the family had spent with Alex. They had been on rations for quite some time, but there had been a large bag of dry roasted peanuts at the back of the cupboard stuck behind two bottles of Mulled wine from the previous Christmas. The nuts had been out of date for six months, but they were the best tasting nuts the family had ever had. Mike remembered how after months of eating plain ration food, Sammy and Jake's faces lit up at the prospect of having snack treats once again. Despite the curfew, despite what was going on in the outside world, that had been a great Christmas. Mike really missed Alex. He had been his best friend. "Blood makes you relatives, love makes you family," he had once told Mike, and it was so true.

Mike and Emma's real dad had been a violent, abusive alcoholic, so even though Alex was their stepfather, he was as close to them as anyone. Mike took another handful of nuts from his pocket, then folded the top of the bag. The rest of them were for Sammy and Jake.

***

Even though Sarah was wearing thick gloves, she kept her hands in her pockets. The sun was out now and the sky was clear, but it was freezing cold and just the feel of her arms and hands pressing against her body gave her the illusion of warmth. She had been walking for what seemed like an age, but had only been an hour. This was the easy part, most of it was on the level or downhill. She knew that when she went around the next turn, the long climb started.

Sarah stopped and looked out to the water. Was that a boat engine she heard? She scanned the bay below and beyond to further depths, but there was nothing to see. The sound was getting louder though, then it hit her, it was not a boat engine, it was a car engine, struggling in the snow, just like she was.

She looked back along the windy track and hoped any moment a vehicle would come around the corner with a spare seat and a heater. A minute later, a smile cracked her chapped lips as she saw Jules in her pickup. The wheels were spinning wildly as they tried to gain purchase on the icy surface, and the engine whirred, but she was making progress. Sarah began to wave her arms and after a few seconds, the lights on the pickup flashed and the horn blew.

"Oh thank Christ!" she said, stamping her feet on the spot, shaking off excess snow before she climbed into the passenger seat.

The pickup skidded to a stop and Jules leaned across to open the door. "What the fuck are you doing out here?" she asked in her Belfast twang.

"Nice to see you too, Jules," said Sarah climbing in.

"Y'know that's not what I meant. Why are you out here walking in this?"

"I was out picking mussels yesterday while Raj was looking after Sammy and Jake. I get back and there's no sign of anyone. By that time the snowstorm was starting, and I couldn't do anything. So, first thing this morning, I set off on my way into the village. I guess he's taken them to the hospital. At least, I hope that's what's happened," said Sarah.

"Well, I'm heading into the village. I think there are a lot of people who'll have been affected by that storm. What a bloody time for them to tell me to look after things," said Jules.

Sarah slipped off her gloves and leant forward in the passenger seat, warming her hands as the hot air blew out of the grills. "You have no idea how happy I am to see you. It was going to take hours to walk those few miles."

"In my life, I've not seen snow like that," said Jules.

"I know, me neither."

They continued their journey for a while, listening to the struggling engine, the skidding tyres and the blowing heaters. A few months earlier, Highland Council snowploughs and gritting trucks would have been out on these roads at the first sign of snow and Jules and Sarah would be able to enjoy the spectacular view of the glistening bay. Now though, things were very different. Everything was a potential hazard, everything had become not just theirs but the whole community's collective responsibility.

"I wonder if George can rig some kind of

snowplough for us?" said Jules.

"If anybody can, he can," replied Sarah. "I mean hell! He built us a load of siege weapons out of odds and ends. He's fixed up a fleet of vehicles for us, I would have thought a snow plough would be a piece of cake for him."

"Yeah! You're right. We'll drop in and see him before…oh shit!" said Jules bringing the car to a skidding stop.

"Oh shit!" echoed Sarah.

A mountain of snow covered the road a few feet away from where the pickup stopped, right to the bend two hundred feet beyond.

"Well, we've had landslides before, I think this is our first avalanche, or at the very least, a snow slide." Jules looked up the side of the hill, where some of the greenery and dark rocks were now exposed.

"There's no way we can get through," said Sarah.

"Nope," said Jules. "Until a thaw starts, they're stuck that side, we're stuck this side. I hope to God they're all okay"

***

"That was my last round," said Shaw, slinging the rifle over his shoulder and taking out his Browning Thirteen.

Barnes continued to take aim and fire. The progress

of the RAMs was slow but relentless. For the time being, no creature had managed to get within twenty feet of Emma, Shaw, Barnes or Beth, but all of them knew, that when the bullets ran out, it would be hand to hand combat, and it was only a matter of time before they were overrun.

The bodies of the RAMs kept falling, dyeing the snow around them pink and red. Often the beasts fell flat, becoming invisible to their assassins as they were entombed in whiteness until the thaw. Creature after creature was stopped in mid-stride by a seventeen hundred mile per hour missile to the head.

"Fuck!" shouted Barnes over the sound of the pistol shots to his left and right. "That's me out," he said slinging his rifle and pulling out his Glock Seventeen.

"I'm out too," shouted Beth, throwing her Glock Seventeen into the snow in front of her and pulling a large knife and a hatchet from her shoulder bag. She stood there for a moment like a statue, with a look of pure hatred on her face. She watched as the hellish beasts continued their advance. This was the end. She always knew her life in this new world would not last for long, but at least she had experienced a little happiness since Leeds. She had fought for everything alongside, Mike, Lucy and the three people she was with now; she had fought for right over wrong, for justice over crime, for everything, for every inch of ground they gained over in Safe Haven, and she was determined to die the same way she had lived...fighting. She took the bag from her shoulder and carefully placed it down on the ground.

The other three kept taking careful aim with their handguns, determined to wipe out as many of the creatures as they could. Then, suddenly they all stopped as they caught movement from the edge of their fields of vision. Beth began to charge. She retraced their snowy tracks, bringing her knees up higher where the snow was deeper.

"Beth! Nooo!" shouted Barnes.

"Arrrggghhh!" she screamed at the top of her voice, diving onto the first RAM, making it lose balance and fly backwards. She brought her hatchet up and hammered it down with a single killing blow, straight through the forehead of the creature. Its grey eyes rolled back, making the eerie pupils disappear behind pallid lids. She pulled the gory blade free and pounced on the next approaching RAM as the sound of guns began to echo once more.

"Beth!" Barnes shouted again, between shots. He began to walk forward maintaining his composure as well as he could and continuing to take down the creatures with precision. "Beth!" His voice was pleading, but each time he shouted the only response was a maniacal scream as his lover unleashed blow after blow on victim after victim.

Shaw replaced the magazine in his Browning and continued firing. "That's me!" shouted Emma, putting the Glock back in her rucksack and pulling out the crowbar and hatchet. She began limping forward to try and catch up with Barnes. Shaw realised, he was the only one standing still, and even though his own leg was in agony thanks to the cold, he began to advance too.

Beth drove the hatchet blade through the temple of

another creature, knocking it sideways to a clumsy, cross-legged finish. She was about to do the same to yet another, when a third came at her from her left. It grabbed a tight hold of her arm, and she yelped as she felt the pressure from its bony, yet powerful grip through her thick winter coat.

She looked into the creature's deathly grey eyes and became almost hypnotised by its black pupils, as they danced like breaking glass held together by invisible elastic. The beast bore its teeth and its head came towards her as she felt the grasp of her other assailant.

Suddenly, Beth was saying her wedding vows at the altar. She looked back and saw her father, Joseph, standing there so proud. She was on her honeymoon, sipping cocktails on the beach. She and Francis went back to their room, and he had arranged for a bottle of champagne to be waiting, and a single red rose lying on the bed. It was the most romantic thing he had ever done. She saw his dead body lying with a bullet in it. She saw the faces of his murderers on top of her as they took turns. She saw the black emptiness of that garage. She heard the sobbing of her little sister. She saw the headlights of the car as the garage door opened. She saw the silhouette come towards her. She heard her father's voice. She saw Mike covered in blood when she thought she would die at the hands of that maniac Fry in the hotel in Candleton. She saw Mike and Hughes in that house where Fry had taken her hostage and tortured her the night of the big battle. She felt her hand wrap around the hand of her new love, when Mike gave his speech, the day they founded Safe Haven. She felt the happiness, she felt the comfort, she felt the feeling of belonging, she felt...

16

Dora bent down and kissed Sammy, then Jake on their foreheads, just above the damp facecloth that had been put there to try and lower their temperature. Dora had a case of flu two weeks before. It put her in bed for a few days, but now she felt fine, and at least she could not get it again. She crossed the hallway to the next room and checked on the patients in there; two elderly women who Dora had seen from time to time around the village but had never had much to do with. They were not anywhere near as poorly as Sammy, Jake, or some of the others, but they had no relatives left alive and so were taken into the hospital rather than left to look after themselves. Their eyes were closed, but that was nothing unusual. Some days they did not stir until midday. Dora went to stand next to the first bed and put her hand close to her patient's nose. She felt warm air against her index finger and smiled.

She went to the next bed and did the same thing. Old Mrs Macleod was fine as well. Dora placed her hand on the woman's forehead. Her temperature did not feel as high as it had the previous day. This made Dora smile again. Lucy, Talikha and one or two part-time helpers had made appearances over the last few days, but Dora had been the mainstay. Lucy had even said without her help, nothing would get done. For the first time in her life, Dora had begun to understand what she wanted to do, where she felt most useful. She wanted to help people like she was now. She knew there would never be qualifications again, but she had always been a good student. She could learn from Lucy and from books. She could become some kind of medic.

In a twisted way, this new world had brought her more happiness and more of a sense of purpose than the old one ever did. She was valued and a vital member of the community. In her old life, she was the deaf embarrassment that was shipped off to one of the best schools in the country for her kind.

She walked out to the main living area of the static caravan and picked up the clipboard at the bottom of the first bed. There was a small square of paper attached to it. It read: *Keep doing what you are doing Dora. I couldn't want a better nurse. You were made for this job. Thank you for everything. Lucy xx*

A look of pure elation swept across Dora's face. She took the note from the clipboard and put it in her back pocket. This would be something for her Happy Memories Box. She really hoped Lucy was okay. If she had taken one of those small tablets, she must have been in a lot of pain with something. She hoped it was not serious.

***

"Are you sure you don't want to come and stop with us at the Old School House?" asked Jules.

"Thanks," said Sarah, "but I'll head home."

Jules looked across at her, "Y'know, Emma and Mike are going to have to wait until this thaws out a bit too, don't you think?"

Sarah nodded. "I'll just keep things ticking over there. Make sure the polytunnel is taken care of and the place is kept warm. Don't want the pipes to freeze."

"Okay," said Jules bringing the car to a stop at the top of the hill. She leaned over and kissed Sarah on the cheek. A few months ago they had been strangers, but they were family now. "You know where I am if you need anything."

"Thanks, Jules," said Sarah, starting to climb out of the car. "Oh, almost forgot," she said, reaching into her bag. "Have one of these," she said, taking out a flask, "It's Sue's recipe potato and onion soup."

"Y'know me. I never turn down free food," said Jules smiling. "Take care Sarah," she said, with a more serious look on her face.

"I will. You take care too." Sarah climbed out of the car and closed the door. She stood there and watched as the pickup pulled away. The sound of the engine continued long after she lost sight of the car. She let out a heavy sigh and a mist of white breath hovered in front of her before disappearing into the icy air.

Sarah started her descent towards Sue's cottage...her cottage. She and Emma lived there as a family with Mike, Lucy, Sammy and Jake. It was their home now. It was her home. She continued her journey, lost in memories. As she walked through the door, placed her bag on the table and sat down on the hard wooden chair, she began to cry. She was in a familiar house, but it was not home. It would not be home again until they were all together, and there was a voice deep inside that was getting louder by the minute. Over and over again it said, *they're not coming back. They're not coming back. They're not coming back.*

***

"For fuck's sake!" spat Mike as the tractor rumbled around another bend. The noise of the engine and the slow progress were more of a danger than he had anticipated. Many times they had passed and driven through the small villages on this stretch of road with little hindrance, but now, Mike was having to fight for every yard.

This time, the beasts had no running start. The fifteen creatures struggled forward through the snow towards the noise, towards their prey. Mike pulled the handbrake on and climbed out of the tractor. This was really starting to piss him off. He took the Glock Seventeen out of his bag and slid in the magazine that Hughes had given him. It clicked into position and he placed it in the back of his jeans. The tractor continued to chug as he stood watching the slow progress of the RAMs in the thick snow.

"I've had enough of this shit," he said marching forward. He whipped the machetes from his rucksack and sped up as much as he could towards his would-be-attackers.

"I!" swipe, one down. "Have!" swipe, two down. "Had!" thrust up, three down. "Enough!" hack four down. Pause. A quarter of the creature's skull sliced clean off, and Mike had not seen that happen before. He looked at the beast lying there in the snow for a second. What remained of its head pulsing just the slightest bit of red.

He looked up again as two RAMs converged on him at once. "Of! This!" five and six down. "You! Motherfucking! Pieces! Of! Shit!" Seven, eight, nine, ten, eleven, twelve down.

Mike reached for the Glock, even he could not miss from this range. He aimed and fired three times, and the three remaining RAMs collapsed, dead in their tracks.

Without pause, he placed the handgun back in his jeans and returned to the spluttering tractor. Mike climbed into the cab and pulled off the handbrake; the vehicle began its forward motion once more. The road was bumpy as the tyres ploughed over his fallen victims, but it was nothing the Massey Ferguson 135 could not handle.

There were still a few villages to go through. Mike felt his temple begin to throb as he negotiated the next bend and saw four more RAMs heading towards him.

***

Dora entered the final static caravan and was about to pull the door closed behind her, but then she noticed a strong smell. She looked towards the windows and someone had shut them all. The Calor gas fires threw out a lot of heat, but it was essential the rooms were kept ventilated. The fumes could often cause headaches, and there was always the risk of carbon monoxide poisoning. She looked towards the beds, Mr Wells and Mr Muldoon were still asleep.

Dora opened the windows a little. The room kept warm, but at least there was some way of dissipating the heavy odour caused by the gas fire. She let the two old men sleep, she would be back around again soon enough when Talikha arrived. Together they would serve the patients breakfast.

Dora went along the corridor and looked inside the rooms. An old man stood by the window in one. He had it open and was spluttering. He waved dismissively at Dora as she approached him. Then she caught a smell of something, smoke.

Despite his protestations, Dora walked straight up to him as he continued to cough, leaning on the frame of the window for support. She grabbed his icy left hand and pulled it back into the warm room from the window ledge. Between his yellow index and middle fingers, he held a thin self-rolled cigarette. Dora snatched it from him angrily and held it up in front of his face.

"I know, I know," he said before coughing again. "I just felt a little better this morning, and I really fancied a puff," said the old man.

Dora pointed to the bed and the old man coughed and spluttered his way across to it before settling beneath the sheets once again. She threw the cigarette out into the snow. The end glowed bright orange as it flew through the air before fading to smoky grey as it smouldered. She wafted her hand for a few seconds to try and get rid of the smell and then pulled the window to, making sure she left it open just a crack to let fresh air in. Dora turned around, put her hands on her hips and frowned, before breaking out into a wide grin to match that of her patient, who started laughing and coughing again. She headed towards the other bed when she saw a patient from the other bedroom stood in the doorway.

Dora was taken aback by the worried look on his face. She watched his lips carefully as he spoke. "It's Jonathan. I think he has stopped breathing," he said, as he supported his weak body on the door frame.

Jonathan, or Mr McGregor, was a strange case. He was in his thirties, strong, fit, no previous ailments. Dora remembered watching Lucy closely when she examined him. Talikha had been with her at the time. And Dora read "This one has me baffled", as it left her lips. He had deteriorated quickly, and this was also puzzling to the doctor.

Dora walked out of the bedroom, patting the other patient on the arm as she passed him. She crossed the corridor and caught a gust of cold from the door she had left open. She would close it when she had tended to Mr Mcgregor. The chances were he was just in a deep sleep, the likelihood of him dying from the flu at his age was slim. Lucy had said that repeatedly.

She walked up to his bed and a little chill ran down her spine. Yes, she was sixteen now, a woman. And yes, she had seen dead people. She had seen all sorts. But this would be the first patient she had lost. Mr McGregor's skin looked like it was draining of colour with each second she stood there. His eyes were firmly shut, no longer fluttering as they had been. *He's dead. He's really dead*, she thought to herself as her heart began to beat faster. She put her index finger up to his nose and felt no movement of air. She placed her hand on his forehead and pulled it back quickly as the skin felt like ice.

Dora drew back the sheets a little and pressed her palm onto his chest, closing her eyes and trying to feel just one small pulse, one movement that told her there was still hope, that he was not gone; but she felt nothing.

She opened her eyes again and sat down on the bed. Tears began to roll down her cheeks, and she pulled out the small handkerchief that she kept up her sleeve to dab them away. *I'm sorry. I'm sorry I let you down*. Her internal voice said to Mr McGregor. She reached out, took his cold hand in hers and looked at his face, as tears continued to trickle.

She felt a presence and turned to the doorway to see the room's other patient leaning against the door frame. He offered a fragile, pitying smile as his head turned respectfully to look at his former roommate. The smile vanished in an instant replaced by a look of horror and suddenly Dora was terrified that the old man was suffering a heart attack. She was about to get up to help him when nothing more than a feeling made her look back towards the bed. McGregor's eyes were open and for a moment Dora felt the most divine happiness, then she focussed on the black shattered pupils firing demonic shards of malevolence towards her.

She let go of the creature's hand like she had just touched a hot coal. A silent scream rose from within her and she began to move, but the beast grasped tight hold of her wrist and pulled her towards him as he pulled himself up. His teeth sank through the knitted cardigan she was wearing and the RAM that a few moments before had still been one of her patients, pulled its head back with a mouth full of wool and bloody flesh.

Dora's head fell back as tears of a different kind streamed from her eyes now. She looked at the ceiling and beyond. Suddenly, a fear rose within her, and her eyes fell shut. She felt the tears continuing to roll down her cheeks. She felt her attacker leap off the bed, she felt a darkness rising from within. Something foreign, something that was not her, something taking over her. She was scared. She had spent her life alone in this silent cocoon now there was something in here with her. Something evil.

17

Beth did not hear the sound of the shots as first one creature then the next fell to the ground like bowling balls. When a hand grasped her shoulder, she swung round like a rabid animal, ready to pounce, but she managed to stop herself. It was Barnes, Dean to her, and no one else. She flung her arms around him and squeezed, possibly the last squeeze they would ever share.

"I love you," she said, pulling back.

"I love you too," he said, and quickly took aim, firing at another approaching creature.

Emma limped up to the side of them, and they formed a line, which grew longer as Shaw joined them. "I suppose the one saving grace is they can't really swarm with that wreck in the middle of the bridge. Should allow us to take out more than we would have got otherwise."

"Never had you pegged as an optimist," said Emma.

"Never too late to change," replied Shaw, and they all laughed, louder than the joke deserved, but they wanted to laugh together one last time.

Shaw and Barnes raised their weapons again and fired at the next two creatures in the endless procession. "There must be close to a hundred just between us and the bridge, nevermind what's on the bridge, and still coming out of the city," said Barnes.

"We do what we can do. We go down fighting. We take as many of them with us as we can," said Shaw, releasing another two rounds. Barnes took aim and brought another down.

"Wait!" shouted Beth, pulling Barnes's gun down to prevent him from firing another round. "What's that noise?"

"That's just their growls, Beth, it's like they sing a bloody chorus when there's a horde of them," replied Barnes.

"No," she replied. "That other noise."

Barnes and Shaw looked at each other, they had been firing shots and their ears were ringing, they did not hear anything out of the ordinary. "Hang on," said Emma, "I hear it too."

The two women looked at each other. "It sounds like an engine, an aeroplane engine, something big," said Beth.

The four of them immediately looked towards the

blue sky. It was clear, no aeroplanes, no anything. But now Shaw and Barnes heard the sound too, it was getting louder. Shaw looked behind. "Fuuuccckkk!" he said as he saw a massive combine harvester heading towards them down the road, churning up the snow and spitting it out of the side pipe like a jet-powered snow-blower.

Barnes began to shoot again, taking down the nearest creatures as they continued their unwavering advance. "It's Hughes!" shouted Beth. "It's Hughes!"

"Fall back!" shouted Shaw, who grabbed Emma's arm and put it over his shoulder, supporting her while the pair of them began to cut through the snow as fast as they could towards the thundering farm machine.

Beth caught up with them. "Give me your gun. Me and Dean will bring up the rear and make sure none of those things get too close."

Without hesitation, Shaw handed over his Browning and concentrated all his efforts into getting through the snow with Emma as fast as he could.

Barnes and Beth kept a close eye on the advancing RAMs, occasionally firing a round, bringing the closest one down, before turning back to speed-trudge through the snow. The rumble of the combine harvester became louder, drowning out the sound of the creatures completely, until, Emma, Shaw, Barnes and Beth could finally see the relieved smile on Hughes's face.

As the blades got closer, the four of them edged around the outside. The combine harvester attachment spread nearly the entire width of the two carriageways. As Beth, Barnes, Emma and Shaw passed, they could feel the immense power of the machine make their very bones tremble. They stood watching as the mechanoid monster continued towards the army of undead that sought to enlist them into their ranks.

The massive rotating blades hit the first two RAMs at the same time and Emma immediately threw up as she witnessed them hacked, sliced, crumpled and then spat out of the side pipe like some grotesque, hellish smoothie. The zombie puree spewed a grizzly trail across the white snow, turning from dark red, to light red to pink, before another RAM and then another was caught and swallowed by the hungry beast.

Emma and Beth stayed put, while Shaw and Barnes began to follow the combine harvester leaving a good space, to make sure there was no chance they could get showered in any of the deathly residue. The blades had demolished the snow, making walking much easier and quicker. The two men were Hughes's backup, ensuring any creature who managed to skirt around the vast blades would be put down. No creature did. Like moths to a flame, they continued to advance and each one was virtually liquidised by the mechanical colossus.

Emma vomited again. She had seen and done all sorts since the outbreak, but this gorefest was one step too far, even for her. Snow, grass, trees, crash barriers, street lights and the dozens of other objects, natural and man-made that create a road siding became coated with the foulest of paints as the gigantic machine rolled on.

Hughes began to slow the huge vehicle down as it approached the bridge. He ignored the army of RAMs that continued to advance and arched his neck to make sure the huge cutter did not hit the crash barriers at either side as he continued. The massive rusted pile-up of vehicles caused by Emma and Lucy a few months earlier was mere feet away as Hughes brought the combine harvester to a standstill. The blades continued to turn and the side pipe continued to spew as more creatures advanced intent on reaching living prey, but each one met the same fate.

Hughes climbed out of the cab and jumped down. Conversation was impossible over the noise of the machine, but he gave each of the men a powerful embrace before they began to head back up the incline. They kept throwing glances back to make sure none of the creatures made it through the narrow gap at the sides. Occasionally one did, and Barnes, a trained sniper, used Hughes's SA80 to put them down with a single headshot.

"In my life, I have never been so happy to see anyone as I am to see you," said Shaw as the distance between them and the massive machine became enough for them to be able to hear their own thoughts once more.

"We heard the shots and it didn't take a genius to figure out what was going on," said Hughes.

"We?"

"Me and Wren," replied Hughes.

"I have never been so glad to see anyone," said Emma as the three men caught up.

"Yeah," replied Hughes, "I get that a lot."

"Where's Mike?" asked Emma.

"He left in the early hours. We got a tractor working, and he headed out. That's where I found this little beauty," he said, nodding in the direction of the combine harvester.

"How the hell did you get them working?" asked Barnes.

"Remember, mate, I'm a bloody magician with anything mechanical, plus, that farm had everything. When things return to normal, we're going to have to pay it a visit. But right now, let's get to some warmth shall we?" he said, pulling Emma's arm over his shoulder and putting his arm around her waist.

"No arguments here," said Beth, as the five of them looked back towards the gory scene, before heading in the opposite direction—to safety, to the future.

***

Even though Sue was fitter than most people half her age, she had often taken a hiking stick out with her on walks. It was the same stick Sarah used now as she made her descent to the bay below the house. She could not remember the contours of the rocky surface beneath the snow, so she felt them out with the point of the stick. The last thing she needed now was a fall, here in the middle of nowhere, all by herself. She had tied a washing rope to the bucket she collected the mussels in and had looped it around her shoulder so she could leave her hands free in case she fell or slipped.

The descent to the small private beach took three times as long as usual, but Sarah finally reached the small grassy incline where Mike dry-docked Sue's upturned small boat. Like everything else, it was covered in snow, but she placed a hand on it to steady herself as she climbed down the embankment and onto the sandy beach. Sue had struck the jackpot when she had found this place. She had pictures up on the wall of the husk the house was before she got hold of it. She had bought it for a song, but now it was beautiful, and the perfect place for this new world. Fresh water was pumped from a well. It had a functioning solid fuel hot water and central heating system, and if that was not enough, it even had a small cove of its own, with a sandy beach, surrounded by huge black rocks that were a magnet to mussels.

Sarah normally loved her trips to this cove, no matter what the weather, but right now, she was just trying to occupy her mind. She was worried about Emma, she was worried about Sammy and Jake, and she was powerless to do anything. The wet sand slopped beneath her boots as she walked towards one of the huge rocks. She was just about to start gathering the mussels when she stopped and looked back across the small beach towards the snow-covered boat. She was not a sailor or a great swimmer, but she had taken it out a couple of times. She took a pace towards it, then stopped again. Seven miles was twice the distance she had ever been. What if something went wrong?

"Screw it!" she said to herself and marched across the beach. Sarah swept, dug and dragged the snow off the white wood. When it was clear, she untied it from the stake that Mike had hammered deep into the earth. She took the bucket from her shoulder, crouched down, bending her knees and keeping her back straight, and then grabbed hold of the bottom edge, lifting it with all the strength she had. She eventually heaved it over, and it flopped, coming to rest on the displaced mound of snow. Two oars were tied together and attached to the underside of one of the seats. She untied them and laid them down at the bottom of the boat. The small motor had not worked for some time. It was going to be a long seven miles, but at least she would be doing something. At least she would not feel so useless. Maybe she could help at the hospital, maybe she could help at the village hall, maybe she could find a way to feel less lost.

**

Hughes entered the kitchen first, and Wolf barked. Without looking around, Wren grabbed the one-handed crossbow from the kitchen counter, turned and pointed. "Oh, it's you," she said, lowering her weapon and placing it back on the counter before continuing to chop the plate full of carrots she had in front of her.

Shaw and Emma stumbled through the door next, followed by Barnes and Beth. They looked towards the girl who was busy chopping vegetables, and in the absence of an introduction, collapsed onto the hard wooden chairs. Hughes closed the door behind them. The heat was almost stifling in comparison to what they had just come from, but nobody complained.

A pot was bubbling on top of the stove and a divine smell accompanied the steam. Wren finished chopping and poured the contents of the plate into the large bubbling pot before lowering the heat a little and placing a lid on. She wiped her hands on a tea towel and turned around as Wolf began to interrogate the new arrivals with his nose.

"I'm making a pot of rabbit stew. I'm guessing you could all do with something warm inside you," said Wren. She looked towards Emma whose face was contorted with pain. "Come with me," Wren said to her as she walked around the table and helped her up. She guided Emma into the living room where a wrought-iron stove radiated powerful heat. Wren helped Emma onto the soft three-seater leather sofa. She looked at the underside of Emma's boots, there was a hole in one. Wren carefully removed it and the sock, which was soaked by a combination of melted snow and blood.

"I don't think the repair held," Emma called out to Shaw.

"Well, I never said I was a cobbler," he called back.

"What size are you?" asked Wren.

"Huh?" replied Emma.

"Shoe size?"

"Five."

"Well, today's your lucky day. I'm a five too. I can

give you a pair of boots, but you're going to have to rest this foot for a while," said Wren. "I've got all sorts of meds and stuff to help, but it's a nasty wound. You might need some antibiotics to stop infection." Wren disappeared and came back a minute later with a large first aid box.

The original dressing on Emma's wound had worked its way loose soon after they had left the carpet showroom. Now the gash was bleeding again. Wren knelt down and opened the box beside her. She pulled out a plastic bottle, and at the same time as tipping it to pour on Emma's foot, she warned, "This will hurt."

"Aghh!" said Emma as the clear liquid ripped at the exposed wound. "Thanks for the warning."

Wren took a wad of cotton wool and poured some more of the alcohol on it before dabbing at the wound. Each time the smarting sensation diminished a little more. "Okay," said Wren, holding a cotton wool pad in place and covering it with gauze before expertly wrapping a bandage around it. She put a safety pin through the loose cloth and secured it into position.

Emma moved her foot around, and the bandage remained tight. "Hey, thanks, you're pretty good at this," she said.

"I'm more used to dressing sprains, but the basic principle's the same," replied Wren.

"You a sporting girl?" asked Emma.

"Heptathlon."

"Cool."

"Would have been if this whole end of the world thing hadn't got in the way," replied Wren.

"Yeah, it was a bummer. Screwed up my plans too," said Emma, and the pair shared a smile.

"You smile like your brother," said Wren.

"You saw him smile? Wow, he must like you. He usually threatens to kill strangers before he gets to know them," said Emma.

"Well, I did save his life," replied Wren.

"That'll have earned you a few points."

"He's a bit…"

"A bit what?" asked Emma.

"A bit mental," said Wren.

"No arguments from me, and I've known him all his life."

"He's nice though," said Wren, and suddenly blushed. She stood up. "It will be a while before the road starts to clear. You can all stay here," she said, first looking at Emma and then looking across towards the others who were still in the kitchen area. "I have plenty of food. There's fresh water from the well, and there's heat."

"Thank you, Wren," replied Hughes. "We really appreciate that."

"It will be nice to have people to talk to," said Wren, as she started towards the kitchen again.

Emma grabbed her hand. "You could come with us when we leave y'know. There are lots of empty properties in Safe Haven still. There is safety and food, and there are people."

Wren looked at Emma and without realising squeezed her hand a little tighter when the word people was mentioned. People were what she missed more than anything. Good people. Not the kind who steal your belongings, try to take advantage of you, try to enslave you…but good people like these. She had worked hard to become independent, but now, maybe it was time to become part of something bigger, to become part of a community again.

"We'll see," replied Wren, "We'll see."

18

Jenny peeked through the gap in the office door. Nobody was looking in their direction, they were just three friends having breakfast together. She pulled out a large hip flask from the inside pocket of her thick wax jacket, unscrewed the top and poured a dash of amber liquid into her chicory. "Fancy a nip to ward off the cold?" she asked, winking at Lucy.

Lucy laughed. "Oh my God, seriously, you're my heroine," she replied, offering Jenny her mug. All three women chuckled and Jenny tipped the flask, making sure Lucy received an ample measure.

Without asking, Jenny poured some into Ruth's drink too, and the three women chinked their mugs together before taking a long drink. "Jura's finest," said Jenny smiling "I've got my own private reserve. The homebrew will do for the customers, but there have to be some perks to the job."

"Oh man, that hits the spot on a day like this," said Lucy.

Ruth coughed, before adding, "here, here."

"Y'know, I've got bottles and bottles of this stuff back at the pub. We could just head across there and leave all the responsible shit to someone else," said Jenny.

"Do you have any better angels calling to you? Or are all the voices you hear demons?" asked Lucy.

"Oh darling, who has fun listening to angels?" asked Jenny, and all three women laughed again. "We'll do an experiment. I'll spend a day with you and we'll listen to your angels. You spend a day with me and we'll listen to my demons, and we'll see which one we prefer. Deal?"

"You are terrible," said Lucy laughing again.

"What can I tell you? I know where my talents lie, and I'm not afraid to use them," said Jenny, unscrewing the top of the flask again and pouring a little more into each of their mugs.

"Y'know, on a serious note, before I forget, we could do with some alcohol across at the hospital. I was going to come and see you," said Lucy.

"Come across whenever you want. You can take as much as you need," said Jenny.

"You're the best," replied Lucy.

Jenny smiled. "It's funny. Remember how we

first…"

"Help!" came the terrified scream as a young woman burst through the swing doors of the village hall.

All three women immediately rose from the table and rushed to the office door. Panic reverberated around the hall as the anxious town's folk waited to hear the reason for the woman's terror.

"RAMs! RAMs!" she screamed.

Ruth, Jenny and Lucy looked at one another in horror, and Lucy instinctively reached round to the back of her jeans, feeling for the Glock that was in her bedside drawer. "Shit!" she hissed. She walked out of the office and headed straight towards the hysterical woman as others continued to look on in panic.

She took hold of the woman's freezing wrists. "Calm down," said Lucy. "Where have you seen them?"

"Outside. They're everywhere," replied the woman.

"What do you mean, everywhere?" asked Lucy.

"The campsite…the hospital. I went to visit my brother, but they were everywhere," said the woman beginning to sob hysterically.

"What do you mean…everywhere?" asked Lucy again.

"I mean they're fucking everywhere! What don't you understand about…"

That second, the swing doors burst open and there stood a forgotten creature. Forgotten, because in the sweet confines of Safe Haven, their kind had not been thought about in a long time. It remained there frozen for an everlasting second looking around the large hall like a starving child in a sweet shop.

Lucy was the only one—the only one—who had a track record against these creatures. She shook her head trying to wave off the last effects of the oxycodone tablets, before grabbing the underside of the nearest rickety canteen table and flipping it through the air like a windmill. The Formica top clattered and all eyes looked towards it. Lucy lodged one foot hard against the underside of the tabletop while kicking her other against one of the metal legs, snapping it from its rusty bolted fitting. Those around her fled as the creature made a beeline for an old woman who remained seated, too shocked and frail to move. Lucy ran forwards, putting herself between the woman and the beast. She swung the table leg like Babe Ruth swung a bat, and the creature went toppling over. She had been up against too many of these things to lose the upper hand. As it attempted to regain its footing, she unleashed another powerful blow on the back of its head, making it collapse face down onto the floor. Then she struck again, and again and again, caving in the back of the skull and revealing brain tissue. It was then and only then that she noticed, the RAM was in pyjamas, familiar ones at that. This was one of her patients from the hospital.

Lucy dropped the black metal leg onto the floor. She was out of shape and sweat had appeared on her forehead. She looked down at the creature, and her eyes closed in on its wound. She had almost forgotten how they bled. This was a relatively new convert to the ranks as the blood flowed more readily, but it still did not flow like that of a living human.

Lucy bent down and turned the beast over, then fell on her bottom and shuffled her feet, desperate to back away from the body. "Oh sweet Jesus!" she said, coming to rest against a wall. "It's Arthur Wells."

Jenny and Ruth rushed towards Lucy while panic swept through the others. Lucy slid up the wall to her feet. "Come on," said Jenny, "we need to figure out what the hell's goi…"

"Aggghhh!" came another high-pitched scream that turned into a gurgle as one woman who had made a bolt for the door was pounced on by a creature seemingly coming out of nowhere. This RAM was younger and more agile. No sooner had it taken a chunk out of the woman's neck than it dived onto another. Before Lucy could even pick up the table leg again, it was on top of yet another victim, tearing a large chunk out of the man's cheek as he screeched with pain and fear.

"Oh shit!" said Lucy, beginning to back up. "Everybody!" she shouted, "Arm yourselves with something. Killing the brain is the only thing that works remember," she added, as the first attack victim sat up. Its hand covered the gaping wound on its neck, despite its brain not understanding why. From sitting, it went to standing, and it turned and looked at the frightened faces as it bore its teeth. The beast launched towards the nearest group, flying through the air like a trapeze artist, grabbing a tight hold of Stacey Kirkbride, a fourteen-year-old girl, who had come to the village hall with her mother after the storm had caved their roof in at home. Mrs Kirkbride let out a haunting wail as the beast's mouth closed around Stacey's face. The creature pulled its head back, taking the girl's nose with it. Stacey stumbled back, gasping, crying and screaming as blood squirted. She put her hand up to the hole and a red fountain sprayed back into her eyes, making her lose vision. Stacey collapsed backwards over a chair, and her mother rushed to her side, while the girl's attacker leapt on a horrified bystander.

Stacey, looked at her mother for a moment through blurry red eyes as the blood continued to spurt, then her eyes finally closed.

"Nooo!" cried Mrs Kirkbride as tears poured down her face. She cradled her daughter, oblivious to the unfolding mayhem around her, and even when Stacey opened her eyes once more, Mrs Kirkbride did not see the deathly, milky grey. She did not see the unnatural, dancing, shattered ebony pupils. She saw Stacey's beautiful blue eyes that could always melt the coldest of hearts. "Oh my baby, my baby," sobbed Mrs Kirkbride, gently removing the blood matted hair from the girl's forehead. The creature laid in Mrs Kirkbride's arms for a brief moment before turning its head and closing its vice-like jaw. Even as it brought its mouth away with a gristly lump of bloody flesh between its teeth, the mother was still seeing the face of her daughter at her fifth birthday party, the first time she rode a pony, the trip to Disneyland for her tenth birthday. It was only as she began to feel the darkness rise inside her that Mrs Kirkbride looked down at the beast and saw the bite shaped crater in her arm. She started to shake uncontrollably, and then, she was no more.

Lucy, Ruth and Jenny all watched on in horror as the nightmare unfolded at lightning speed. People panicked and a large group fled out of the entrance, no longer interested in breakfast or the warmth of the village hall, all they wanted now was to be away from this new horror. It was not until their feet crunched into the snow of the car park and they saw three more RAMs closing in on them that they realised there was no escape.

"We need to contain this!" shouted Lucy, unleashing a hammer blow on Mrs Kirkbride's head, killing her instantly before the transformation had even occurred. "Ruth! Jenny! Help me with this!" she said, looking towards her friends.

Lucy stood in the middle of the hall. Nobody had listened. Nobody had armed themselves, they were only interested in looking for escape. But the beasts were too fast and the space was too confined. Another two creatures burst through the double doors, their grey faces decorated with the blood from their last kill.

"Oh dear God!" said Jenny, as she finally acknowledged that there would be no miracles, that there would be no rescue, and if she wanted to live, she had to fight. She and Ruth rushed to the upturned table and began grappling with the metal legs, trying to pull them loose, trying to arm themselves.

"Oh fuck!" said Lucy, remembering back to her dream. "I missed it," she said it out loud. The RAM who was now tearing into another hapless victim was McGregor. It had not been a case of flu, he had been scratched, that's all that made sense. "I missed it."

They had become complacent. They still gave full medical examinations to all Safe Haven newcomers, but they had never checked the men and women who returned from the scavenger missions. How could she have been so stupid? She snapped out of her thoughts as the creature that had been Stacey Kirkbride just a few moments before began to run towards Lucy with cheetah-like speed. She was on her before Lucy had a chance to swing the table leg. She grasped it in both hands, as if she was holding a bell bar, and shoved the metal into the RAM's gaping mouth breaking eight teeth, and sending the beast flying back with the force.

It landed heavily on its coccyx and then fell onto its back. A living being would have been in agony, a living being would have struggled to get back up, but not feeling any pain, the beast flew to its feet again like a breakdancing champion and charged towards Lucy. The gap where its nose had been sent a chill down Lucy's spine and as it opened its mouth once more revealing broken teeth and bloody gums, Lucy no longer saw Stacey Kirkbride, just a hideous, wretched monster.

This time, she was able to swing the table leg, and the side of the beast's temple caved, stopping its attack instantly. It fell to the ground.

Lucy looked around, numerous people were being attacked. She looked back towards Jenny and Ruth who were both still struggling to free one of the table legs to use as a weapon. She headed across, stepped onto the upturned table, then pressed her boot hard against one leg, then another, sending the metal supports clanging onto the hard floor.

"Thanks," said Jenny picking one up.

Ruth bent down to grab the other, and the three of them formed a small back to back triangle as they watched the terror unfold around them. One of the newly turned RAMs ran towards Jenny, Lucy caught the blur out of the corner of her eye, the creature leapt the final two metres, almost flying. Jenny tried to swing like she had seen Lucy do, but she could not get enough momentum and the creature, was deflected slightly, but not damaged. It landed in a crumpled mass at Ruth's feet.

"Oh God!" screamed Ruth as she booted the monster in the face. The RAM flicked its head back round straight away, the kick not phasing it, and it bit into her boot like an angry dog. Its teeth clamped around the rubber and Ruth let out a deafening scream. Lucy whipped around, saw what was happening, and unleashed a crushing blow with the table leg. For a second the RAM's teeth locked even harder around her shin and Ruth began to cry, before falling backwards onto the floor.

Another beast came towards the three of them like a juggernaut, Ruth and Lucy were too preoccupied, but Jenny timed her swing perfectly this time, and the black metal bludgeon snapped the creature's jaw from its hinges. It stood there dazed for a moment, with its bottom jaw at a forty-degree angle to the rest of its face. Blood began to trickle where bone protruded through skin, and Jenny had to stifle the urge to vomit.

"Oh my God!" gasped Jenny, horrified by what she saw. The creature tried to move its mouth in a biting motion, but despite a loud clicking sound that could even be heard above its growls, only the minimum of movement occurred. Its daze was temporary and it lurched towards its victim once more, flailing its arms wildly. Jenny raised her stylish high heeled boot and kicked, sending it back a few paces, before swinging the table leg and hooking the creature against the side of the head as it made another attempt to grab her. This time it collapsed to the left in a hopeless pile. The body spasmed before falling still. Jenny shoved the base of the table leg down and rested on it trying to catch her breath.

Ruth remained on the floor, a chunk of leather had been ripped from her boot. Lucy raised the table leg above her and even though the RAM was motionless, she unleashed blow after blow on its head. "You M-O-T-H-E-R F-U-C-K-E-R," she screamed, before dropping her weapon to the floor with a loud clang and crouching down to look at Ruth's leg. The boot was tight around her jeans and Lucy couldn't see the bite beyond the cosmetic effect it had on the librarian's clothing. "Fuck!" she yelled, picking up the table leg again and at the same time, grabbing Ruth beneath the arms and dragging her across the floor towards the small back office the three of them had shared breakfast in just a few moments earlier.

"What the hell are you doing?" shouted Jenny.

"Cover us, I need to see Ruth's leg," shouted Lucy, pulling her friend through the doorway. The unfolding scene was the stuff of nightmares. RAMs were attacking young and old, adding to their ranks, their legion.

"Jenny! Behind you!" shouted Lucy as another creature ran towards them.

Jenny twirled, instinctively raising the table leg, and as the beast made its leap, she swung with all her might. The already bloody end of the bludgeon sliced through flesh and cracked through bone, catapulting the creature over tables and chairs into a useless heap.

The librarian was continuing to moan and cry, and Lucy was terrified that she was going to have to kill her friend. Jenny stormed into the small room after them and immediately shoved the large desk up against the door.

Lucy dragged Ruth into a corner, she knew time was everything. If the skin had been breached, Ruth would turn any second now. The doctor ripped the boot from her friend's foot and the librarian shrieked again. Lucy rolled up the jeans and saw teeth marks, but the skin was not broken. At the worst, there would be a bruise there.

"Oh my sweet Jesus," said Lucy collapsing backwards as the screams and growls continued outside in the village hall.

Ruth looked down at her leg. "I'm okay? I'm okay?"

Sweat was pouring down Jenny's face as she leaned the table leg against the wall. "Yes love, you're fine...for the moment," said Jenny looking towards the door.

Lucy brushed her fingers through her hair, "I have

to get to the hospital," she said.

"What? What the hell are you talking about?" demanded Jenny.

"Sammy and Jake. I need to get to them," replied Lucy.

"Love!" said Jenny. "They're gone. Don't you realise? The hospital has gone. It's all gone."

19

Humphrey stopped and his body went rigid. "Come on boy," said Raj, it's too cold to…"

The dog began to growl. Growls were a form of communication like no other, and both Raj and Talikha felt chills colder than the snow beneath their feet at the sound of this one. They stopped dead in their tracks, and Talikha instinctively reached over and took hold of Raj's hand.

Raj looked back across the short snowy pier to the small rowboat, and beyond to their yacht out in the deeper bay. He trusted Humphrey's instincts more than his own, and he knew that growl. That growl meant RAMs.

"I think we should go back to the boat," said Talikha.

"I think you are right, my love," replied Raj, who gave a small tug on Humphrey's collar. The three of them headed back along the dock. When they were all on board,

Raj untied the rope from the cleat, while Talikha picked up her oar and pushed it into the water.

Humphrey began to bark as first one, then two RAMs appeared at the end of the pier and started trailing through the snow towards the small boat. The volume of Humphrey's barks increased with each step the creatures took. Raj bent down, grabbing an antique sword from beneath his seat. The item had been a Sikh weapon, and Hughes had very proudly given it to Raj after one of his scavenging trips. Raj had not had the heart to tell Hughes he was actually Hindu, not Sikh, and now he was glad.

He stood poised with the sword, ready to strike if the creatures reached them before the boat pulled away from the dock. He felt gradual movement and looked down as the gap between the snow-covered pier and the rowboat gradually began to widen.

"Thank goodness!" Raj whispered, as the creatures got nearer and Humphrey's barks became more intense.

Raj looked to his side and saw Mike there. He had been transported back in time to the hotel in Candleton when he, Mike and Lucy fought off a group of the rampaging creatures. A lot had happened since then. As the boat drifted further from the dock, and the creatures came to a withering stop, at the end of the pier, he looked down at Humphrey.

"I really hope our friends are safe boy," he said.

Humphrey looked up at him and let out a small whine.

**

Jenny walked the filing cabinet over to the desk, then used all her weight to push it over. The sturdy nineteen eighties creation clattered on the hard floor. She placed her back against the wall and used her feet to push the cabinet against the desk. The remaining gap between the filing cabinet and the wall was filled with various pieces of office furniture, fittings and accessories. The construction wedged the door solidly. The door would have to break to move.

"You girls sit tight," said Lucy as she stood on a chair to open one of the high, narrow, frosted glass windows.

"This is madness," said Jenny.

Lucy looked back at her friends, "I've got to see at least."

"Lucy, sweetheart, please, don't risk your life. They're gone, love. We should assume the whole campsite is gone. You saw how quickly all that happened. The only hope is to stay locked up and pray help comes," said Jenny.

"Help? What help? Mike and the soldiers are eighty miles away. The whole coastline is covered in thick snow, so even if we could raise the alarm, no one would be able to get to us. It's going to be a few days before vehicles can start to travel properly again. Right now, there's just the three of us," replied Lucy.

Ruth pulled herself up using the desk. "Go Lucy. If there's a slim chance they're okay, you should go, but please be careful."

Lucy climbed back down from the chair and hugged both the women. "I need to know. Plus, I might find some survivors out there."

"Please be careful," said Jenny.

"It's not like I've got a lot of choice, is it? If I'm not careful, I'm dead."

Lucy zipped her coat up tight and climbed back onto the chair. She placed the table leg on the window ledge and heaved herself up and through the narrow gap. She squeezed through the opening, and unable to get purchase on the lip of the ledge, fell the eight feet to the ground on the other side. The snow had drifted against the wall and her landing was soft if not cold. She stood up, brushed herself down and spotted a RAM already running towards her.

"Oh shit!"

"Are you okay out there?" asked Jenny through the window.

"No! Jen, pass me the table leg, I left it on the ledge," said Lucy.

"Hang on, I'm just taking my boots off, these heels aren't doing me…"

"Now Jen! Now!" demanded Lucy as the creature stormed through the snow towards her.

There was clattering from inside and Lucy heard the window creak a little before the table leg emerged. "Oh my God!" cried Jenny as she caught sight of the beast charging towards Lucy.

Lucy grabbed the table leg and braced herself ready to take a swing. She recognised the RAM as one of the newcomers who had shown up just a few days before the storm. He was a nice man, quiet, polite, but not anymore. Lucy swung the table leg with all the force she could muster, and there was a loud crack as it made contact with the creature's skull, but the beast did not go down. It stumbled and then continued, albeit much slower.

Lucy leaned back against the wall and booted the RAM in the chest, forcing it in the other direction. It staggered and then fell flat. She took advantage of the fall and began to pound the beast's head mercilessly, causing a red spray to spread over the surrounding snow. She stood there for a second, looking at the creature, making sure all movement had ceased, then she looked back at Jenny. "Close that window, stay quiet, and hope help comes."

The window closed and Lucy headed across the rear car park, hoping she wouldn't see Sammy or Jake before she reached the hospital. If she saw them, it meant they had turned.

***

Another piece of the heavy loader bucket from the front of the tractor fell to the floor of the huge corrugated barn with an echoing clatter. Hughes turned the welding torch off and pulled his mask up.

"You want me to take a turn?" asked Barnes as Hughes wiped the sweat from his forehead.

"Nah, I'll be done soon enough," replied Hughes.

"I can't believe we didn't find this place before on one of our trips," said Barnes.

"We usually gave Inverness a wider birth than this, and even if we did head out this far, it's not somewhere you see from the main road, we could have missed it. I know one thing, when the thaw comes, we're going to get everything we can out of here," said Hughes.

The pair surveyed the huge outbuilding. Corrugated plastic windows on the roof were still partially covered with snow, letting in less light than usual, but the two of them could see the machinery and barrels of red diesel lined up on the large shelving units. This had not been a small family run business, this had been a huge farm.

The side door to the building opened and Shaw limped in. "How's it going?"

"Not much more to cut now," said Hughes.

"You sure this is going to work?" asked Shaw.

"Hey, give me a welding torch and I can perform miracles, my friend," said Hughes smiling.

"Have you managed to get the tipper working?" asked Shaw.

"Oh yes!" Barnes climbed into the big green Volvo tipper truck and turned the key. The engine coughed, then rumbled to life, and smiles lit up the three men's faces.

"How?"

"There's a storage cupboard stacked with new parts for all sorts of vehicles. New batteries, wiper blades, nuts, bolts, the whole lot. An operation this size probably had a full-time mechanic making sure everything ran smoothly," said Hughes.

"Sweet," replied Shaw.

"George is going to be over the bloody moon when we take some of this stuff back to him," said Hughes, signalling to Barnes to cut the engine as the fumes started to irritate the back of his throat.

"So how long do you think?" Shaw asked.

"I don't know, another couple of hours or so. We might need everybody here when it comes to fitting the plough on," said Hughes.

"Okay, well just give us a shout. I'm not sure what use Emma will be at the moment, but Wren will give us a hand," replied Shaw heading back out.

Barnes climbed down from the tipper. "I still don't know how you had this brainwave," he said smiling.

"Because I couldn't just twiddle my thumbs and wait for the thaw. Our mate's out there. Anything could happen. The tractor could break down, he could go off the road, he could get attacked. At least if I'm doing something... I wouldn't be able to live with myself if something happened and I'd tried nothing Barney." Hughes lowered his mask and ignited the flame on the welding torch once more.

***

Lucy climbed over the back fence of the village hall car park and kept low through the bushes. She hoped the majority of the RAMs were on the other side of the village hall opposite the campsite, but she was not going to chance anything. She could feel the cold and wet as she headed through the snow-laden branches, and when she came to the edge of the thicket, she crouched down and popped her head out just a little, checking in each direction. There was a row of beautiful painted white cottages and today they had white roofs too. The middle one was where Ruth, Richard and David lived. There was no sign of any creatures in the street, so she made a break from the trees and ran as fast as she could through the thick snow and into the garden, choosing to leapfrog the gate rather than taking the extra time to open it. She ran around the back of the house and opened the kitchen door, pulling it to firmly behind her.

"Ruth? Ruth, is that you?" asked David. "I could do with a fresh hot water bottle, this one is lukewarm."

"I could do with one too," muttered Richard.

"Yes. Yes, Ruth, Richard could do with one too. And Ruth, could I have a fresh jug of water? I knocked the other over. Oh, and could you fetch a cloth, there's water all over my bedside table," said David.

"I'd like fresh water," said Richard, quietly.

"Oh, and Ruth, could you bring some fresh water for Richard too? Oh, and could you put a mint leaf in like you did last time? In mine and his," said David.

"I don't want a mint leaf," said Richard.

"No. No, Richard doesn't want a mint leaf, Ruth. But I'll have two. Put two mint leaves in mine please."

"How the hell does she live with these guys?" Lucy asked, under her breath.

"Ruth? Ruth?" said David.

Lucy headed up the stairs and into their bedroom. They both looked shocked as she walked through the door.

"I'm not Ruth, and you can get your own damn water," said Lucy.

Despite having pyjamas on, both men instinctively pulled their quilts higher as if they were blushing brides on their wedding nights embarrassed to show their skin.

"Lucy? What are you doing here? Where's Ruth?" Asked David.

"Listen, how sick are you guys? Seriously?"

"We're sick. Not doctor sick, we just need time to rest, that's all," said David.

Lucy rubbed her hands over her face. "There are RAMs. Lots of them," she said.

"What? Where?" asked both men at the same time, forgetting their coyness and sitting up in bed.

"There's been an outbreak at the campsite, and then there was a big attack in the hall. Ruth and Jenny are barricaded in the back office. I need to get across to the hospital. Sammy and Jake are there."

David pulled the quilt back, climbed out of bed and went across to the window. He stood back, looking through the lace curtains. "I don't see anything," he said.

"There'll be a lot of them in the village hall still, and I think there'll be a lot across at the campsite and the area in between. They'll slowly start to spread. That's what they do," said Lucy.

"Oh my God. I didn't think this would ever happen here, not in Safe Haven," said David.

"You n' me both, sweetie," said Lucy. "So, how sick are you?" she asked again.

David looked a little sad that being waited on hand and foot by Ruth was over. "What do you need us to do?"

"That door in the village hall won't last forever, and Ruth and Jenny are sitting ducks in there." Lucy walked to the window and looked across to the thicket and trees beyond, shielding the village hall rear car park from view. "I have to get to the hospital. You need to get to them."

"What? Us?" said David.

"Hey, both of you. Stop being pussies and remember who you are. You're not the same guys who entered a suicide pact back in Skelton. You're important members of this community. You have done amazing things. If it wasn't for the two of you, do you think for a second we would have been able to build the siege weapons that took down Fry?" she asked, looking at both of their reddening faces. "If it wasn't for you, we wouldn't have a school. We wouldn't have the hope that this place gives us. But right now, it's not your minds, it's your actions that are going to count."

The two men looked at Lucy, and then David walked across to the chest of drawers and pulled out some fresh underwear, socks and outer clothing. "I'd do anything for Ruth, we both would," he said almost mumbling.

"Attaboy," said Lucy. "Now, I need weapons. What have you got?"

"Not much," replied Richard, coughing. "We've got some sharp knives in the kitchen. There are spades and pitchforks in the garden. Ooh, we've got a rake too!"

"Seriously? A rake? I'll help myself to a knife if that's okay with you," said Lucy.

"Take whatever you want," said Richard climbing out of bed and coughing again.

"Thanks guys. Be careful, and if you've got a set of steps, you might want to consider taking them, it's quite a drop from that window."

David turned around to look at Lucy, "You be careful too," he said and took hold of her hand.

"I meant what I said. You're not the same guys you were in Skelton. Ruth and Jenny need help, I turned to the only people I can trust". She leaned in and kissed him on the cheek. "I have to go," she said and headed out of the room and downstairs.

"She's right, you know, we're not the same people we were in Skelton," said Richard.

"I suppose we're about to find out, aren't we?" said David.

Lucy walked into the kitchen and headed straight to the knife block. She removed a well-made piece of Sheffield steel and placed it in her belt. She bent down and looked under the kitchen sink, there was nothing in there of any use. She picked up the table leg which she'd left at the side of the door and headed into the back garden, unlocking the shed and pushing enough snow to one side with her boot to open the door. She stepped inside and immediately breathed in a lungful of creosote. She coughed a little, although the smell was not unpleasant. She looked at the pitchforks and the spades, then she zeroed in on a lawn umbrella. It was part of a set of four white chairs and a white table. The table had a hole in the centre and the umbrella pole went through the hole and unfurled over the table to stop the heat of the sun. The umbrella itself was basically a big metal spike that stabbed into the ground with a large fabric top which opened up when a small switch was pushed.

Lucy removed the knife from her belt and hacked the fabric off, then bent and ripped the thin metal ribs that supported the cloth from the pole too. After a moment, she was left with what was ultimately a white spear with one sharp end and one end covered by a plastic cap with the Home and Garden Depot logo emblazoned on it.

She placed the knife back in her belt, left the table leg leaning next to the pitchforks, and exited the shed, closing the door behind her. She would never give up. No matter the odds, no matter how outnumbered she was. This was her family. Nothing was more important than family.

20

The yacht sat off the shoreline with Humphrey remaining vigilant. His eyes stared towards the dock even though he could no longer perceive the details. Raj and Talikha stood on deck, the sea was calm, the landscape was white, and at any other time, this would have been a day where they counted their blessings and bathed in the beauty that surrounded them. This was not any other day though, this was today, and something they never thought would happen had happened.

"Can we call for help using the radio?" asked Talikha.

"I have no idea of the frequency the lookouts use," replied Raj. I think the best thing to do is head up the coast to see Jules. She may be able to rally some troops, although, I fear by then we will be too late and all the damage that can be done will be done."

Talikha placed her hand over Raj's. "We control

what we can, let fate take care of the rest. Let us set sail. Let us get word to Jules."

He nodded. There was pain on his face, and Talikha knew why. He admired Mike more than anyone he had met. Mike was his best friend. Mike was the bravest man he knew, and Mike would not waste time going for help, he would head into the village alone if he had to. He would fight every last creature himself. He would not think of the danger, he would just do it. "I…"

"I know what you are thinking. He is not here. He is brave, but he is rash. You have a wife, and you have a dog who love you and need you. You are brave, but you temper bravery with thought. Our friends need our help. The best way for us to do that is to get to Jules as fast as we can," said Talikha.

"You are right. But then again, you always are."

***

"Mother," thwack, "fucking," slash, "piece of," slice, "shit," said Mike, leaving another four creatures in his wake as two more approached. They struggled through the deep snow towards him, and not for the first time, he lost more than his patience. Mike charged towards them, churning the snow beneath his feet as he went as fast as his legs could carry him. He swiped at both beasts simultaneously, hacking through their skulls. Both of them fell in unison, and Mike stood there like a vicious animal, looking around himself waiting to see where the next attack would come from.

This journey was taking an age. Without fail, every time he approached one of the larger villages, the RAMs were already heading in his direction. The noise of the engine was like banging a dinner gong for them. He bent down and wiped the blades of the machetes clean in the snow before placing them into his rucksack. He dabbed the sweat from his brow and headed back to the rumbling tractor. Usually his anger came in bursts, but he had become more and more infuriated every time he had to interrupt his journey. He knew every delay was one step closer to the point of no return for his sister.

Mike climbed back into the tractor and the wheels began to turn once more. He hoped he was not too late. He hoped all this was not for nothing.

***

Even Emma had limped out to the huge barn to lend whatever support she could. Barnes, Shaw, Beth and Wren pulled their trolleys out from underneath the plough as Hughes shut off the welding torch and pulled his mask up. The attachment stayed in place.

"How the hell did you do this?" asked Emma.

"It was easier than it looked, Bit of welding here, bit of hooking there and Bob's your uncle, you've got yourself a snowplough," said Hughes.

"Say what you like. It's brilliant Hughesy. I never remember seeing this shit on Blue Peter," said Shaw, and they all laughed.

"So, when do we head out?" asked Beth.

"Soon as," replied Hughes. "I want to grab a few bits from in here, we'll take some supplies for the road and then we go. Twenty minutes? Half an hour?"

"I'll get some food together," said Wren, heading straight out. She had played it cool up until now, but the prospect of being part of a community, interacting with people, decent people, was too much for her to contain her excitement. She just wanted the journey to be underway now.

The five of them watched her as she left, and then all smiled. "She's really sweet," said Emma.

"Yeah," replied Hughes, taking the heavy welding mask off his face completely. "Her bloody dog scares me to death, but she's a real sweetheart."

"Do you think she'll stay in Safe Haven?" asked Emma.

"Dunno. I can tell she's missed company. She'd become very independent, but the poor kid's craving attention. I mean, she went from having her family surrounding her, supporting her, to having no one in the blink of an eye. She travelled from Edinburgh to Inverness by herself…by herself for Christ's sake. A sixteen-year-old, out there, alone. She can look after herself, but I think that when she sees what we've got, she'll want to be a part of it," said Hughes.

"Let's hope," said Emma, "We need people like

her…like us."

"You mean fighters?" said Beth laughing.

"I mean…we've had a lot of new people joining us. Not all of them would have taken up swords against Fry," said Emma.

"Fry is dead and gone, thank God," said Beth.

"Yeah, but we never know when another Fry might come along. We never know what the future holds, and while it's great that we've got a few builders and a few farmers and teachers and fishermen, we need fighters. We need warriors, so if the day ever comes that we need to take up arms again, we know we'll have enough of us in our ranks to do it," said Emma.

"I think we're in pretty good shape," said Barnes. "We've got a small militia. We've got a good-sized group of volunteers who man the look-out points, we've got a good group of people who stood side by side with us against Fry and who would again."

"Yeah, but out of all the newcomers, how many of them have signed up for lookout rotation? Granted, they give in other ways. We are really developing as a community, but I think if we had to go to war again, we'd struggle. That's all I'm saying. That's all I was saying—it would be good to have a fighter like Wren joining us," said Emma.

"I don't want to even think about any of that crap. Let's deal with one problem at a time. Let's get home," said Beth.

Hughes remained silent, but locked eyes with Emma. It was like she had read his thoughts, and despite the sweat still running down his back, his skin prickled with goosebumps.

***

Lucy crept back down the garden path, keeping a close eye on the quiet street. There were three possible routes to get to the campsite, and all of them were just as dangerous.

"Eeny, meeny, miny, moe," she said in nothing more than a whisper, and suddenly she was no longer standing in Ruth's garden, she was back home with Sammy, Jake, Mike and Emma. It was a Sunday afternoon, and Lucy had made Sammy a pendant from a beautiful shiny piece of quartz she had found on the beach. She held two fists in front of Sammy, telling her to guess which one her surprise was in, and the young girl recited the same little poem that had just come from Lucy's own lips. It was the same poem millions of children said when faced with a decision, it was the same poem her own daughter had said. Her Charlie. Her sweet little innocent Charlie. Sammy was like her in many ways. She had already lost one little girl, she could not lose another.

Lucy snapped out of her daydream and back to the cold reality. She reached down to her pocket and felt the bulge of the pill bottle. She had only taken one tablet, but the effects were sticking with her much more than the old days. She kept zoning in and out, and this really was not the time for that to be happening.

Lucy climbed over the gate and turned right, choosing not to cut back through the thicket and small wooded area to the village hall. Richard and David would need all the help they could get to rescue Ruth and Jenny, and if Lucy got to the village hall and had to make a quick backtrack, that would ruin their chances. She trudged down the empty street in the deep snow. The sea was blue, and the sun was getting higher with each passing minute, but sunny was not the word she would use to describe the day.

Lucy knew that when she got to the end of this street, all hell would more than likely break loose. It was a feeling she'd had numerous times before, but unlike before, she was facing it alone.

"Nooo!" came a high-pitched scream that tore through the air.

Lucy looked behind her, there was no sign of anyone or anything. She carried on walking and her grip tightened around the spear she had fashioned from the parasol. She reached across and felt the butt of the kitchen knife with her other hand, as her breathing began to speed up, and perspiration started to trickle down her back despite the frigid weather. She reached the end of the road and crouched down, first looking left, then right. It was all quiet. She headed left. The beautiful water glistened to her right and a small park with a climbing frame and slide stood eerily quiet on her other side. The arc of trees shielded what was beyond from view and her from what was beyond.

Another scream cut through the cold air, and as Lucy approached the junction, familiar growls began to drift through the breeze. She crouched down once again and peeked around the corner. This time, Hell was waiting. The scream had come from a young girl, and four RAMs each knelt down around her, their mouths full and bloody. The girl's body spasmed for a moment before falling still, then slowly at first, it began to reanimate.

The snow in this street had drifted, but on the road itself was shallow. The upside to this was Lucy would be able to move faster, the downside was so would the RAMs. She got up from her crouch and took in the wider area. The five creatures were all she could see for the time being.

"Screw it! We've all got to die of something," she said and kicked through the last few feet of thick snow before beginning to jog down the middle of the street.

The two beasts facing in her direction were the first to charge, almost knocking their counterparts over as they began to head towards Lucy. One had been an old woman with a badly deformed leg. She trailed behind the other, but with all the venom and malevolence of the first. The other creatures finally reacted and soon, all five were heading straight for Lucy.

Lucy stopped running and planted one leg behind her. She held the spear in both hands and waited. The second the sprinting creature was in range, she thrust the weapon towards its head, the dirty white point sunk into its left eye, punching through the brain and cracking through the beast's skull on the other side. In a fraction of a second it ceased all movement and Lucy dragged the spear back out, scraping it against bone. It left the creature's body with a popping sound, and before she had time to think, the second and third RAMs were nearly upon her, having overtaken the lame one by a good few strides.

This time, Lucy twirled the spear above her head, using it to smash one creature across the side of its face, making it veer and lose its balance while at the same time, bringing her right foot up and booting the other square in the chest. She heard its ribs crack as the heel dug in, and the beast went flying backwards onto the snowy ground.

Not wasting a second, Lucy turned and drove the point of the spear straight through the back of the skull of the first fallen beast before spinning around and staking the other straight through its temple. Both creatures fell motionless, while the growls of the fourth warned her she was still in immediate danger.

Lucy caught the RAM's movement out of the corner of her eye, and while she pulled the spear free from her third victim's temple with her left hand, she snatched the kitchen knife with her right and ducked a flailing arm before standing straight and plunging the long blade of the knife up through the beast's chin and into its brain.

It dropped like a concrete block revealing the final creature, still limping towards Lucy, relentless in its endeavour to feast, to infect.

"Oh God!" said Lucy, realising it was one of the old women from the hospital.

What Lucy had thought was a long coat from a distance, was actually a navy blue dressing gown. The doctor braced herself, then forced the spear through the eye of her former patient the second she was in range. The RAM fell backwards onto the ground, and that's when Lucy began to shake uncontrollably. "Oh God. Oh no, please, God," she said as she looked at the RAM's face and was suddenly sure it was that of one of the women in the room across from Sammy and Jake.

***

"You guys okay back there?" asked Hughes releasing the speak button of the walkie-talkie and waiting for a response as the plough made short work of the snowy lane.

"Go screw yourself," said Beth.

The occupants of the cab of the truck burst out laughing. There was very limited space for Shaw, Emma and Wren, especially with Wolf curled up underneath the heater of the footwell, but at least they were not out in the freezing cold.

Beth and Barnes sat in one corner of the tipper. They wore wool hats, gloves and had a quilt wrapped tightly around themselves. Barnes grabbed the radio from Beth and hit the talk button. "We're fine, thanks mate," he said.

Hughes smiled and placed the radio handset into the cup holder. The pair of walkie-talkies were little more than toys that Wren had scavenged on one of her trips to

Inverness. They ran on AA batteries of which she had a large supply, and Wren had checked through the different preset frequencies often in the hope she may hear another voice, but she never did.

"So how did you survive on your own for so long?" asked Shaw.

"What do you mean?" replied Wren.

"I mean... against the RAMs? Against the people?" he replied.

"I ran when I could run. I fought when there weren't any other options. I stockpiled food. I taught myself the skills I needed. I did what anyone would who wanted to survive," she replied, still a little puzzled by the question.

"But..." continued Shaw, and then broke off.

"But what?" asked Wren.

"But you're only sixteen," he said.

"Why does that make a difference?" she asked.

"Because..." he broke off again, now he was the one struggling to understand.

"Look," she said, "I'm an athlete...was...sometimes I'd train over six hours a day. I know how to push myself, I know how to focus. I set myself goals, and I work towards them. I still train to stay fit, but now I teach myself other stuff, Like with the crossbows. I practice skills. I got lots of books from the library until those, those thugs set fire to it," she said, almost spitting the last words.

"Who?" asked Emma.

"The flat dwellers. The lowlifes who take what they want without thought for others. Thieves and worse."

"Flat dwellers?" said Emma.

"There are some luxury condos, they took them over, a big gang of them. I had a few run-ins, a few near escapes. They found me in the library once. They tried to...a group of them tried to...but I fought them off. Then there was another time they caught me leaving with a satchel of books, but even with a full satchel, I could outrun them. When I went back a few days later, though, the building and the one next to it were burnt to the ground," she said, with a look of sadness sweeping across her face.

"Well, we've got a library in Safe Haven," said Emma.

"You have?" replied Wren.

"Yeah, it's not huge, but it's growing all the time. We've even got three qualified librarians," said Emma.

Wren watched Emma's face for a moment, and then turned away, looking hurt. "It's not nice to make fun of people."

Emma grabbed the young girl's hand and squeezed it. "Wren, I'm not teasing you, I'm serious. We've got a library and three librarians, who came up with us from Yorkshire."

Wren leaned across to look at Hughes, "Is she kidding me?"

Hughes chuckled. "No, love. We brought a shed load of bloody books up from Yorkshire, all selected by the nerdiest librarians you're ever going to meet," he said smiling. "Mike insisted we have a library. He said it was the only way we were going to survive and build ourselves a future."

"Mike said that?" asked Wren.

"Yeah," replied Hughes.

"Oh," replied Wren.

"Oh, what?" asked Emma.

"Erm, he didn't really strike me as a book sort of person," she replied, and Emma, Shaw and Hughes all laughed.

"Yeah well, my brother is full of surprises."

21

Lucy hopped over the wall that bordered the campsite. There was a healthy wooded area all the way around, protecting the inhabitants from the vicious Atlantic winds that battered the coastline in winter months. She stayed low until she was out of sight of the road and then stood straight, keeping close to the trees as she walked. There was little snow on the ground as most of it still decorated the foliage, but she stepped lightly, careful not to break twigs or branches to alert any RAMs to her whereabouts.

The four static caravans, or trailers as she called them, that constituted the hospital were annexed off by a small, shrubbed square. There were three more sets of four trailers, then about twenty four-berth caravans that had been scavenged to provide temporary housing to newcomers until more permanent accommodation was arranged. The campsite was key to Safe Haven's plans for growth, and even though a fair few of the inhabitants would have been having breakfast across in the village hall when they were attacked, Lucy anticipated there would be a good number still at the campsite.

She stopped when she got closer to the edge of the tree line. She closed her eyes and placed her forehead against the rough bark of an oak. It was just as she had feared. There were dozens of RAMs laying siege to the caravans all over the campsite. Their fists were battering doors, their bodies smashed against the sides of some of the smaller ones making them shake and even lean. She could hear muffled screams from inside some as children and mothers were trapped by the ghoulish beasts hell-bent on reaching them.

Lucy opened her eyes again and looked across the site to the cordoned area of the hospital. The door to one of the trailers was open. A small handful of creatures had climbed the steps to batter against the doors of the others. Eventually, they would gain access, the trailers were not the sturdiest constructions, but for the time being, they were holding. The caravan Sammy and Jake were in was at the furthest end, opposite the tree line.

"Shit!" said Lucy, looking at all the creatures attempting to gain access to the hospital trailers. "Okay," she said taking a deep breath, "I can do this. I can do this."

She retraced her steps a little to make sure she had cover while she skirted the perimeter of the campsite, then continued her journey to the hospital. When she knew she was close to the four large trailers that housed her patients, she moved forward once again until she came face to face with the rear of one. All the activity was at the front. She could hear the growls of the creatures. She could hear the bangs against the sides of the large mobile homes, but for the time being, she could not see any RAMs, and that was a good thing. In her short journey, she had formed a plan and the element of surprise was everything.

Lucy jumped up to look in the first bedroom window. There were two older men and one middle-aged woman sat close together on a bed, looking towards the bedroom door. Lucy reached up and tapped lightly against the glass, then jumped up again. All three heads had turned to look in her direction. A moment later, the woman had opened the window.

"Lucy! Thank God!" she said.

Lucy passed her spear to the woman, then took hold of the window ledge and jumped again, pulling herself up. The woman grabbed hold of Lucy's jacket and helped her into the room, before closing the window. The woman was one of the few patients at the hospital not being treated for flu. She had been having frequent dizzy spells and during the last, she had banged her head causing a concussion. Lucy wanted to keep her in for a couple of days just to keep an eye on her. Now she wished she had sent her home. At least she might have stood a better chance at home.

"Where are the others?" asked Lucy.

"The others?" asked the woman.

"The other patients," replied Lucy.

"There were two. They tried to go for help earlier when there weren't so many. I saw them get caught. I saw them...turn."

The two old men were looking better than they had a few days earlier. Lucy remembered they had been in the opposite room. They looked towards Lucy with long, drawn faces.

"Listen to me," said Lucy. "You're going to have to make a break for it."

"What are you talking about?" said one of the old men beginning to cough.

"It's a matter of time before they get in here. I'm saying on the other side of those trees is the pub, the dock, the road. I'm saying it might not have hit over there yet. The caravan to the side of us, the door is wide open. You are the only ones who have a chance of escaping this."

"Don't you mean we?" asked the woman. "You'll come with us if we go, won't you?"

"I need to get to Sammy and Jake across the way," replied Lucy.

"That's mad. You'll never reach them," said the woman.

"That's my problem," replied Lucy walking back to the window and opening it.

"I'd prefer to stay here," replied the woman.

"Sorry, sweetie, I'm not giving you a choice. In five minutes this place will be RAM central. You're going now. All three of you."

"What do you mean RAM central?" asked the woman.

"You don't wanna know," replied Lucy. "Now I need all three of you to get out."

"But…"

"Now!"

"I really don't feel well enough," said one of them.

"See how you feel when you've got someone taking a chunk out of your neck," replied Lucy, who for the first time actually heard what she was saying. She took a breath and paused for a moment as she saw the looks of confusion on all three of their faces. "Look. I'm sorry. I need you to go. It's the best chance you've got. What I'm about to do is dangerous, I don't want to risk anyone's life but my own."

A few minutes later, Lucy was watching the mismatched trio stumbling through the woods away from the campsite and hopefully to safety. She caught a final glimpse of them as they drifted from her view, then she took a deep breath before heading out of the room. The moment she opened the door, the thuds and growls began to shake her very bones, and the butterflies started to flap wildly in her stomach.

She stepped into the kitchen, grateful it was at the

rear of the mobile home away from the view of the wolfish crowd of ghouls. Lucy reached into one of the drawers and brought out a reel of fishing line. They had a good supply in the village, not just for catching fish. She used them to suture wounds. In the absence of proper medical supplies, they were a near-perfect alternative, but right now, she needed them for something else. She took a pair of wire cutters from a drawer and went back down the hall, crouching before entering the living room area. The clattering against the front door was even louder now, but that was the least of her worries. She looked towards the two beds that stood on opposite sides of the room, then crawled towards the first. She unravelled a length of fishing line and tied it about two brick widths above floor level. She crawled across to the bed on the opposite side and did the same. She repeated this until there were multiple tripwires dotted around the living room area. When she was satisfied she had done all she could, she placed the fishing line back in her pocket and took a deep breath.

"Okay! Here goes a whole lot of nothing," she said standing up and walking across to the window. She looked at the terrifying creatures and felt the familiar icy chill run down her spine as the malevolence intensified in their eyes and they bore their teeth like wild animals. She opened the small narrow window above the main picture window and began to yell.

"Hey! Hey! That's right! Over here! Hey!" she bellowed, gaining the attention of the creatures from the surrounding trailers too. Suddenly there was a rampage towards her, and she felt the thud as two dozen more

RAMs smashed against the side of the mobile home in unison. Lucy gulped, as she realised just how much of a Hail Mary she was about to play. She shuffled along, making sure to keep all the beasts in view as long as she could before leaving the line of sight afforded by the large window panes. She opened the inner door to the small entrance hall and heard the creatures battering against the outer door. Even though the door opened outwards, she could see it shaking in its frame, and the outlines of the creatures through the UPVC squares and frosted glass looked just as menacing as the ones she had seen in their full glory seconds earlier.

She was amazed that the glass had held as the beasts smashed against it, but maybe that was the one last piece of good luck she would ever enjoy. She stood back, raised her foot and then booted the door handle down and out as hard and fast as she could. It burst open, knocking the creatures behind it through the weak wooden bannister of the small veranda, and sprawling onto the snow.

Lucy immediately turned tail and began to run through the living room of the trailer as the first half dozen creatures sprinted up the outside steps after her. She leapt over the first fishing line hurdle, then the second, then the third, all without looking back. She ran down the hall as she heard the table drag and crash as the first beast tumbled to the floor, followed by a second, then a third and fourth. She shot a glance back to see more creatures piling through the entrance, and she paused to make sure they did not lose sight of her.

One of the creatures somehow managed to bypass

the second boobytrap and Lucy seized the handle of the knife in her belt with her right hand, ready to fight. The third piece of fishing line caught it just as it brought its foot up however, making it trip and fall while still more behind it began to topple. She remained there while RAMs continued to pour through the entrance, and the fallen creatures began to scramble to their feet. Finally, she opened the bedroom door and ran through, closing it firmly behind her and pulling one, then the other bed against it before tipping over the wardrobe and wedging that against the beds. The door began to open and the creatures' barges and shoves began to push the furniture across the floor in small increments at first.

Lucy turned and opened the window, lowering her spear out, then lowering herself down into the snow before grabbing the spear and pushing the window closed. She kept down as she headed past the living room windows opposite the door where the creatures were still storming in, then she stopped as she peeked around the corner, making sure there was nothing waiting for her. The noise was even more pronounced out here in the open as dozens of the beasts converged on the one dwelling. Seeing the coast was clear she edged around and headed along the breadth of the trailer, keeping low. She stopped several feet before the corner, pressing her back against the wall, and angling her head forward as far as she could. She could see the bodies of the creatures pressing against the wooden railings as they reached the top of the steps and squeezed against other beasts through the door and into the trailer. She looked across at the opposite mobile home. It was identical to this one, apart from the fact, there was not a single RAM anywhere near it now.

The first part of her plan was complete, she had lured the beasts away from Sammy and Jake, now for part two. That would make part one look like a walk in the park.

***

"Is that a rowboat?" asked Talikha as she picked up the binoculars and began to focus the lenses.

Raj squinted into the distance and then looked towards his wife. "What do you see?"

"It is. It looks like Sarah," she replied.

"Sarah? What is she doing in a rowboat?" asked Raj.

It was not long before the two vessels closed on each other's positions and Raj used a pole to guide Sarah's small boat in to join them. He lowered the swimming platform and helped her onboard.

"Am I glad to see you?" said Sarah, "I think my arms were about to fall off."

"What are you doing out here in a boat?" asked Raj.

"I wanted to get in to see Sammy and Jake."

"But in a boat?" said Raj.

"There was a landslide...avalanche... I don't know, but it blocked a big stretch of road. It's impassable by car or on foot for that matter," said Sarah.

"Oh my!" said Talikha, grabbing hold of a rail to

steady herself.

"That is not good," said Raj.

"We'll be able to clear it when it starts to thaw, but right now nobody can get through," said Sarah. Raj started to massage his temples. He closed his eyes and tried to clear his head. "I don't understand," said Sarah, "It's not the end of the world."

"Sarah, there has been an outbreak in the village," said Raj.

"I don't understand," she replied. "An outbreak? What do you mean an outbreak?"

"RAMs, Sarah. There are RAMs in the village," said Raj.

A nervous smile appeared on Sarah's face which quickly disappeared. "How?"

"I don't know, but I saw them with my own eyes. We were heading to your place so we could get to the Old School House and tell Jules."

"I was with Jules not long back. We saw the landslide together. She turned back. I don't think Jules will be able to do much. Her brothers are stuck at the east ridge. Mike and the soldiers are gone. The road is treacherous and even if she could get up and down the coastline, I doubt there would be too many people who would volunteer. But even if they did, there are only so many we can transport by boat, and it could all be too late by then," said Sarah. "Oh God, Raj! This is a nightmare!

What are we going to do?"

"I think the only option, for the time being, is for us to continue to see Jules. She may be able to think of something," said Raj. "And just for good measure, I think we should all start praying for a miracle."

***

Mike looked up to the ridge as the tractor continued to chug. He had no idea who was on watch, but he knew right this second, they would be radioing someone to tell them an unidentified tractor was heading towards the Safe Haven coastline. He was not home yet, but he was getting there, and his nightmarish journey was nearly at an end. He continued along the road, losing sight of the ridge. The tall woods on either side of the track held the majority of the snow, so the tractor was able to travel faster.

He had formed a plan on his long journey. Stan Collinshaw, a Lancastrian who Mike loved arguing with about cricket, lived just a couple of miles from where he was. In the summer, Mike had helped him paint his motorboat. It was not the newest or the fastest vessel on the waves, but it would get Mike back home a lot quicker than the tractor, and every minute counted.

The trees began to thin out and the snow began to thicken beneath the massive tyres of the tractor. Mike looked to his left to see the huge loch where Hughes and Barnes often went fishing. He smiled to himself, but the smile did not last, as nerves began to jangle in his stomach.

He knew his Lucy would do everything she could to

keep Sammy alive, but now as he got closer to home, the reality of the situation was dawning on him. He had been so wrapped up in getting the drugs, in getting back, that he had not considered for a moment that it could be in vain. But now, as he finally pulled the heavy wheel round and turned the tractor left onto the coast road, doubt began to shroud him.

***

The bodies of the RAMs thudded against the plough as the Volvo lorry continued to make good progress along the A835.

"Bloody 'ell, our Mike was busy," said Hughes as he looked into the mirror, seeing pink-red mounds of snow and broken bodies piled up in banks against the side of the road.

"I didn't think the tractor would have had the speed to run them over," said Wren.

"It wouldn't, and they weren't," said Hughes.

"I don't understand," replied Wren, looking in the same mirror, watching the gruesome debris cascade and settle.

"I mean, Mike took all these out by hand," replied Hughes.

Wren laughed, "Yeah, right," she said.

Hughes looked across at her. "He's not joking you, Wren," said Shaw. "Look at the wounds, they're clean, from a single blade. These things haven't been hit by a vehicle," he said, as another one thudded against the plough. "Well, that's not what killed them anyway."

"But…" Wren sat for a moment, thinking back to when she was standing on the roof of the pharmacy. She had watched Mike take out a number of the creatures before he looked like he was going to fall to them. He was an impressive fighter, but to kill this many was the stuff of make-believe.

Hughes reached across and took hold of Emma's hand. "He'll be okay, love. There's not that many villages left and then we'll be in the final straight. If anybody was going to make it through this alone, it was Mike. I bet you my last pack of fags that he's back home, and Lucy is giving Sammy an injection of the antibiotic right this minute."

22

Richard and David kept low as they shuffled down the garden path with the tall step ladders. Richard sneezed and dropped the end he was carrying into the snow.

"Shhh!" said David.

"I can't help it if I sneeze," he said, taking a handkerchief out of his pocket and wiping his nose.

"They'll hear you," whispered David.

"I said I can't help sneezing," replied Richard.

"Well just try to do it quieter."

"How can I sneeze quieter? Sneezing is an involuntary action," said Richard.

David put his end of the ladders down too. "Look we both know that sneezes can be stifled a little. Granted, we can't stop them completely, but…"

A bone-chilling scream sliced through the cold air. "Look," said Richard picking up his end of the step ladders again, "Maybe we should have this discussion later."

"Yes. Yes, I think you're right," replied David, picking up his end as well. The pair of them scurried out of the gate and across the road, easing the set of steps over the wall, before climbing over themselves. They picked the ladders back up and began to weave through the trees until they reached the perimeter of the rear car park of the village hall. The brown brick building had only three windows at the back; a frosted glass toilet window to the right-hand side, and two long slim frosted office windows, quite high off the ground, towards the left. The two of them crouched down and surveilled the area for a moment. The growls of the creatures rose high into the blue sky sending chills down the spines of the two librarians.

Richard turned to look at David as he sensed his friend being overcome by the same fear. He reached into his jacket and pulled out a long kitchen knife. "It's Ruth in there. She wouldn't leave us. We can't leave her," he said, handing him the weapon.

"Damn it! You're right," said David, picking up his end of the step ladders. "Let's do this."

"Yes, let's do this," Richard replied, picking up his end too.

Another scream shredded the stillness of the air and both men flopped down behind the bushes once more.

***

"You can do this. You can do this. You can do this," whispered Lucy as she sprinted as fast as the snow would let her around the side of the trailer and to the one housing Sammy and Jake. She was a few metres across before the RAMs that had not already gained access to the trailer she had just escaped noticed there was fresh meat running through the courtyard. Seven of the creatures immediately began to race after her. Lucy reached Sammy and Jake's trailer, took the three steps in one leap, turned, grabbed the handrail with one hand, while still holding her spear with the other, and kicked with all her might, smashing the first beast in the chest, and causing it to fall back against the others. This gave her the extra time she needed to pull open the front door before banging it shut once again and locking it behind her. Seconds later, the first of the creatures began to smash against the UPVC frame and batter their fists against the glass squares.

Lucy opened the inner door. The living room was empty. She leaned her spear up against the wall, and closed all the curtains, blocking out the images, but not the noise, not the fear. She went across to one of the beds and dragged off a mattress, pulled it across the floor and leant it up against the front door, before heading back in and doing the same with the bedframe. The metal shrieked on the linoleum, and it banged and clanged against the door frame as she stood it up and walked it through, eventually wedging it against the rear wall of the small entrance hall and the frame of the outer door.

She backed up and closed the inner door, before

unzipping and removing her coat. Perspiration glued her clothes to her body, and she noticed the Calor gas heater still burning in one corner as the heavy fumes filled the air. She switched it off, but the fumes and the heat would take some time to dissipate.

Lucy combed her fingers through her damp blonde hair and looked around the interior of the room. There was no sign of disturbance other than what she had caused herself. She made her way to the hallway and placed her palm on the butt of the kitchen knife that rested in her belt. Lucy peeked her head around the corner of the open door. All she saw were two empty beds. Her eyes moved to the closed door, opposite. She could feel her breathing beginning to speed up as she placed her fingers on the door handle and pressed. The door parted from its frame to reveal an old woman sitting at the base of Jake's bed. She held a scalpel in front of her, pointing it towards Lucy. The silver of the metal glinted as it trembled in her hands.

"It's okay," said Lucy, "it's me."

The old woman dropped the scalpel and began to cry. "The others tried to make a run for it," she said, sobbing even louder. "How ridiculous. Three ill pensioners thinking they could escape. What was wrong with them? How could they leave these little angels behind to fend for themselves?" asked Mrs Macleod in her soft West Coast lilt.

"Not everybody has what it takes when it's needed," replied Lucy, crouching down in front of the old woman and taking her hand. "It's Mrs Macleod, isn't it?"

"Donalina," she said nodding.

"Well, Donalina, you did a great thing here today. You protected two children while everyone else watched out for themselves," said Lucy smiling warmly.

"They all died. I watched it. I watched it happen. Those...those things attacked them, one by one. They move like wildcats. So fast. So fast they are. There's no way anyone stands a chance. We're done for, you know?" she said.

"I don't intend to stop fighting anytime soon," said Lucy.

"I don't mean us. I mean as a species. But yes, I do mean us, I suppose too," Mrs Macleod bent down and picked up the scalpel.

"Don't worry, sweetie, I think we can find you a better weapon than that," said Lucy looking at the thin precision blade.

"Better weapon? I don't need a better weapon," said Mrs Macleod as she rammed the blade straight through her left eye and collapsed to the floor, dead.

"Jesus Christ!" squealed Lucy, falling back onto her buttocks and scooting away from the pooling blood. She sat for a moment with her back against the wall watching the flow of red from Donalina's eye dying the carpet. "Oh my God! What did you do?"

***

Raj and Sarah controlled an oar each as they rowed the boat back into shore. Humphrey sat in front of Talikha, his tongue hanging out, his face happy as ever.

"I wish I knew his bloody secret," said Sarah, looking towards the Labrador Retriever.

Raj smiled. "Animals have the greatest gift of all. They live in the moment. He is happy to be with his family, in the sun, having an adventure. He is not worrying about the danger he has just seen. That was in the past."

"I'll have to start doing that," replied Sarah.

"Alas, my friend. We carry a burden we cannot shake. No amount of wishing can make it go away," replied Raj.

"Tell me about it," said Sarah. "Things were going so well here. I just can't believe everything has turned on its head so quickly. This is the end you know. Whatever happens. However this plays out, this is the end of our project, of Safe Haven. We won't recover from this."

Raj did not say anything, he just kept on rowing until eventually the water became shallower. They jumped out of the boat, and despite all of them wearing winter boots, they could feel the icy chill as they waded the shallows. Snow still clung to the top of the black rocks surrounding the small cove. Raj and Sarah heaved the boat to the small snow-covered grassy verge where it had laid not long since. They tied the rope around the stake and the four of them began their journey up the steep incline.

***

Richard and David travelled in slow motion across the car park, desperate not to stumble or make a sound that would alert the creatures to their position. They carefully leaned the aluminium steps up against the wall and planted the feet firmly in the thick snow. David stepped onto the rungs while Richard held the ladder.

"It's me, David," he whispered as he tapped on the window. He could not make out much through the frosted glass, but after a few seconds of nothing, he saw activity. A figure moved across, then he saw a blurred face appear. Seconds later, a latch squeaked and the window was levered up.

Jenny's eyes met David's, and she put her hand through the gap to grasp his. "Thank God," she whispered.

"Can you and Ruth climb through?" David asked.

"Ruth hurt her leg, but between the two of us I think we can get her through the gap," she replied. She released his hand and disappeared.

A few seconds later, Ruth's fingers reached through and her grateful eyes came to rest on David. "You came for us," she said smiling.

"Did you ever think we wouldn't?" he asked.

"No, never," she replied.

"If I take your arms, do you think you can climb through the gap?" he asked.

"I think so, maybe," she replied, reaching her second arm through the window. David grasped hold of both her hands while he heard a strained sound from Jenny as she took Ruth's weight and pushed her upwards. Ruth's face contorted in pain as her ribs clunked across the brow of the windowpane, but as she came through the other side, she grabbed hold of the top of the steps and swung herself round. David guided her and when her feet and hands were safely on the aluminium he retreated down the ladder, making sure she followed him step for step.

When Ruth's feet were settled in the snow, David went back up for Jenny, who was already halfway through the window. Her knee-length zipped leather boots swung out, and David had to parry backwards to avoid being hit in the face. He jumped down the last couple of rungs and Jenny followed closely behind stumbling a little. David put his hands out in an effort to stop her toppling and accidentally caught her breasts.

"Oh my God. Oh, I'm so sorry. Sorry Jenny!" he said with a horrified look on his face.

Jenny burst out laughing. "You're fine, the least you deserve is a quick feel after what you just did for us," she said. David's face went bright red, but Ruth let out a small giggle.

"Come on, we'd better go," said David, beginning to lift the steps.

"What are you doing?" asked Jenny. "Do you really think we're going to need these again right now?"

"Erm, no," said David.

"Then let's just get the hell out of here," she said grabbing his hand and starting to follow the trail back towards the woods and safety. Ruth and David joined them, and they had almost reached the tree line when a familiar growl rustled through the otherwise still air. All four of them turned immediately and there they saw it. Its clothes were clean, but for a bloody red bite mark on the shoulder. Its pallid skin was not as grey as some, but its eyes gave it away as a creature of death...a RAM.

It began to charge, kicking up snow as its feet thrust forward. "Oh God!" cried Ruth.

David and Richard looked at each other, this is what they had spoken about, this moment would define their future. They both swallowed hard and pulled the kitchen knives from their belts.

The pair stepped forward, shielding Jenny and Ruth from the beast storming towards them. They stood with their legs apart, trying to remember the few basic tips Mike had given them one time about what do if they ever got into such a situation. "Distribute your weight and maintain your balance," said David.

"I remember, I remember," snapped Richard.

Both men tensed their fists around the knife handles as the beast got closer. It was Richard who moved first, ducking low, avoiding the creature's outstretched arms. The librarian forced his shoulder into the RAM's hip, and weaved his left arm around the rear of its thighs, making it stumble backwards and fall flat onto the snowy ground, taking him with it. The knife went flying out of his hand and into the deep snow as he fell. As they landed, Richard released his grip and leapt on top of the beast's torso, pinning its arms below the elbow as its mouth began to snap and its upper body tried to wriggle free.

Richard felt the creature's legs kick and writhe, but he held on like a rodeo cowboy. The beast's eyes began to hypnotise him with their evil intent. The cavernous black pupils made him think of nothing but his own demise, and chill after chill rippled down his spine. Each time the creature lunged, it broke a little more of the strength from Richard's grip, and its gnashing teeth edged closer to his arm.

Richard let out a small cry as the beast's chin made contact. But just then, a flash of metal caught his eye and his grip around the creature's arms softened a little as David brought the blade of his knife down with all the power of a road drill.

The blade cut through the beast's temple like it was being plunged into an overripe pumpkin, and the RAM stopped struggling instantly. David remained frozen in his pose for a moment, as still as the creature he had just slain. He locked eyes with Richard, and they both exhaled deeply. A knowing passed between them, an understanding, a feeling, that they had both taken charge of their destinies once more, that the regression was over.

It was time for them to realise the people they could be, the people they always wanted to be.

David removed the long blade of the knife which made a slopping sound as it popped out of the beast's head. He wiped it first in the white snow, then on the creature's clothes before standing up and offering a hand to his friend.

Richard grabbed hold of David's forearm and pulled himself to his feet. He walked across to the thin hole in the snow where he had seen his knife disappear and fished it out, placing the blade back in his belt. "We'd better get going before any more arrive," he said and turned, heading towards the woods. David followed him, while Ruth and Jenny just watched, dumbstruck.

"What just happened?" asked Ruth.

Jenny looked as the two male librarians stopped at the edge of the woods and beckoned her and Ruth. "I think your two boys just became men," replied Jenny.

23

"I won't forget this Stan," said Mike, as the two men swept big handfuls of snow from the tarpaulin covering the motorboat.

While Mike finished clearing the green cover of white, Stan began to dig around the jack and tongue of the boat trailer so it could be lifted and wheeled down to the water. Within a few moments, the freshly painted wood was floating on the calm, blue, salty Atlantic and Mike was climbing in.

Stan stood with his hand extended, "I hope Sammy's alright mate, she's the sweetest little thing," he said.

Mike firmly grasped Stan's hand and shook it. "Thanks Stan. I appreciate it mate. I'll see you soon."

"See you soon," replied Stan, pushing the boat hard into deeper waters and turning it to the direction of travel.

"Good luck," he said letting go and watching the vessel drift for a few seconds before the motor kicked in.

In less than a minute, Mike had lost sight of Stan. He was on the final leg of his journey and he would soon know whether it had all been in vain. Despite, the friendly faces and the reassuring words of Stan and his wife, the nerves had not left Mike, nor would they now; not until he knew one way or the other how Sammy was, and how she would be. He looked out at the rippling sea, then up to the blue sky and white clouds. He turned his head and viewed the wintry landscape of the Highlands, in their majesty. All these things made this such a special place to live. All these things made this place like no other. All these things made this place like a home. But home was a who not a where. Home was his family, and if something happened to any of them, then his home would be gone.

"Hold on, Sammy. Please, hold on."

***

"We're screwed," said Jules as she looked at Raj, Talikha and Sarah. Logs crackled in the fire and Humphrey laid down on the wool rug, happy to close his eyes for the time being.

"I don't understand," said Raj.

"I can't get anybody. The pick-up went off the road earlier. It's on its side in a ditch. I've got the radio, but the weather must have messed things up because I've not been able to get hold of anyone since yesterday afternoon, and even if I could, I can only talk to the north and east ridges, and they're more cut off than anybody. The snow hit the higher ground even harder than us. The few houses in the village are mainly lived in by people who've spent their entire lives there. Most of them are pensioners, none of them are fighters" said Jules. "That's what I mean by we're screwed."

Sarah stood up. "I'm going," she said. "Sammy and Jake are there. Dora's there. Lucy's there. Ruth, Richard and David are there. I've got to do something," she said, zipping her jacket and standing up.

"Listen, you're springing this on me," said Jules. "Just give me a minute." Sarah sat back down. The thought of her having to do anything by herself scared her, so she was grateful when someone else took charge. Jules leant forward in her chair, placing her elbows on her thighs. Her loose dirty blonde curls fell over her ears as she inhaled the peat fumes and scoured her thoughts.

"I think the choices are straightforward," said Raj.

"Oh yeah?" said Jules, "and what would they be?"

"We stay here, do nothing, and hope for the best, or the four of us head to the village and fight," he said.

"I don't really rate our chances," replied Sarah, "but I'd rather die fighting, than live knowing I didn't even try."

Raj looked towards Jules. "If I am not mistaken, this house is one of the safe houses for weapons, yes?"

The battle for Safe Haven had been a gruesome affair. Buses and vehicles carrying the enemy had been thrown onto the rocks and into the sea as manmade landslides had swept them from the cliff roads. Across on the farm where the second part of Fry's army had gathered, RAMs had waged their own war, turning it into a hellish tinderbox. Mike, Hughes, Shaw and Barnes had led scavenging expeditions, first in boats to see what arms could be salvaged from the wreckage at the bottom of the rocky cliffs, then, after a few weeks, when the RAMs had spread further afield, at the farm. They had assembled a wide variety of guns, swords, knives, even a working mortar, as well as a healthy supply of ammunition. Fry and The Don before him had raided barracks, police stations and anywhere there was a supply of weapons in order to build their huge army.

Now the weapons belonged to Safe Haven and they were stored at strategic points up and down the coast, ready and waiting if trouble ever reared its ugly head again.

Jules let out a deep breath realising what she was about to commit herself to. "Yes. Yes it is," she replied standing up. "Follow me," she said, and as she walked out of the warm room, she picked up the radio handset by the door.

Raj, Talikha and Sarah did as she asked and followed her. Jules proceeded down the hall and turned a corner. She paused and brought the radio up to her mouth, depressing the speak button. "If you can hear this, it's me, Jules. There are RAMs in the village. Repeat, there are RAMs in the village. I'm heading there now. Rob, Jon, Andy, I love you. Look after each other." She took her finger off the speak button and closed her eyes hoping for a response, but none came. She let out a heavy sigh.

"You never know my friend, they may have heard you," said Raj.

Jules opened a panelled oak door and grabbed a lantern. She pulled a lighter from her pocket and lit the wick, before placing her left foot on the first clunky wooden step. She proceeded down the staircase and the others followed her. When she reached the bottom, she hung the lantern on a hook and crouched down on the floor while the others gathered behind her. Jules opened three sturdy green plastic fruit crates, the kind they used in supermarkets, revealing an assortment of firearms and ammunition.

"Okay, choose your weapons."

***

Lucy took one last look at the quilt covered body and closed the door behind her before walking across the hall and into Sammy and Jake's room. The children's breaths were erratic and shallow and their eyelids were no longer fluttering. Their bodies were losing the battle against the infection.

Lucy slumped into the chair in the corner of the room. She had been deaf to the growls and the bumps and bangs against the frame of the static caravan for the last few minutes, but now they flooded the air. She looked towards the two small frail figures lying in the beds. They weren't going to make it out of here, any of them. This would be the end, but if nothing else, she was going to die with her family. Lucy reached into her pocket and pulled out the small brown plastic bottle of pills. She lined up the arrows on the safety cap and levered it off, before tapping three of the small white tablets into her hand. She placed the pills in her mouth, cocked her head back and swallowed, wincing just a little as they caught on the back of her tongue and the bitter powder sprawled over her taste buds.

There was a muffled crash as the sound of a glass panel broke behind the mattress Lucy had leant up against the front door. She sat there, breathing in and out deeply, waiting for the effects of the powerful tablets to kick in.

"It's okay babies, it will all be over soon. It's okay Sammy, it's okay Jake, it's okay Charlie, it's all okay," said Lucy as she closed her eyes.

***

Richard and David stopped at the tree line. Their house was in sight, and it was David who braved the small exposed space first. He kept low and finally popped his head over the black stone wall to look up and then down the street to make sure the coast was clear. After a short time, and only when he was happy, he waved his arm to signal for the others to join him as he clumsily vaulted the wall. He landed heavily and awkwardly on the other side.

He heard the thud of Richard's feet crunch into the snow behind him, then stood up and offered his hand first to Jenny, then to Ruth as he helped the two of them over.

"I haven't heard any screams in a while," said Ruth,

"Surely that's a good sign."

"That's a really bad sign," said Richard.

"I don't understand, why?" replied Ruth.

Richard was about to respond when David spoke. "It means, they're probably all gone. They've all turned."

"Oh God!" said Jenny. "I hope Lucy and the kids are safe at…" she broke off, realising how she sounded. How selfish was she? The village had fallen, but all she was concerned about was her friends.

Ruth held out her hand and took Jenny's, "It's okay, it's natural to feel this way," she said. "Mankind is tribal, and we are a tribe. I hope they're safe too."

"C'mon," said Richard, let's get across to the house, then if nothing else, we're not sitting ducks. The two women did not argue, but ran across the road and into the familiar, yet snow-covered garden.

As they headed up the path, the neighbour to the left opened her front door. She was a woman in her fifties who had not been in Safe Haven long and had struggled to make friends, but she was on speaking terms with Richard, David and Ruth at least.

"I heard screaming earlier, what's going on?" she asked, crossing her arms for warmth.

"You need to get back inside Jill, there's been an outbreak in the village, the place is crawling with RAMs," said Ruth.

"What?"

"We think it started at the hospital. Get inside and close your curtains, lock your doors and pray," said Ruth.

Jill stood there for a moment, looking at Ruth in disbelief. "Can… can I join you?" she asked, her voice quivering.

Ruth paused for a few seconds, then said, "Yes. Yes, of course."

"I just have to get some things," said Jill disappearing back into the house.

On entering their home, Richard and David went straight to the black wrought iron stove. One began to fold some newspaper like he was practicing origami, while the other opened the door of the stove and put in a couple of pieces of wood kindling.

"I'll get the smokeless coal," said David, heading into the kitchen and returning with an unopened plastic sack. "We don't want to take any chances."

"Good thinking," said Richard.

"What are you doing?" asked Jenny, watching Richard fold the paper.

"George showed me this. It's easy to light, but it burns for ages, and helps get the fire going properly."

"Erm, okay," she replied, blowing into her hands and rubbing them together hard.

David lifted the kettle on top of the stove and judged it to be almost full from the weight and heavy sloshing sound. Finally, Richard's creation was ready and he placed it carefully next to the log, before putting some of the kindling over it. David crouched down, took a match and struck it against the rough stone of the fireplace. A small flame ignited, and he carefully guided it through the stove's door and rested it against the artfully folded newspaper. The flame caught and spread slowly at first, but then it began to burn brighter. Richard and David both smiled.

"The place will warm up in no time," said David, closing the door and walking to the window. "Jill's got a box with her," he said as he watched her trudging up her snowy garden path.

The four of them watched as she awkwardly rested the box on a fence post while trying to displace some of the snow that was stopping the gate from opening smoothly. Eventually, she managed, but then struggled as she tried to close it again.

"I'll go help her," said Richard, heading towards the door.

"Nooo!" screamed Jenny, as from out of nowhere, a blur of movement shot towards Jill.

The scream froze Richard in his tracks, and he turned in time to watch the beast launch through the air and tackle Jill. The pair dropped out of sight behind the hedge and Richard, David, Ruth and Jenny gaped in horror as their blood turned to ice.

After a minute, two figures rose from behind the hedges. They both looked around the white landscape, surveying the area for prey. Jenny, Ruth, Richard and David continued to watch on in terror, the lace curtains shielding them from the view of the creatures. The beasts heard a sound from somewhere and like rats following the Pied Piper, began to wander towards it.

Richard finally broke his daze and moved to the front door. Slowly and gently, he slid the bolt across and put the security chain into its slot. When he was sure the creatures were far enough down the road, he turned the key, clunking the heavy lock into position. He rested his forehead against the wood, then took a deep breath and rejoined his friends in the living room.

"Well," he said, "Hell has finally found us."

***

Mike figured out there was something wrong long before he pulled the motorboat onto the beach. The second he had navigated the final crease in the shoreline and seen Raj's yacht, he knew trouble lay ahead. His muscles clenched as he dragged the boat through the sand. When he had pulled it far enough away from the lapping waves, he began to run up the incline.

He burst through the back door, and bypassing the rooms on the lower level, immediately charged up the stairs, "Luce?" he shouted as his feet hit the landing. The soles of his feet pounded across the carpeted floorboards and stopped at the entrance to Jake's room. When he saw the duvet rolled back and an empty bed, he advanced to

Sammy's room more hesitantly. He looked around the corner, already knowing the answer to his question.

What did logic say? If they were not here, if Lucy was not here, there were only two possibilities. The first was unthinkable, the second was that she'd taken them to the hospital. Maybe it was to give them better care, maybe it was to keep an eye on them while looking after the other patients, but that was where he would head next. He ran back across the landing and down the stairs, jumping the last five and making a shuddering bang on the floorboards.

Mike sprinted out of the house, and realising there was no vehicle parked in the drive, he began to head back down the slope towards the beach. Leaping over the top of the snow-covered wall, something made him pause. At first, he could not identify what it was, but as he drifted from the kaleidoscopic wheel of terrifying realities that may or may not await him, he came to his senses and realised it was a sound...a voice.

"Mike!" Jules's voice trembled through the gentle, wintry breeze and vibrated in his ears. He looked around and finally his eyes fixed on the road beyond the gate, and to the five figures coming down the hill. A friendly, but deep bark sounded, which Mike recognised instantly.

"Jules? Raj? Sarah? Talikha? He said as the outlines against the landscape became clearer.

The first figure creaked the large metal gate open just enough to squeeze through and beat a path towards Mike. Sarah flung her arms around him. "Oh thank God!" she said, kissing him on the cheek. "Where's Em?"

"Em, Bruiser, the rest of them, they're following. I had to get back here as quick as I could." Mike did not see the point of going into the specifics. All he wanted to do was get the medicine to his little sister.

"I'm so glad to see you. It's all gone to hell," blurted Sarah.

Mike pulled back from her. "What do you mean? Where are Sammy and Jake?" he asked as the others caught up. They each gave him, powerful hugs, but he kept looking at Sarah, as her eyes dropped to the floor.

Jules kissed him on the cheek. "Don't worry," she said, "We're heading there now, and our chances just got a whole lot better."

"What...what are you talking about?" asked Mike.

Jules grabbed him by the shoulders. "Mike... there are RAMs in the village."

He shot a glance to Sarah, then, Talikha, then Raj. All their faces looked sorrowful. "This is my fault," he said.

"What are you talking about?" asked Jules, amazed by his lack of surprise.

"This is my fault. I didn't piece it together until it was too late. This is all my fault," he said, hanging his head. "Where are Sammy, Jake and Luce?" he asked almost in a whisper.

"I took Sammy and Jake to the hospital when Jake's

condition took a turn for the worse," said Raj.

"Jake's condition?" asked Mike, looking up.

"Yes, my friend," replied Raj.

"But...they're both still alive, yes?" asked Mike.

"Yes," replied Raj.

"We're cut off, Mike, there was a landslide and we don't have a vehicle. We can't get anyone else. It's just us. We're the only ones who can do anything," said Jules.

Mike noticed the weapons they were carrying. They had all opted for pump-action shotguns, the surest bet for a bad shot. Mike picked up a hand of snow and rubbed it over his face. It began to melt on impact with his skin as the rage within him boiled his blood.

He headed to the house, not saying a word to his friends. He entered, climbed the stairs and pulled the small loop that brought down the loft ladder. Mike climbed a couple of steps, then reached in and pulled out the sturdy holdall, placing it on the landing floor and removing a box of shotgun shells. He pulled the pump-action from his rucksack and loaded it, putting the spare shells in his jacket pocket. He replaced the magazine from his Glock with a fresh one, then grabbed a second Glock and six spare magazines from the holdall. He shoved the spare mags into his rucksack and stood up, wedging both Glocks firmly between his belt and the back of his Jeans.

"Mike?" called Jules as she entered the house. "Are you okay?"

Mike did not answer, but picked up the holdall, put it back in the loft, raised the ladder and headed downstairs, meeting Jules in the entrance hall. "Couldn't be better, why do you ask?" he said walking by her with a wild look in his eyes.

"I'm not sure I like that look," she said.

"I didn't come this far to fail now," he muttered under his breath.

"What?" asked Jules. "I didn't hear what you said."

"I said, I didn't come this far to fail now!" shouted Mike.

"Mike!" yelled Jules, worried for him as the look on his face surpassed any anger, any rage she had seen before.

"How many times? How many times do I have to be tested? What do I need to fucking do?" He looked up to the blue sky. "You put me in harm's way, that's one thing. You put my fucking family...my brother...my sister...my Lucy...you put them in harm's way? How fucking dare you? How dare you?" he yelled with tears appearing in his eyes.

"Mike," said Sarah, softly.

"You bring your hell to Safe Haven? I'll show you what hell is."

24

"I wonder who's on duty," said Emma as the truck thundered through the small valley. She looked up towards the ridge, and despite everything, despite the worry about her brothers and sister, despite the pain radiating from her foot, a warm feeling cloaked her. They were home. They were back where they belonged.

"On duty?" asked Wren.

"We have lookouts. This place is like a fortress," replied Emma.

"Wow! I thought I was paranoid," replied Wren.

"Hang on," said Hughes, bringing the huge truck to a skidding stop. He pulled on the handbrake and jumped out looking up at the ridge as a light flashed on and off. Shaw looked too and climbed out.

"Barney!" shouted Shaw as he jumped down from

the cab. Barnes climbed down from the bed of the tipper and joined them.

"Bloody hell, it'd be quicker if they just came down here and told us," said Hughes as he watched the signal play out in slow motion.

"S-A-F-E-H-A-V-E-N-F-A-L-L-E-N-R-A-M-S-S-A-F-E-H-A-V-E-N-F-A-L-L-E-N-" said Shaw.

"Oh Fuck!" said Hughes.

"Fuck!" repeated Barnes.

"Jesus!" said Shaw. "We need to move, now!"

The three men jumped back into the vehicle and in a flash, the wheels were turning once again. "What is it?" asked Emma, sensing the urgency.

"Safe Haven," said Shaw.

"What about it?" replied Emma.

"It's gone, Em," said Shaw.

Emma shifted round in her seat. "What the hell are you on about?" she demanded.

"RAMs. RAMs have taken our home."

***

"Can't we make this go any faster?" asked Jules.

"Not really," replied Raj. "We're at full power now."

"What the bloody hell's wrong with him?" asked Jules fighting to hold back tears of frustration.

"We do not have enough time for me to answer that question fully and accurately," replied Raj, "suffice it to say, there is a lot wrong with Mike. But there is even more right with him. However, please do not misunderstand me, right this minute I would like to hit him over the head with a cricket bat...repeatedly."

"I'm with you there," said Sarah. "The bloody fool's going to get himself killed running off like that."

Raj turned towards Sarah as he adjusted the wheel. "I have been at Mike's side when he has fought, and I know that if there is anyone who can turn a tide, it is he, but on this occasion, I hoped he would show some restraint and at least allow us to face the danger with him rather than facing it alone. He is unpredictable, fiery and dangerous, but he is my friend, and I believe in him now the way I always have."

"What possessed him? We were all heading there. What possessed him to jump in that bloody boat and go off by himself?" asked Jules.

"There, my friend, you have asked the single most important question," said Raj.

"I don't understand," replied Jules.

Raj remained silent and fixed his eyes on the waters ahead.

***

Mike killed the engine and the motorboat drifted into the dock. He took the rope and moored it around the cleat. No sooner had he stepped onto the snow-covered wood when two creatures came charging towards him, alerted by the sound of the engine. Mike pulled one of the pump-action shotguns from his rucksack and raised it to his shoulder. He fired first at one and then the other, making most of their heads fly into the breeze in a burst of red.

Mike was not on a stealth mission. He had decided the more creatures descended upon him, the less risk there was to his family. This would be an absolute battle, full-on war, the last one standing was the victor.

As the second creature fell into the snow, Mike pulled two shells from his pocket and topped up the shotgun chamber before screaming at the top of his voice, "Luuucccyyy!!!" The scream echoed around the whole village and across the water too.

He began to walk down the snowy pier, turning his head from side to side as he went, surveying the entire area in front of him. He heard the growls before he saw the creatures, and from the sounds, he could tell there was a small army making its way towards him.

"Luuucccyyy!!!" he yelled again. The pier was narrow and no more than three people, living or dead, could walk or run side by side at any one time, so halfway down and in the absence of a better idea, Mike stopped, raised the shotgun to his shoulder once again and waited.

***

"Those were gunshots," said David. He and Richard looked at one another, then looked towards Ruth and Jenny. "I... I think Richard and I should go check."

"What? Are you mad?" asked Ruth. "If they were gunshots, whoever is shooting has a distinct advantage over you or Richard. They're armed. Why would you possibly want to go towards a sound that won't do anything but attract more of those creatures, with nothing to defend yourselves but a couple of knives?"

"I'm with Ruth," said Jenny. "It would be dangerous and foolhardy to head out there again."

David visibly deflated. The adrenalin was still surging through him, but suddenly, he had been made to listen to the voice of reason once more. "I suppose you're right he said," sighing deeply.

Seeing his reaction, Jenny walked across to him and held his arm gently. "I don't wish to sound selfish, but if you two go, who will protect me and Ruth? Like Ruth said, whoever is out there has a gun which is more than we have."

"Jenny's right," replied Richard. "We need to stay here for the time being. We need to stick together."

Another two booming shots echoed and David looked out of the window once again. "I hope to Goodness whoever it is knows what they're doing," he said and closed the curtains.

**

"I swear to Christ, I'm going to slap that bloody idiot upside his thick skull when I get my hands on him," said Jules, pumping the forend of her shotgun as she stepped off the swimming platform and into the small rowboat.

"I still don't understand why we can't take the yacht all the way up to the dock," said Sarah as Talikha untied the rope and Raj eased the oars into the water and took the first strokes.

"Because," he said, lifting the oars and placing them back in the water before stroking once again, "It's too shallow," he continued, repeating the rowing action. "We'd run aground."

"Fair enough," said Sarah as she scooted over and took one of the oars from Raj.

The small boat made steady progress as more and more booms echoed through the otherwise still air. Jules closed her eyes and held the shotgun close to her chest. "This is going to end badly. I know this is going to end badly."

Within two more minutes, the dock was in sight. "Oh fuck!" blurted Sarah, catching full view of the unfolding mayhem.

A lone figure stood halfway up the wooden pier as dozens of creatures forged a path towards him. Mike kept aiming and firing, blasting bloody tunnels through the beasts' heads as creature after creature fell. The fallen bodies created an awkward hurdle for the RAMs to negotiate, giving valuable extra seconds to aim and fire.

He emptied the shotgun, then reached into the back of his jeans for the first Glock Seventeen. He started to fire shot after shot, but the accuracy needed was more than Mike could achieve from that distance, so he walked forward, closer to the massing horde. Their growls amplified with each stride he took towards them, and suddenly, those familiar grey eyes were no longer just abstract visions in his head, but there, plain to see. The cavernous, demonic, broken ebony pupils shot malevolent beams of hatred towards him.

Two beasts climbed to their feet from the clambering mass that crawled over the already downed bodies. The creatures began to run towards Mike, their feet kicking through the snow like it was bath foam. Their speed took him by surprise, and he could not get a good aim on either. More RAMs rose to their feet and ran towards him. All of a sudden, he had lost his advantage.

"Shit!" he said beginning to back up. Realising, the skill needed for the Glock was more than he possessed, he slotted it in the back of his jeans and reached round taking tight hold of the machete handles. The first two RAMs tore towards him. They had similar colouring, in life, they may have been mother and daughter, but now, they were just monsters, freaks of nature, hell-bent on recruiting Mike into the ranks of the undead. They were both on him at the same time, and he pushed his foot out hard, catapulting one backwards through the air, making it collide with another advancing ghoul. He raised his right hand and made the machete whistle as he brought it down with a crack through the skull of what he assumed to be the first creature's daughter. The young body flopped to the side like a puppet with cut strings, and that was when Mike looked up and saw that at least nine RAMs had made it over the mound of lifeless bodies he had created.

Mike began to back up again, but the creatures' forward momentum outpaced his retreat. He raised his machete, whatever was going to happen, he was not going to stop fighting until his last breath, but suddenly, a shudder of panic ripped through him as something grabbed him tightly, the jerky movement almost strangling him before he felt the ice-cold fingers and nails scratch against his skin.

***

The lorry skidded a little as Hughes negotiated the bend. Emma, Wren, Shaw, and even Hughes himself took a deep breath. A few months before, the craggy rocks below them had seen the demise of countless men that had tried to take their home, and they knew that just because virtue was on their side, it did not leave them impervious to the sharp blade of Death's scythe.

"Do you think we could slow down a bit?" asked Wren.

Hughes looked across at her. "Sorry about that, love, it's a bit of a tricky bend that one, I should have taken it better than that, sorry."

"So, that's a no then?" she said, beckoning Wolf, who obediently leaned up and rested his head on her lap.

"We need to stop at Jules's place," said Hughes.

"What? Why?" asked Emma.

"Restock ammo," he replied.

"We can go to mine, we've got a cache there too," said Emma.

"Seriously?" said Hughes looking across at her. You expect me to get this rig around that tight bend and down that track with all this snow on the ground? Don't get me wrong, it's a nice compliment that you think I can do it, but I don't have your faith in my skills."

"I wasn't thinking," replied Emma.

"Yeah well, I think you can be forgiven under the circumstances, don't you, love?" said Hughes looking across at her. "Look, I think you should sit this one out? I'll drop you off at the end of your road and you and Wren can make it down to your place. Sammy and Jake are going to need all the support they can get. We'll head to Jules's, get the supplies we need and then crack on to the village."

She gave him a fleeting look then stared straight ahead, knowing any sign of affection from anyone would make her burst into tears. She waited a moment to get her emotions under control before speaking. "Mike will go with you, I know he will."

"I'll give you one of the radios, there's only a few hundred yards between Jules's place and yours, they should work fine, but my bet is Mike's already on his way. Knowing Lucy, she's probably with him. My guess is when you get home, there'll be Sarah and the kids, and that's it."

Emma pulled out the hip flask from her jacket and took a drink. "I don't know what will be waiting for me when I get back home, but there's no way I'm not going to join you. Safe Haven is more than just a place. It's an idea. I won't let it fall without putting up a fight."

"But Em..." began Hughes.

"No buts, that's what's happening."

***

Lucy's eyes scratched open. She knew she had a tendency towards the most horrific nightmares, but as she woke and heard the growls of the creatures and the bangs and clatters against the side of the trailer, she knew this was no nightmare. Despite the peaceful daze that the oxycodone allowed her to bathe in, she remembered everything up to the point that she had drifted off to sleep. She wished she could forget, but there was no drug on the planet that would allow her to do that.

She looked at the two small figures in their beds. It was a miracle they had held on this long. Even from this distance, she could still make out their shallow breaths. This family were all fighters.

Lucy swallowed and tried to piece together what had dragged her out of her deep sleep. She had shut herself off to the white noise of the growls and hammering long since, but something had burst into her dreams like a thunderbolt.

Boom! There it was again, and again, and again. It was gunfire. She straightened a little in her chair and wiped her eyes free of sleep. Lucy leaned forward and held on to the arms of the chair, gripping tighter with each subsequent boom. It sounded like a shotgun, but who was firing it? Her mind flashed through all the scenarios, but none made sense.

Finally, she stood and crept towards the window. She peeked around the corner of the curtain and through the holes in the lace to see the throng of RAMs unwavering in their pursuit to get to her. Whatever the noise was, they were not interested, because right here in this little sardine can, they knew there was live prey. Anything else could wait. Lucy continued to observe the determined beasts as she heard a second then a third glass panel shattering in the front door.

***

Just as quickly, the cold grasp and scratch of the fingernails became forgotten as Mike fell backwards into the snow. As his head hit the icy cushion, he caught the blur of Jules raising her shotgun and firing. Another boom sounded to his left. He turned his head to see Raj. Someone else stepped over him, Sarah, she fired, then pumped the forend of the shotgun and fired again. Mike heard barking and angled his head to see Humphrey standing at the end of the wooden pier, desperate to join his family in the fight against these creatures, but not daring to disobey the last orders from his master.

Mike scrambled back, placing the machetes in his rucksack and pulling out the shotgun. He delved into his pockets and grabbed the spare shells, hastily reloading it, before climbing to his feet and joining his friends.

"Looked like you could use a hand!" shouted Jules as Mike joined her.

"Nah! I was just lulling them into a false sense of security," he said, continuing to fire while Jules dropped the shotgun and pulled a Glock from her waistband. She brought the handgun up and closed one eye, before taking headshot after headshot. Mike watched on in amazement as she put six RAMs down in a matter of a few seconds. "That...is...impressive!" he shouted over the sound of the shots.

"Well, I've been practising, haven't I?" she replied, aiming for a couple of the creatures further back, without the same success. "Problem is, once I go past a certain range I can't shoot for shite. I think I might need glasses," she said, as Mike aimed the shotgun in the direction of the two creatures Jules had tried to hit and blew half of one's head off, while obliterating the face of the other.

"Nice," said Jules. "Shame I don't have my phone, that would make a lovely pic for my Christmas cards," she said as she turned to watch Sarah bending over and throwing up.

"Death is never pretty, Jules," said Mike, as Raj and Talikha brought four more creatures down between them.

The final three beasts stumbled over the mountain of bodies. Mike put his hand up to signal the ceasefire and everyone lowered their weapons as he walked up to the lumbering creatures, replaced the shotgun in his rucksack, took out a machete, and one after the other, slashed and stabbed until there was no further movement.

He wiped the blade clean in the snow and put it back in his rucksack. Jules went and stood beside him, "So what now?" she asked.

"First of all, I need to fish out the nails you sunk into my neck when you pulled me down onto my arse."

Jules shook her head. "You're such a little crybaby. I save your life and that's the thanks I get. Okay, and then what?"

"We head to the campground," said Mike. Not even waiting for a reply, he pulled some of the bodies to one side to make a clear path, then marched down the pier.

"Good talk," called Jules after him. "Glad we got that cleared up anyway. Planning is so important."

25

Lucy's pulse began to race as she heard the sound of multiple shotguns. *Who would try and take the town back without the soldiers? Without Mike or her?* She had no idea, but a switch flipped inside. She headed out of the room and immediately the sound of the creatures' guttural growls from the doorway filled the air like a demonic choir in full song.

A chill gripped her, and not just the one caused by the missing panels of glass from the front door. She went to the kitchen and began to search the drawers. She pulled out a knife from one, just a little longer than the one she had brought from Richard and David's house. All the weapons they had back home, and this was the best she could manage. It might be in vain, but if there were people prepared to put up a fight for the town, then she would too.

Lucy poured some of the icy water from the jug by the sink into her cupped hand and splashed it on her face.

She drew some more and took a drink, helping to alleviate the furry coating on her tongue caused by the dissolved tablets from earlier. She could still feel them in her system, but adrenalin had kicked in countering a lot of the oxycodone's effect.

She opened the medicine supply cupboard and bypassed all the small containers, grabbing a translucent plastic bottle with a white cap, just a little bigger than a standard soda can. In the absence of any other weapons, she would have to make her own. She opened the food cupboard and pulled out a large bottle of vegetable oil, placing it next to the alcohol.

She then searched the other cupboards, slamming the last door hard as she couldn't find the glass bottles she was looking for. The coated wood bashed against the frame and slowly swung open again, while Lucy leant back on a countertop. The growls continued to reverberate down the hallway. She looked around, desperate for inspiration. There had to be something in here, something she could use. Then her eyes drifted back towards the open cupboard door. Tucked behind the mugs and plates were three tall hi-ball glasses. Lucy tiptoed and reached in for them, placing them carefully on the countertop. She stood there for a moment with her arms folded, looking at the glasses, then burst into action. She poured alcohol into each of them, filling them just short of two-thirds of the way up. Then she poured in vegetable oil which she watched sink to the bottom until there was a gap of just an inch at the top of each glass.

Lucy opened the double doors beneath the sink unit

and pulled out a box of wax candles. She removed the gas safety lighter from the cutlery drawer and lit one of the wicks. Within a couple of seconds, the first drops of liquid wax appeared. She tilted the candle carefully and watched as the wax dripped onto the surface of the alcohol in the first glass. She moved it round very slowly, praying that no errant strand of flaming wick fell into the concoction.

"Oh, Mikey, you have been such a bad influence on me," she said, as she watched the droplets fall onto the surface and solidify, joining together like waxy lily pads on a flammable pond. Within two minutes, a solid layer had coated the whole surface. She made sure the wax dripped down the inner sides of the glass too so there would be no leakage. When she was content that the covering was deep enough, she leant the candle up in a coffee mug and lifted the hi-ball glass from the sink.

She waited another moment and looked at her creation like a child looking at a magical snow globe. She leaned over the sink and slowly tipped the glass further and further. Any second she expected to see a gush of fluids flow down the plughole into the waiting bucket below, but none did. The liquid was trapped beneath the solid wax. A satisfied smile crept onto her face.

Lucy quickly got to work doing the same thing with the other two glasses. As the first drops of wax fell on the surface of the last glass of liquid, another crash sounded, this time accompanied by a creaking groan. "Oh shit!" she said, realising the door frame was beginning to give way.

There was another smash which rumbled through the air making Lucy shudder. Her hand shook and she watched in horror as a glowing piece of wick drifted from the candle like a tiny feather from a phoenix.

Lucy leapt back as a ball of flames exploded from the sink. She watched and limboed as the heat singed the air around her. Her back hit the kitchen floor hard and her head banged making her bite her tongue. She shimmied towards the door as she watched the window blind, the walls, and the cupboards all catch fire. Lucy leapt to her feet and grabbed the other two glasses, before running out of the room.

***

"Shite!" shouted Hughes as he brought the truck to a skidding stop once again. He pulled on the handbrake and climbed out, followed by Shaw. When they'd been stopped for more than two minutes, Barnes and Beth jumped down from the back of the lorry to join them. They all stood looking at the snowy landslide. Small branches and rocks stuck out of the dirty grey snow, and Hughes grabbed hold of one of the leafy tendrils and tugged, uprooting a small weedy shrub.

"What do you think?" asked Barnes.

"I think we don't have a choice," replied Shaw. "What do you think, Hughesy?"

"It's not tightly packed, and it looks like it's more snow than rubble. I say we should make an attempt to plough through," he said. "I'll take it slow and if it looks like it's getting too hairy, I can always back up, but we've got to try."

"We'll do whatever you think," said Shaw. The four of them looked towards the debris-filled snow slide one last time before returning to the truck. Hughes climbed back into the driver's seat and looked across as Shaw grimaced through his leg pain to struggle back in. Then he looked towards Emma and finally Wren, who was still stroking Wolf's head.

"Y'know, you really don't have to do this, love. We could drop you and your dog at the next place we come to," said Hughes.

Wren looked past Emma and across to Hughes. "By the sound of it, you need all the help you can get, and it's not like I'm new to this. I've been fighting these things since the beginning."

"I just thought…" began Hughes.

"I know what you thought, and I appreciate it, but it's not necessary. I've looked after myself this long, I can look after myself now. I wasn't going to stop in Emma's empty house alone, and I don't want to stop with some strangers while I could actually be doing some good." Wren turned her head back to view the road ahead and Hughes and Emma exchanged a smile.

Hughes pulled off the handbrake and the huge mechanical beast began to move forward once again. Snowy debris was pushed from the road and down the rocky cliff face as the engine roared louder and louder.

***

"What the hell are we heading up here for?" asked Jules.

"We can go in the back way," replied Mike. "We can head around the pub, through the woods, then we're right on top of the four hospital statics."

"Okay," she said. "Fair enough."

Sarah, Raj and Talikha travelled along with them in silence as they marched through the crunching snow. The road was eerily quiet, when normally it was one of the busiest places in Safe Haven. Ever since the stills had begun to produce, and Jenny had taken over the running of the pub, it had become the main meeting place up and down the coastline.

All of them froze as Humphrey began to let out a growl from the back of his throat. He stood there with one paw raised, his teeth gritted, and his lips peeled back in a snarl as he looked beyond his own field of vision, through the beer garden walls to the back of the pub.

Mike pulled the machetes out of his rucksack and sped up, breaking away from the others. Jules ran a few steps to catch up with him, and raised her shotgun in readiness, but Mike put his hand over the barrel and lowered it. She furrowed her brow and was about to ask why when he put a finger up to his mouth. In the open, he was happy to make his presence known, but heading into the woods, the less RAMs, the better. They needed quiet now more than ever. The next steps were crucial, as he edged around the corner of the rear of the pub and found three creatures on their knees in the snow feasting on a fallen body. They took a final bite each before the newly born creature began to twitch to its second life. The RAMs had not heard Mike's approach above the sound of their own gnashing bites.

Mike raised the two machetes high and whipped them through the air, dropping them on the nearest two heads with freight train power and speed. He flipped the handles back, bringing the gory blades with them, then, brought the weapons down again on the other two creatures, extinguishing them of all life, never to rise again.

He wiped the blades clean and placed them into his rucksack, before carrying on through the woods behind the pub. Jules glanced back towards the others who just followed in silence. After a short time, they reached the edge of the trees and saw the rear of the first two static caravans that constituted half of the four hospital wards. They all crouched and Raj put a hand on the back of Humphrey's neck who had been growling constantly for several minutes. The hand was the only encouragement the Labrador Retriever needed to stop.

They all stayed there, with one knee in the cold wet snow as they listened to the cacophonous growls from the beasts in the campground. Slowly, Mike got to his feet, pulling one of the machetes back out of his rucksack. He ran from the tree line to the rear of the bottle green static caravan and pressed his shoulder blades against it for a few seconds before beginning to edge to the corner. Jules was about to call something after him, and he put his finger up to his mouth. As he sneaked along, he got lower and lower until he reached the corner on his bended knees.

Mike crawled the last few feet and dropped his head down low. There was no sign of any of the creatures, but from his new position, the noise was amplified massively. He looked back to his friends once again but did not say a word as he began to scuttle down the side of the caravan. Long before he got to the front, the sound told him there were dozens of RAMs, possibly a lot more. The day they had founded Safe Haven, there had been just one hundred and thirty-eight residents along the whole coastline. Since that time the population had swelled to nearly seven hundred. The old village was where the newcomers were put up until more permanent accommodation could be sorted out. There were ample mobile caravans in the campground and when Safe Haven got a large influx at the same time, they erected camp beds in the village hall too.

Mike really had no idea how many creatures would face him if he popped his head around the corner, but the noise stopped even him from acting rashly. He retraced his knee prints in the snow before running back over to the tree line and crouching down with the others.

Humphrey began to growl again, sensing Mike's unease. "Well?" said Jules.

Mike winced, before answering. "There are tons of them," he said.

"What do you mean tons?" asked Jules.

"I mean I got halfway down the side, and heard enough to know what we're going to face. We're not talking about a handful that can be taken out with a few well-placed rounds. We're talking about a bloody army of the things," he said, as he began to make sure all his weapons were fully loaded.

"So what do we do?" asked Sarah.

"I'm still thinking," replied Mike.

"Well, take your time. It's not like we're in a rush or anything," said Jules, reloading her weapons as well.

***

Lucy ran back into the kitchen to see even more flames catching the cupboards and fittings. She had a small powder fire extinguisher and two bath towels with her. She dumped the bath towels in the doorway as another crash came from the entrance, followed by a shriek of metal.

"Oh fuck! They're in," she said to herself as she pulled out the pin from the extinguisher and pressed the trigger, aiming it at the base of the flames. The liquid had erupted in several directions at once and although some of the small fires had joined together, there were spots of flames spreading everywhere. The powder quickly began to suffocate the licking tendrils of fire and within a minute, the flames that had been lashing the walls and cupboards were doused. The small extinguisher coughed and spluttered its last magic powder, and Lucy threw it to the ground, quickly gathering up the towels. She grabbed the jug of water and poured it over them, ringing them just a little before using them to pat, brush and scrape the last scorching flames away.

She coughed as the acrid, perfumed smoke lingered

in the room and drifted into the lounge area causing the smoke detectors to erupt into their disturbing high-pitched song. There was a heavy thudding coming from the entrance hall now, and Lucy knew it was the sound of the creatures battering against the wood of the inside door. The last barrier. Timing was everything. She rushed to the cupboard under the sink and opened the blackened scorched doors. The coated wood was warped and smelled of burning chemicals as the vapour of the paint continued to rise into the air. Lucy coughed again and wiped her mouth, then through stinging eyes she looked to the back of the cupboard to see a tote bag. They were always in good supply as she and Dora would often need to take equipment or supplies from one ward to the next. She put the knives in it, the gas lighter, and headed back into the hall to put her homemade Molotov cocktails in, but then she stopped.

"Shit!" she said, "The fuse. Shit," she said again, rushing back into the kitchen and grabbing a large wad of cotton wool and the remaining alcohol from the cupboard.

Lucy took one of the knives and carefully drilled a small hole through the wax. The hole gradually became bigger as she twisted the point from side to side. When it was just big enough to put her middle finger in, she tore off a good-sized piece of cotton wool and carefully screwed it into the gap. She repeated the procedure for the second cocktail, before carefully placing them, along with the alcohol and the knife she had used back in the bag.

Lucy headed out of the smouldering kitchen, paused in the doorway of Sammy and Jake's room to throw them one last loving glance, then closed the door firmly. She rushed down the hall to the bathroom, and climbed onto the edge of the bath, reaching up to the snow-covered skylight, she pulled the release lever, but the weight of the snow was too great and the hinges that would normally raise the light by a couple of inches did not even budge.

"Son of a bitch!" she yelled and jumped down to the floor. She ran back into the living room with her heart in her mouth as she saw the wood of the internal door shake with each bang from the creatures. The smoke detector continued to wail its warning, agitating the RAMs even more. Lucy grabbed a tall stool from the breakfast bar, and as she weaved around the now abandoned patient's beds, she saw the large red fire extinguisher. It held water and would have spread the fire further if she had used it, but now, it was just what she needed. She threw the strap of the bag across her other shoulder and dragged the stool with one hand and the extinguisher with the other, clumsily hitting door frames and walls as she ran down the hall.

Lucy placed the stool directly beneath the skylight, then picked up the heavy extinguisher. She climbed onto the side of the bath, then stepped onto the tall stool, pausing for a second to get her balance. She heaved the extinguisher up to her chest like she was lifting weights, then thrust it with all her might at the first hinge. The rusted metal buckled, and with the second hit, tinkled to the floor. She carefully turned to the next hinge which smashed with a loud crunch. Lucy dropped the heavy red canister which banged on the bathroom floor and rolled to meet the side of the bath. She put both of her hands against the skylight and pushed with every bit of strength she had. For a second, nothing happened, but then it began to budge and the snow slid away making the reinforced Perspex lighter with each inch it travelled higher.

When Lucy felt she had enough momentum, she pushed hard, and the thick plastic disappeared from her view, leaving nothing but blue sky above her head. She crunched her fingers through the icy snow and grabbed hold of the skylight surround, before swinging herself up through the hole like a gymnast. Lucy grimaced as her arm muscles supported her full weight, but a relieved breath burst from her lungs as first one foot made it through the hole and onto the roof, quickly followed by the second.

The sheen of perspiration on her forehead felt cold out in the open, and as the growls of the creatures surrounded the very air around her, Lucy shuddered. She noticed that the shooting had stopped. She had not heard a single shot for several minutes. All the activity, all the confusion had deafened her to the facts. There was no one coming for her. She was by herself.

She stood up and the growls almost sounded like roars as the creatures saw their prey in all her splendour. Lucy looked across the caravan park and realised every single beast was heading towards her. The dinner gong had been rung, and New England steak served rare was on the menu.

26

"Bollocks!" spat Hughes as he brought the truck to a halt once again.

"I'll get Barney," said Shaw, opening the door and jumping to the ground.

A moment later, Shaw and Barnes were digging underneath a tree that had been brought down in the landslide and was now blocking the entire road along with several tons of snow. The pair of them dug and scraped with their gloved hands and improvised tools until there was enough of a gap beneath the trunk to weave the heavy rope through.

Barnes fed the line around before tying a firm knot. Shaw took the other end and walked back to the truck, feeding it up and over the right-hand bracket that held the plough in place. He tied it around and pulled hard. Once he was happy it was secure, he looked up into the cab and nodded at Hughes, who began to back up the lorry, carefully checking the mirrors, making sure that he did not veer from the road and send them all crashing down to the craggy rocks below.

At first, the truck juddered, but then, the tree shook free from its snowy cocoon and began to glide across the icy surface, eventually coming to rest on the verge. Even with his limp, Shaw did not struggle to keep up to the lorry. He untied the heavy rope, and he and Barnes wound it and threw it back onto the tipper bed. Barnes climbed up to join Beth, and Shaw got back into the cab. He peeled off his gloves and warmed his hands in front of the blowing heater.

"Looks like we've got through the worst of it," said Hughes, arching his neck up a little to see if there were any more major obstacles in sight.

"Let's just hope it's not all for nothing," replied Shaw. Emma shot him a scowl. "I'm sorry," he said, "I wasn't thinking."

She turned back to look at the road, but inside, she was thinking exactly the same thing.

***

Lucy stood there, looking at the sea of grey malevolence as the demonic gurgles of hate vibrated in her ears. She could feel the structure shift as creatures from all sides pounded at it. She looked across to the next trailer. There was a ten feet gap between the two of them. She could not risk any of these monsters getting in to Sammy and Jake. She would not allow them to be turned.

Whatever else might happen, she would not allow that.

Lucy began to kick a pathway through the snow. It did not take long, but all the time, she felt the eyes of the beasts boring through her as she chiselled out her track. When she was done, she zipped her coat, made sure the bag was secure around her shoulder, and she began to sprint as fast as she could along the flat roof of the trailer, taking off into the air just a couple of inches before the start of the gutter. She landed heavily on the other side and deliberately twisted round and fell on her back, making sure the bag with precious cargo in it was well protected.

She stayed there for a second, with the freezing white snow surrounding her body. She turned her head and felt it against her face. The ice scraped at her skin, and she let out a relieved breath as she stood up and walked first to one corner and then the other. All the attention was still on her and had now shifted away from the first trailer. She smiled. Lucy stayed put as she watched the horde of creatures swarm below her. The ones that had broken into the entrance hall of the other trailer fed out of the doorway as excited growls lured them into the cold.

Lucy began to walk around the edge of the roof, making sure she had the full attention of every single beast that was in view. The creatures reached out with grasping fingers. They pulled empty handfuls of nothing out of the air, and Lucy looked down at them solemnly. She recognised quite a few of the faces. This was different to the last time she had faced a crowd of these things. Some of these people were acquaintances. She had shared conversations and laughter with them.

"So cruel," she muttered under her breath.

***

"Hello? Is there anybody in there?" asked Jules.

"Just give me a minute, please, Jules," he said, looking straight into her eyes. "Please, just give me a minute."

Jules took hold of Mike's hand and dragged him to his feet, pulling him away from the others. "Listen Mike. We don't have a minute darlin'—I wish we did. We need to make a decision, right fuckin' now!"

"I... I..." suddenly there was a loud whooshing sound that made them both look towards the gap between the two static caravans. Flames reflected on the metallic surface and Mike shook free from Jules's grasp and ran to get a better view, diving onto his belly before he reached the opening between the two statics.

He edged up, mounding the snow in front of him, and raised his head. For a second, his brain struggled to compute what he was actually seeing, as what looked like a hundred RAMs were massed around the static caravan, otherwise known as ward two. They pounded and shook the metallic frame to its very foundation, and there, standing on the roof of the structure was his Lucy. She looked down at a small handful of the creatures who were coated in flames, barging into others and lighting them up too in the same flammable sticky residue.

Two of the burning beasts ran through the open

door, colliding with door frames and furniture. Eventually, they became fully consumed by the licking flames and collapsed, acting as inhuman kindling to curtains, upholstery and a wide selection of internal fittings. The inside of the static caravan lit up like a flame grill as flickering ribbons of fire climbed the inside walls.

"Oh, no!" said Mike, looking on in horror as Lucy, stood on the roof with no idea of what was going on beneath her. He watched as the living room got brighter and the creatures outside became more excited. All the time Lucy stood there, blissfully unaware, getting ready to launch a second missile into the ghoulish crowd.

Mike rolled over onto his back and pressed his head down into the deep snow. He did not feel the cold. He did not feel the icy white of winter cling to his skin and begin to melt against the side of his face and his ears. All he felt was despair.

He became deaf to the growls of the creatures, and it was in that freezing, solitary silence that it all became clear to him. A pinprick in time, he remembered the exact moment that he realised Lucy loved him. It was that second back in Skelton when he led the RAMs away from the rest of the group. He took them through the streets of the town like the Pied Piper, and that's what he needed to do now. Whatever the outcome for him, it did not matter. He had been given extra time already by Wren, now he needed to make use of it.

Mike sprang to his feet and ran back to the others. Jules was apart from the rest of them where he had left her. He reached into his rucksack and gave her a carrier bag full of boxes. "These are the antibiotics Lucy needed. When I'm out of sight, get to her, get her, Sammy and Jake back to the yacht, and get out of here. When Shaw, Barney and Bruiser get back, they'll sort this mess out, but right now, you need to run."

She looked at him with her mouth half-open. He kissed her and held her tight. "I love you, Jules," he said, relinquishing his grip and heading towards the others. He hugged Raj and Talikha, repeating the same message to them, then grabbed hold of Sarah's hands. "Make sure you and Em take good care of each other," he said, kissing her quickly before kneeling down in the snow to kiss Humphrey. The dog panted happily. "Look after all of them boy," Mike said, before jumping to his feet and running back towards the sound of the growls. Before anybody could reply he was out of sight, and Jules, Raj, Talikha and Sarah just looked at each other as they heard Mike's battle cry echo around the campground.

Mike quickly followed it up with a shotgun blast which made two of the creatures' heads explode like paint-filled balloons. Suddenly, all eyes were on him. For a split second, he drew his gaze away from the mob of ghoulish horrors and looked up towards Lucy.

Their eyes locked, just like they had that fateful day back in Skelton. She felt then what she felt now. Hopelessness.

"Mike! No!" she screamed falling to her knees as tears began to stream down her cheeks. "No!" she yelled again, but this time it came out as nothing more than a croaky rasp.

It was the thundering of feet that dragged Mike from his sentimental reminisces, and back to the stark reality.

"I love you, Luce!" he yelled at the top of his voice. "I always will."

She mouthed 'I love you' to Mike, but now her sad cries were the only sounds she could make as the mass of creatures began to storm towards the love of her life.

Mike pumped the shotgun and paused momentarily to fire another shot, bringing down his leading pursuer and causing three of the subsequent followers to stumble. At the same time, he saw a flaming object arc through the air and smash into the crowd of creatures, spreading a burst of flames over half a dozen of them. He turned around and ploughed through the snow as fast as his legs could carry him.

The growls and noise of the beasts added momentum to Mike's strides as he tried to put as much space between himself and Lucy as he could. He looked back again and saw a spearhead of RAMs form behind him, tearing through the snow like a jet-powered plough.

Mike exited the campground and headed diagonally across the road, through the village hall car park. He paused again, making sure the creatures kept sight of him, then skirted around the building to the back. He saw the bloody remains of a RAM and pondered who would or could have done it.

He looked back again and locked eyes with the

leading beast. There was no danger that it would lose interest in its pursuit as Mike headed across the rear car park towards the trees. He ran into the shadowy blanket of the snow-covered branches with the speed of an Olympic sprinter. The snow was no obstacle as Lucy's very survival depended on each stride. Within seconds, he was sprinting flat out as the floor of the woods was virtually snow-free thanks to the thick branches above. He reached the other side in double quick time and leapfrogged the stone wall, skidding onto the path as his feet landed on someone else's icy footprints.

His eyes followed the multiple trails across the road to the librarians' house. As tempting as it was to see friendly faces, Mike knew the large bay windows would be smashed in no time if he led the creatures there. He carried on down the street, but his progress slowed once again as the snow was much deeper on this stretch of road.

He looked behind him. A handful of the creatures had made their way over the wall to continue their pursuit, but others were in the woods. Three of the six beasts that had caught fire were running between the trees, lighting the way for the others. They were gaining ground fast as they did not have to fight through the same depth of snow Mike was contending with.

"Oh fuck!" he said, angry with himself for not thinking his actions through. He kept going a few more seconds before shooting another glance to his side. Mike saw one of the burning beasts fall to its knees and onto its face. Its brethren surged passed it and gradually angled their steps closer to the wall and the road beyond. As the first stumbled over the waist high black stone wall, followed by a second and a third, Mike brought the shotgun up and fired again, bringing a fourth down before it even had chance to reach the pavement on the other side.

The other two burning creatures collapsed as the bright orange flames melted their clothes and skin, but they were a drop in the ocean compared to the mass of figures charging into the clearing and over the wall.

Mike could not run any faster than he was, but his lead had been cut from forty feet to half that. He kept going, even though the sweat was pouring down his back, even though his legs were beginning to feel like jelly as they pushed hard against the deep snow.

He reached the bottom of the street and turned right onto the road out of the village. It was uphill and would slow him even more, but a left turn would mean heading back towards his loved ones. He cast another glance behind him and saw his lead had been cut further, as the creatures came tearing around the corner after him. He stopped, brought the shotgun up to his shoulder, held his breath, and squeezing the trigger twice, he made two of the beasts collapse to the floor. Others fell and stumbled over them causing a small pile-up and breaking the pack's momentum. Mike turned again and started sprinting flat out, knowing he needed to take full advantage. He looked around again to see a number of the RAMs were back in hot pursuit having clambered over the fallen ones or just bypassed them completely. More and more surged around the corner, but the shots had given him valuable seconds and maybe, just maybe, he had given his family and his friends the precious time they needed to make an escape.

Suddenly, he skidded and went sprawling. His body and face hit the ice hard, and frozen jags spiked at his skin. He slid again trying to get to his feet and then began to run with everything he had. He didn't look back, he could feel the presence of evil, its freezing hand reaching out for him. His lungs hurt, his leg muscles pulled and strained, but he kept going. Mike pumped the shotgun, and not bothering to stop, turned the top half of his body and fired.

The beasts were closer than he thought, but the one shot blasted into the faces of the first two creatures causing a mini pile-up, and gaining him a small amount of precious distance once again.

Mike finally made it to the brow of the first hill. The horde of creatures were now about thirty feet behind him, but showing no signs of slowing down. He turned back to his direction of travel, and suddenly lowered his head, closed his eyes, and dropped to his knees, as tears began to fall from his face into the snow.

27

Lucy heard the glass break and saw the smoke rising in front of her at the same moment. She realised immediately what it meant. There were still ten RAMs in her line of sight. There could be more dotted around the campsite, but these had materialised shortly after the main army of creatures had followed Mike.

Tears still streamed down her cheeks. It was Skelton all over again, but this time, there was thick snow on the ground and so many more pursuers. A lot did not make sense, the confusion only added to Lucy's sadness. How had Mike got back? Why was he alone? She looked down at the beasts still shooting malevolent stares straight at her, and heard another windowpane break as the heat from inside expanded the glass.

Time was running out for her, she needed to make a decision. Leaping back across to the other roof would put Sammy and Jake at risk. Staying put would mean she would either become asphyxiated by smoke fumes or burn to death, which left just one option. She would have to jump down, and on the off chance she did not break her ankle, she would either need to fight the beasts with nothing but two kitchen knives, or she would try to run. Either way, she did not rate her chances.

Lucy was about to head to the other side of the trailer and jump when she caught something out of the corner of her eye. She looked across and saw Jules, Raj, Talikha, Sarah and Humphrey heading towards her. Seconds passed as she watched them, wanting to make sure it was not a hallucination, then she clicked into action, running to the far side of the roof and jumping down into the deepest snow she could find. She looked one way, then the other, expecting to see RAMs heading towards her around each corner, but none did.

Lucy ran around to the front and saw all the beasts converging on her friends. Another two appeared from behind one of the smaller caravans and charged towards them. Jules started firing and Lucy's shouts of warning and hand gestures went unheard and unseen. She had no other choice, the doctor grabbed one of her knives and started running as fast as she could towards the two RAMs that were closing in on her friends.

Jules was the only one who had real experience fighting, from all the time she had spent at the Home and Garden Depot. Raj, Talikha and Sarah did the best they could to follow suit, but Sarah's first shot took out a window of the burning structure, missing all the creatures completely. Talikha managed to remove one beast's arm with a blast that came from her shotgun, but Raj, less panicked, took aim and although the thrust knocked him back a pace and sent a jolt of agony through his shoulder, he blew the head clean off one of the advancing beasts.

Humphrey had been relegated to stand behind his master, but catching sight of the same two beasts Lucy had seen, he began racing towards them. The two RAMs were closing in fast on the small group and commands or not, Humphrey would defend his pack with everything he had. Almost as if they were choreographed, the Labrador Retriever and Lucy leapt into the air at the same time. Humphrey's large paws landed on the first RAM's chest, knocking it from its feet like it had been hit by a freight train. Both the creature and Humphrey went tumbling into the snow.

Lucy, with the kitchen knife raised, let out a scream as she smashed the second creature to the ground. Her cry drew the attention of Raj and Jules, who realised what a near-miss they'd escaped. Their eyes lingered for a second as they watched Lucy plunge the knife through the eye socket of her victim, before leaping back to her feet and pouncing on the beast Humphrey had brought down.

Knowing they were by no means out of the woods, Raj and Jules turned back and continued to fire at the other RAMs. When Jules took the final shot, everyone's eyes followed the explosion as the creature's head blew apart in a bloody splash.

When the echoing crack finally died, the friends, unfroze and rushed towards each other. Lucy embraced each of them before bending down and kissing Humphrey who was now limping a little after his brave assault on his master's would-be attacker. Then she suddenly came to her senses. "We need to go after Mike. We need to help him."

"Here," said Jules, handing Lucy the bag. "It's the medicine."

Lucy looked inside, then looked to Raj. "Please," she said pointing to the trailer that Sammy and Jake were in, "I need to help Mike. Please, you know how to give them the shots."

Without saying anything, Raj took the bag, then he and Talikha ran towards the doorway and began removing the obstacles to gain entrance. Humphrey limped after them, still determined to defend his family despite his own injury.

Jules started reloading her shotgun and paused to hand Lucy a Glock Seventeen and three spare magazines. "You're a much better shot with one of these than I am."

"You don't have to do this, Jules," said Lucy, placing the gun in the back of her jeans.

"Don't be fuckin' daft," replied Jules. "We're family. All of us. You don't think if that was me out there, Mike wouldn't be the first one to come after us? Y'know he would. We stick together, so come on, let's go find him."

Sarah looked longingly towards the doorway of the static caravan where Raj and Talikha had just disappeared, then she looked across towards the campsite exit, where Mike had led a horde of vicious beasts just moments earlier. She pumped the shotgun and desperately wanting to sound like an action heroine from a Hollywood blockbuster, but in fact sounding more like Popeye's Olive Oil, said, "Let's do this!"

***

Mike did not feel the chill and stab of the snow and debris as it hit him. He heard the engine rev harder as the huge truck sped up, and he felt the cold wind suck at his face as the loud mechanical beast powered past him and towards the crowd of bloodthirsty creatures.

As the beasts began to smash and thud against the plough, Mike took a deep breath and climbed to his feet. He wiped away his tears and reached into his pocket for more shells to refill his shotgun. Turning, he watched as the broken bodies of RAMs were scattered in red and white mounds of horror.

The odd creature managed to skirt around the roaring truck and Mike was about to take aim, when one, then another collapsed to the floor. He looked towards the bed of the tipper where Barnes was knelt, taking kill shots despite the movement of the vehicle.

At the bottom of the incline, the lorry came to a stop and first Barnes, then Beth jumped down. Two RAMs appeared from around the side of the truck and Beth raised her Glock, while Barnes brought up his SA80. They each put one of the creatures down, before heading towards Mike, who was now jogging down the hill to greet them. Hughes and Shaw rolled down their windows and as the RAMs began to batter against the sides of the stationary vehicle trying to get to the fresh prey that sat within, the two soldiers took their time and carefully aimed their weapons, placing shutters over the wild flaring pupils forever.

"We've got to get to the campsite," said Mike, hugging Barnes and then Beth.

"Why?" asked Beth pulling back.

"Lucy, Sammy, Jake, Raj, Talikha, Sarah, Jules...they're all there. That's where I left them," replied Mike.

A look of determination swept over Beth's face, and she took her Glock in both hands and began to walk back to the lorry, aiming and firing at the diminishing crowd of creatures as she moved. Barnes looked towards Mike briefly, then ran to catch up with her and began firing too. Mike paused and took a breath, looking towards the mass of falling figures, before catching up with the others. He headed down the driver's side of the lorry while Barnes and Beth went down the passenger side. Mike fired once, twice, three times, but then there was nothing left to fire at. The majority of the damage had been done by the snowplough as it had crushed, mashed and pulverized the throng of beasts. The remaining ones had lined up like mechanical ducks on a fairground stall to be picked off one by one by the two experienced soldiers in the cab.

The lorry started up and pulled forward. Shaw took another three shots at staggering creatures that had lagged behind the rest of the horde, they each went down. Hughes brought the huge truck to a stop once again, making sure that he and his passengers would not be stepping out onto a mound of decaying corpses. He opened the door and jumped down into the white snow. Mike weaved round the bloody bodies to meet him, and the two hugged like long lost brothers. Not even waiting for Shaw to climb down from the other side, Emma clambered across and stumbled down into Mike's waiting arms. They kissed and held each other close.

"We need to get to the campsite," Mike said, "Our family's there."

"Okay," said Hughes, "let's go."

Emma broke away, and the smile left her face immediately. She had blocked out the reality for a moment while her arms were around her brother, but now she remembered, the day was far from over, the danger was far from behind her. She grimaced as she took the first step back up to the cab, and when she was up and had sidled across to her original position, Hughes climbed to join her. He leaned across and shut the door.

"Climb in the back with Beth and Barney," he said to Mike, as he eased off the handbrake.

Mike nodded, and ran around to the back of the open-box bed, grabbing hold of the edge and using some of his remaining strength to pull himself on board. He stood holding onto the side while the truck navigated the bends and turns on the short journey to the campsite. The lorry pulled to a stop once more before the turn for the campground, and Mike, Barnes and Beth heard the cab doors open. They shot glances towards each other before checking their weapons and jumping down to the ground.

They walked around from the back of the truck, and a wave of happiness washed over each of them to see the familiar faces. Barnes and Beth continued, rushing towards their friends and grabbing them in loving embraces. Mike froze as he laid eyes on Lucy. Hughes had her in a bear hug, the relief apparent on both of their faces. The soldier eventually released his grip, and Lucy pulled away smiling before feeling compelled to turn her head, almost as if she felt eyes on her. Suddenly, her face lit up in an expression beyond joy to see Mike looking at her. She ran towards him and as the two of them met they joined in a kiss that blocked out everything but their own world. After a minute, Lucy pulled back for breath, and the two of them laughed.

"You're a mad fuckin' bastard," said Jules, pulling Mike around to face her.

"Good to see you too," said Mike, smiling and throwing his arms around his friend.

Emma climbed down from the cab of the truck and almost fell into Sarah's waiting arms. "I won't kiss you," said Sarah. "I've thrown my guts up a couple of times," she said.

"Nice," said Emma laughing and pulling Sarah towards her. "You have no idea how happy I am to see you."

"Ditto!" replied Sarah, nuzzling her face into Emma's neck for reassuring warmth.

The rest of the group came around the truck to join

them, Wren followed with Wolf, and Mike pushed past Shaw, Barnes and Beth to reach her. "Hi," she said quietly, "glad you made it."

"Me too," he said smiling and giving her a hug. Wolf began to growl, and Wren told her canine protector to calm down, which he did.

Mike looked towards Lucy, Jules and Sarah. "This is Wren. She saved our lives back in Inverness."

The three women greeted her warmly, but within a few seconds, Jules's brow began to furrow. *There was something familiar about this girl. What was it?*

"Okay!" said Mike. "There could be a load of stragglers around the village, we're going to have to do a sweep to make sure this place is safe."

"God, Mike! Can't we just have one minute?" asked Sarah.

"Look! If there are more of them out there, each minute that goes by is a greater distance they can put between us, it's a greater risk that they can attack someone else. It's…"

Mike cut off as the loud horn of the lorry beeped, bursting through the stillness of the air like an air raid siren. Emma kept her fist depressed on the horn and eventually RAMs began to shamble towards them. These were the slow movers. Creatures that had been decrepit in life and now in death. One by one they were taken down.

There was no point wasting bullets on these beasts.

They were too slow and too fragile. Mike, Barnes, Beth, Hughes and Jules slashed and sliced and chopped as creature after creature fell. Eventually, Emma removed her hand from the horn as the last of the RAMs were finished off. As she did, more familiar faces appeared at the bottom of the road. The librarians and Jenny rushed towards their friends and greeted them all with hugs.

"We really need to see Sammy and Jake," said Emma looking towards her brother and Lucy.

Emma took hold of Sarah's hand and the two of them began to walk the short distance to the campground entrance. Lucy and Mike did the same, while Hughes, Shaw and the others gathered together as their adrenalin levels gradually returned to normal.

Emma and Sarah walked through the campground entrance, and Sarah's face lit up. "Oh thank God!" She said as a figure was heading away from them towards the broken door of the static caravan that Sammy and Jake were in.

Sarah broke her grip from Emma's hand and began to run towards the young woman. "No!" thundered Mike as he raced to catch up with his sister's girlfriend. He caught her by the shoulder and she stopped. Confusion was painted all over her face, but before she even got chance to ask Mike why he had stopped her, he reached down, made a snowball and pitched it at the figure's back.

The snow exploded against the light blue wool of the cardigan, and suddenly, the figure whipped round. It remained frozen for a few seconds, poised in a menacing stance, it's legs apart, its grey hands looking more like claws, as its mouth dropped open in a silent growl. The creature bore its already blood-stained teeth as it began to charge towards the woman who had just collapsed to her knees crying.

"Dora," sobbed Sarah., "Oh...my Dora!. Not you. Not you, sweet girl." Tears streamed down her cheeks and blurred her vision to the ghoulish horror storming towards her and Mike. Sarah became deaf and blind to everything but her own pain.

Emma and Lucy stood in silence, unable to break their horrified gaze from the unfolding terror. Mike pulled one of the machetes from his rucksack and took two paces forward, making the creature veer towards him. He raised the blade as he had so many times before. He brought it down with the power of Thor's hammer, like he had so many times before. He looked into the creature's eyes like he had so many times before, but rather than the opaque grey and flaring black malevolence of the pupils that usually greeted him, he saw the deaf girl who had nursed Sammy and Jake, who had helped when his gran died, who had always been there for everybody, who had never wanted, never put upon.

Dora closed her eyes for the last time and the monster that had taken over her body fell back into the snow. Mike flung his machete to the ground, and tears began to run down his face too. He stumbled back to where Sarah was kneeling and dropped to his knees. He put his arms around her and held her close, kissing her head over and over, saying "I'm sorry. I'm so sorry," in-between his own baying cries. "She was the sweetest kid. I'm so sorry."

***

It was Barnes who climbed into the driving seat of the huge snowplough, Beth sat by his side. Jules had asked to go with them to see if she could get her hands on another vehicle. The lorry rumbled away, leaving Hughes, Shaw, Wren and Wolf in the middle of the snowy road. The path had already been cleared when the plough had made its entrance into the village, so the truck made good time on its return journey. They soon left the bloody, beaten remains of the creatures behind, and once again, the hills and rocks were coated with the purest white as the lorry wound along the Highland road. Annie and John came running out to greet them as the truck pulled into the forecourt of the large garage and workshop that sat next to George's house.

Beth and Barnes hugged and kissed the children before leading them into the warmth of the cottage, and Jules threw her arms around George. "How you doin', old man?" she asked, kissing him roughly on the cheek before pulling back with a loving smile on her face.

"I'm just fine, poppet. How are you?"

"To say it's been a very long day would be an understatement," she replied.

"Why? What's been happening?" asked George.

Jules took George's arm and the two of them went

inside while she told him the potted version of the day's events. Beth and Barnes remained in their own happy family world, sitting on the old fashioned but comfy settee with Annie and John telling them every detail of the past couple of days they had spent with George.

Jules and George looked on smiling, until Jules said she needed to go to the toilet. As she walked down the hall, she paused at a photo. George looked a good few years younger, and he was standing with all his family. He had a look of pure glee on his face. Jules stepped into the kitchen and looked at the photo more closely; she smiled a warm smile. He had loved his family. The memory of them was too painful, he did not talk about them often, but once in a while he would mention something before bottling up his feelings again like a lot of men from his generation.

"Have you got a four by four for me?" asked Jules when she returned from the toilet.

"Where's the pickup?" asked George.

"Long story," she replied. "Have you or haven't you, old man?"

"C'mon" he said, getting up from his comfortable armchair and placing his pipe back on its stand. "Let's go see."

"You guys are okay here, aren't you?" asked Jules looking towards Beth and Barnes.

"Course we are," said Beth, still in a state of elation to be back safe with her family.

"Won't be long," said Jules, before following George out to the big workshop.

George pulled back the long slide door letting the afternoon sunlight up the inside of the large workshop. "How will this do you?" he asked, pulling a tarpaulin from an ex-army Land Rover.

"Let's take it for a spin," she said, climbing into the driving seat.

"What? Now?" asked George.

"Yeah! No time like the present. There's going to be a lot of repairs needed in the village, you may as well get a look at them now so you know what you're going to need and who you're going to need to help you," said Jules.

"How is it whenever there are repairs, I'm the one who ends up doing them?"

"Ahh, quit moaning, old man. You know you enjoy it." The two friends shared a warm smile, and George walked around to the passenger side and climbed in.

George shuddered as Jules crunched the gear stick into reverse. She backed out of the workshop and quickly spun the steering wheel, making the Land Rover skid and spin a little in the small court area. "And suddenly, the mystery of the missing pickup becomes less of a mystery," said George under his breath.

"I heard that," said Jules as she straightened the wheel and slowly pulled away. Within a few minutes, the devastation became apparent, and George's face dropped with the heavy weight of sadness as he saw the shattered bodies of RAMs piled up by the side of the road. Familiar faces looked towards him in deathly gazes, and he turned his head away.

"Dear God!" he said.

"I don't think he had anything to do with this," said Jules.

Jules took the bend faster than she should have done and the back end of the Land Rover skidded again. She pulled up the car near the entrance to the campsite, and then looked across to the village hall. Hughes and Shaw were standing outside, deep in conversation. As Jules pulled the Land Rover into the car park, they stopped and went over to greet their friends.

"Y'alright, mate?" said Hughes, shaking George's hand as he climbed out of the car.

"I am now we've stopped," said George with a thin smile.

"Ahh, give it a rest. We'd have a ten mile an hour speed limit if it was up to you," said Jules.

A deep bark broke them from their banter, and they all looked towards Wolf as he held a big red ball in his mouth before running back out of sight.

George frowned, he had never seen that dog here before. He began walking to the side of the building, and Jules caught up with him. "The guys picked somebody up in Inverness, the dog is theirs."

"Oh, I see," said George, "it's a fine looking thing isn't it?" he said as they walked around the corner.

"It is that," said Jules, taking hold of George's arm as they went.

The ball flew in the other direction this time, and Wolf chased after it. "Hi," said Jules.

The girl who had thrown the ball for her dog turned around. Her mouth dropped open.

The silence went on for seconds before George finally broke it. "Wren?"

"Grandad?"

EPILOGUE

How many times had this kitchen been the venue for gatherings governing the future of Safe Haven?

Mike, Lucy, Emma, Sarah, Jules, Beth, Raj and the three soldiers stood with hot drinks in their hands. Lanterns and candles lit the room, and the fire in the range roared away warming them all. They leant back against walls and kitchen cupboards as the shrill laughter of Sammy, Jake, Annie and John filled the house from the other room. Despite the seriousness of what they were discussing, they paused and all of them smiled. They knew how different things could be right now.

Save for their actions, Sammy and Jake would not have made it. They did it by working together, that's the way they always did everything.

Four weeks had passed since that blackest of days. It would always scar them, but time is a good healer, and it was not as if they did not know how to deal with sadness.

"We're not placing blame. We all make the decisions here, it's never just one of us," said Shaw.

"I'm the doctor, I should have insisted," said Lucy.

"We've been over this," said Mike. "I should have figured it out. He was acting weird on the journey back, I should have known something was wrong. But look, that's in the past now. This is all about the future. We're putting down the rules to make this a safer place," said Mike.

Sarah sat at the table with a collection of pens and a legal pad in front of her. "Okay, so how do you want me to word this?" she said.

"Anyone entering or reentering the boundaries of Safe Haven will be subject to a full physical examination," said Emma. Sarah started writing.

"I'm going to need a lot more help," said Lucy.

"You'll have it," said Mike. "We rested on our laurels too long, and we paid the price. We need to look at the way we do absolutely everything."

"How do you mean?" asked Lucy.

"We've done amazing things, but Safe Haven is growing way too fast for just a few people to be depended upon time and time again," he replied.

"So, what's the answer?" asked Lucy.

"The answer is if we need nurses to help you, we recruit and train nurses. If we need more soldiers to fight, we recruit and train more soldiers. If we need more farmers to farm, more builders to build, then we recruit and train them. There will be no free rides. We have a lot of skilled people in Safe Haven. They can pass on their knowledge to others, we can build this into something great, but everybody has to play a part like they did when we started this thing. None of us knows what lies ahead. All we can do is prepare the best we can, and that's got to start today with the people around this room." Mike looked at each of them before continuing. "This is only our first winter, and it's been pretty shitty so far, but it's taught us a lot too. We can't just plan for next week or next month, we need to look to next winter and the one after that, and the one after that too. We need to prepare for all eventualities."

Mike finished his mug of tea and put it down on the counter. "We thought we'd never face an enemy worse than Fry, more powerful than his army. We were wrong. Nature just opened up a can of whoop-ass on us, and I'll be damned if I'm ever going to let that happen again." He headed for the door.

"Where are you going?" asked Hughes.

"I'm going to find Lucy some staff."

"It's nine o'clock at night," said Hughes.

"We've lost enough time already. I'm not wasting another minute," he replied, and walked out into the cold darkness, closing the door behind him.

THE END

A NOTE FROM THE AUTHOR

I really hope you enjoyed this book and would be very grateful if you took a minute to leave a review on Amazon and Goodreads.

If you would like to stay informed about what I'm doing, including current writing projects, and all the latest news and release information; these are the places to go:

Join the fan club on Facebook

https://www.facebook.com/groups/127693634504226/

Like the Christopher Artinian author page

https://www.facebook.com/safehaventrilogy/

Subscribe to the newsletter at

https://christopherartinian.org/

Buy exclusive and signed books and merchandise:

https://www.christopherartinian.com/

Follow me on Twitter

https://twitter.com/Christo71635959

Follow me on Goodreads

https://www.goodreads.com/author/show/16438874.Chr istopher_Artinian

Follow me on Amazon

https://amzn.to/2I1llU6

Other books by Christopher Artinian:

Safe Haven: Rise of the RAMs

Safe Haven: Realm of the Raiders

Safe Haven: Reap of the Righteous

Before Safe Haven: Lucy

Before Safe Haven: Alex

Anthologies featuring short stories by Christopher Artinian

Undead Worlds: A Reanimated Writers Anthology

Tales from Zombie Road: The Long Haul Anthology

Treasured Chests: A Zombie Anthology for Breast Cancer Care

Trick-or-Treat Thrillers – Best Paranormal 2018

CHRISTOPHER ARTINIAN

Christopher Artinian was born and raised in Leeds, West Yorkshire. Wanting to escape life in a big city and concentrate more on working to live than living to work, he and his family moved to the Outer Hebrides in 2004.

He released his debut novel, Safe Haven: Rise of the Rams in February 2017. This was the first instalment of a post-apocalyptic zombie trilogy. Book two, Safe Haven: Realm of the Raiders continues the fast moving and often terrifying story and book three, Reap of the Righteous concludes the first chapter in the gripping saga. In July 2018 he released A Zombie Novella – Before Safe Haven: Lucy, featuring one of Safe Haven's most loved characters. A Zombie Novella – Before Safe Haven: Alex came out in August 2018. There are several more Safe Haven works currently in progress.

In October 2017, he won the prestigious Zombie Book of the Month Award for Rise of the RAMs. In December 2017 he was also awarded with the prestigious, "Best New Author" prize by the Reanimated Writers group. In addition, Safe Haven won the "Best Series" award in the popular   Good   Morning   Zompoc   members   poll.

For fans of the Safe Haven books, a standalone short story featuring one of the main Safe Haven characters was published as part of an anthology (Undead Worlds). Christopher was also featured in the Treasured Chests anthology and another of his stories, "Condemned" was released in the Zombie Road anthology.

Printed in Great Britain
by Amazon

18717134R00180